## "DO YOU WANT ME, AMANDA?" SLADE ASKED SOFTLY.

Her mind understood the danger in his question, but her body would not obey its command to escape his sweet threat. Before Amanda could think further, Slade's mouth found hers again in a long, mind-fogging kiss. Her breath, when she remembered to breathe, came in short little gasps. Her whole body throbbed with a painful ache. Opening her eyes was a mistake. She was immediately lost in the dark, passion-filled depths of his gaze.

"Yes. Yes. I want you, Slade," she whispered. "Please."

Harper
Monogram

# The Lady and the Lawman

## ⊰ BETTY WINSLOW ⊱

HarperPaperbacks
*A Division of HarperCollinsPublishers*

This is a work of fiction. The characters, incidents, and dialogues are products of the author's imagination and are not to be construed as real. Any resemblance to actual events or persons, living or dead, is entirely coincidental.

HarperPaperbacks   *A Division of* HarperCollins*Publishers*
                   10 East 53rd Street, New York, N.Y. 10022

Cover illustration by Joseph Cellini

First printing: June 1995

Printed in the United States of America

HarperPaperbacks, HarperMonogram, and colophon are trademarks of HarperCollins*Publishers*

❖ 10 9 8 7 6 5 4 3 2 1

To the Tuesday Morning Ladies:
Betty, Chris, Connie, Lynne, Nora, and Rosie.
You made me believe that dreams really do come true.

# 1

**Texas, 1859**

*Amanda Jefferson clutched* the leather strap beside the open window of the swaying stagecoach in an attempt to keep her slight frame on the hard seat, and out of the lap of the bespectacled, balding man seated across from her. Each time she swayed in his direction, she noted the light of anticipation that flared in his eyes. He reminded her of a cat waiting to pounce on a canary.

She thought of the derringer tucked into the reticule dangling from her wrist. She probably wouldn't have time to retrieve it if the man became aggressive, but she could darn well smack him in the head with the heavy bag. The gun's weighty presence was a great comfort.

The men of the West she'd encountered during this trip had been, for the most part, a rough-looking, ungentlemanly lot. Perhaps it was the lack of single ladies on the frontier that made them so.

The man on the opposite seat had introduced himself as Samuel Griffin. The way he looked at her made her feel uncomfortable in the extreme. Not that she was much to look at at the moment, she thought wryly.

She'd seen her reflection in a badly clouded mirror at the last rest stop and, to put it bluntly, she looked a sight. Her dove gray traveling dress was wrinkled and dust-covered, the feather on the small matching hat perched atop her coiled auburn hair had long ago drooped, and her black, high-buttoned shoes were scuffed and dirty.

She hadn't had a decent meal or a full bath or slept in a really clean bed in the four days and three nights since she'd begun the last leg of this horrid journey. Her head ached from breathing the dust stirred up by the coach, and her stomach churned from all the bouncing. She thanked God that the end was nearly in sight.

Another jolt bounced her off the seat and plopped her down again. She felt an urgent need to rub her smarting backside. One look at the leering man across the coach stifled that impulse.

In truth, she did understand the necessity for speed. At the last rest stop the station man had informed the driver that a band of Comanche were roaming the area.

Their driver, who said his name was Shorty, told them this stage might well be the last to get through until the Texas Rangers could round up the Indians. His last bit of advice after fresh horses had been hitched to the stage was "Hold on to your hats, folks, 'cause I'm gonna whip up the horses."

The next jolt bounced Amanda up so high that her head hit the ceiling, causing her hat to slide forward over her eyes.

Griffin snickered.

Amanda righted her hat. Shorty, she decided, was a man who knew what he was talking about.

Leaning back, she closed her eyes against the penetrating stare of the man seated across from her and tried to ignore her discomfort.

She would not allow anything to distract her from the job ahead. Robert Commings, her father's business partner in the private investigation firm of Jefferson and Commings, hadn't been able to talk her out of making the trip, though God knew he'd tried.

Robert didn't think she was qualified to handle the investigation into Cecil Jefferson's murder, and he was probably right. Although she *had* worked on cases with her father on a few occasions, she had never worked undercover alone before. But, although she might not have been the most logical choice, she certainly was the most determined, and the least likely to be detected.

Admittedly, she was terrified. But she had vowed to avenge her father's murder and finish the investigation of the Knights of the Golden Circle—an organization of Southern sympathizers—that Mister Lincoln had hired him for. It was imperative that the North prevent the Knights from supplying the South with arms, and come hell or high water, she would do her part in this effort.

Someone had betrayed her father the night the shipment of guns was stolen from the Armory in Washington, D.C. Papers she'd found in her father's desk indicated the guns would change hands in the small Texas town of Three Wells. Her father had planned to make this trip. Now she would do it for him.

Still, if the fates hadn't intervened she probably wouldn't have gotten Robert to agree. The letter informing Amanda of her mother's death and of the inheritance awaiting her in Three Wells had come a week after her father's funeral. She now had a legitimate reason to be in Three Wells and the cover she needed to begin her investigation.

Amanda didn't care a fig about the inheritance or the mother who'd placed her in a convent school at the age of five. She barely remembered the woman or the house she'd lived in, except for a child's impression that it was big and the woman was beautiful.

If her father hadn't rescued her from the Sisters when she was twelve, she probably would have taken her vows by now. She would always be grateful to him for offering her an alternative.

She'd never been sure if he'd come for her out of love or duty. He wasn't a man who allowed his emotions to show, but he had cared for her for the past ten years, and she owed him for that. She would pay the debt, no matter what the cost.

She'd finally managed to convince Robert that no one would suspect a proper young lady, who'd come to town to settle her mother's estate, of being an investigator. And she already had a contact in Three Wells. Her father's notes mentioned a man called Hawk Hawkins, a Texas Ranger already working on the case. She would find him and get this job done so she could return to civilization.

Thunder rumbled in the distance, intruding on Amanda's thoughts. She roused herself enough to peer out of the stagecoach's small window. A fast-moving line of storm clouds was approaching from the west.

The size and emptiness of Texas awed and frightened Amanda a little. It was a hot, dry land, flat and treeless, broken only by the occasional low hills or creek, where welcome shades of green could be seen. The silence and the space gave one room to think and breathe, she supposed, but it would take some getting used to.

The stage careened around a sweeping curve, and Amanda would have been thrown across the seat if she hadn't been clutching the strap. Griffin smirked as she anchored her hat with her free hand and, taking a cue from him, braced her feet against the base of the seat opposite her. They raced down the dusty main street of the tiny Texas town and came to a teeth-rattling stop.

"Mercy," Amanda muttered, with a sigh of relief.

"You got that right, little lady. It was quite a ride," Griffin replied.

In the time it took her to catch her breath, Griffin had opened the door and stepped down. Turning back, he offered her his hand. Good manners required that she place hers in his. His palm was hot and sweaty, his grip a bit too tight as he assisted her from the coach. He held her hand a moment longer than necessary before releasing it. Amanda chose to ignore the impropriety.

The driver tossed down Griffin's bag and then handed him Amanda's small trunk. Griffin placed it on the boardwalk in front of the stage office.

"Thank you, Mister Griffin, you've been most kind," Amanda murmured, then politely discouraged him when he offered to help her find a hotel.

A gust of dust-laden wind, kicked up by the fast-approaching storm, whipped Amanda's dress about her ankles and almost dislodged her hat as she made her way to the stage office door. The man behind the counter smiled warmly as she crossed the threshold.

"Afternoon, miss. Can I help you?"

"I really hope so. May I leave my trunk here? Just until I'm sure where I'll be staying?"

"Sure thing, miss. I'll see to it. Won't be no trouble at all."

"I was told that this is the place to leave letters and messages. Is that right?"

"Right as rain, miss," he replied, his chest puffing up with pride. "We're the post office and stage stop all rolled into one."

Amanda debated with herself about leaving a message for Hawk, but decided to wait. She would get the inheritance business settled first, and then concentrate on the guns.

The letter informing her of her mother's death had been signed by a man named McAllister, who said he was her mother's partner and that he was handling her affairs. She would see him first.

"How convenient, Mister . . . I'm sorry. I don't know your name."

"Adam Griswald, miss."

Amanda extended her hand. "Amanda Jefferson. I'm pleased to meet you, Mr. Griswald. Could you possibly tell me where I might find a man named Slade McAllister?"

Adam Griswald dropped the hand he was gingerly shaking as if it had burned him, and appraised her now with unfriendly eyes.

"You'll find him at the big white house on the east edge of town," he responded tightly. Turning away, he mumbled something under his breath about Baton Rouge.

What a strange man, Amanda mused. She left the building and was nearly swept off her feet by another gust of wind. Glancing up at the darkening sky, she muttered an unladylike oath. She didn't relish the idea of getting wet. In her grimy condition, she figured, she would probably turn to mud.

She was unaware of the tall, thin man before her until she collided with him, sending his hat flying.

"Oh! My goodness, I'm sorry."

He stooped to retrieve the wide-brimmed Stetson before the wind could whisk it away. "My fault entirely, miss." His blue eyes contained admiration and his smile was charming. "Where did you come from?" he drawled.

Amanda couldn't help smiling back. "We—the stage and I, that is—literally blew into town together."

The man laughed pleasantly and then looked up to scan the darkening sky. "We're going to get rained on soon. My name's Davis, miss. Sheriff Jim Davis. Let me escort you to wherever you're going." His gaze swept over her. "There's so little of you, this wind is likely to blow you away."

Because of the shiny star pinned to his shirt, Amanda didn't object when he took her by the arm. She smiled up at him.

"I'm Amanda Jefferson. Thank you for the offer, sir. It seems I'm not getting very far on my own. I need to get to Slade McAllister's house at the end of the street."

The sheriff's hold on her elbow loosened and his smile faded. His voice sounded sharp when he asked,

"Would you mind telling me what business you have with McAllister?"

Amanda couldn't fathom why she was getting this reaction to McAllister's name. None of the information she had on the man gave the impression that he was anything out of the ordinary. But then her information was sketchy. Perhaps there was something in the reports about him that she'd missed.

Amanda smiled up at the sheriff. "Of course not. I have some business matters to conduct with him and I want to have a look at the house. I'm thinking of buying him out."

A look of astonishment crossed the sheriff's face. His grip on her arm tightened as he propelled her forward along the boardwalk at a very rapid pace. Minutes later, he stopped before the gate of a stately white house. Amanda was panting from the effort of keeping pace.

He released her arm, and the look he gave her could only be described as assessing. "I'd be very careful when dealing with McAllister if I were you, miss," he warned. "Good day." Then he turned and left her standing on the walk.

Amanda tried to think of a reason for the man's odd behavior, but couldn't. The men in this town, she concluded, were certainly a strange lot.

Opening the gate in the white picket fence, she paused to admire the structure before her. It resembled the Southern plantation houses she'd seen in pictures. Four ornate columns supported a balcony that ran the width of the upper story. Double windows flanked a massive front door.

Thunder rumbled again, and a few fat raindrops

splattered on the brick walk. Amanda scurried forward to avoid getting wet and climbed the three wide steps to the porch.

A brass knocker, in the shape of a heart, caught her attention; it was definitely unique and rather quaint, she thought. She knocked and the door swung open to reveal the largest man she'd ever seen. He stood at least six and a half feet tall and was nearly as wide as the door he held open.

He was impeccably dressed in a black suit, white shirt, and black string tie. His black hair was graying at the temples. His pale blue gaze met hers. Thinking that in this strange place he might well be the butler, she swallowed back her surprise and tried hard not to stare.

"May I help you, miss?" he asked as he took in her rumpled state without a blink.

With as much composure as she could muster, she answered, "I certainly hope so. I wish to speak to Mister McAllister, please."

"This way, miss. We've been expecting you. How was the trip from Baton Rouge?"

Amanda didn't have the slightest idea what he was talking about, and decided not to ask. The size of the man held her spellbound. She silently followed him past a curving walnut staircase and along a polished hardwood hall to a set of open library doors.

The man behind the desk looked up from the papers he was studying. His dark gaze swept over her.

"Thank you, Sampson," he said, quietly dismissing the giant.

He didn't stand to greet her, and that irritated her, but the smile he gave her soothed her sensibilities and for some reason set her pulse to racing.

His hair was dark and wavy, his eyes—the color of rich coffee—were magnetic, and his smile was disarming. He had to be the most ruggedly handsome man she'd ever met.

"Are you the new girl from Baton Rouge?" he inquired, taking an inventory of her person in such a flagrant manner that she felt her face flame.

So much for good looks, she decided; they would never replace good manners. His behavior was deplorable. The headache that had developed in the swaying coach pounded and her temper flared.

"No, I am definitely not the girl from Baton Rouge," she informed him coolly. "Whatever that means."

Standing as straight and tall as possible, she tried to maintain as much dignity as she could in her dirty clothes and disheveled state.

"If you're looking for employment, we're not hiring."

Amanda stood stiffly as he looked her over again and then favored her with another heart-stopping smile. His attention seemed to linger on her bosom.

"But you've sure got everything in all the right places, lady. Leave your name and where you'll be staying and if the other girl doesn't show soon, I'll look you up."

Amanda bit her lip and counted to ten before she answered. "I'm Amanda Jefferson, and I am not looking for employment, Mister McAllister." Not waiting for his reply, she continued. "How long were you my mother's business partner?"

"Your mother! Sweet Jesus," McAllister shot to his feet. "Your lawyer could have handled this for you. Holy hell!"

Running a hand through his brown, wavy hair, he

pushed the unruly locks off his forehead. "What do you think you're doing here?"

A frown wrinkled Amanda's brow; her headache was getting worse by the minute.

"I think, Mister McAllister, that I'm here to claim my inheritance. I also think that I will have to ask you to refrain from swearing in my house. I am not accustomed to crude language, and I find yours offensive." She felt a tiny tingle of victory at his openmouthed expression of astonishment.

McAllister rounded the desk so quickly she gasped in surprise. He towered a good foot over her five-foot-two-inch frame. His wide shoulders and broad chest were emphasized by an expertly tailored gray suit.

He glared down at her, and the dark scowl on his face put the black storm clouds gathering outside to shame.

"That may very well be, but until I know you're capable of running an operation the size of this one, I'm not taking any orders from you. You got that?" On the last sentence, he jabbed a finger at her for effect.

Amanda squared her shoulders. She would not be intimidated. It was very important that she establish her place here immediately.

Pointing her own finger at him for effect, she answered, "Now you listen to me, Mister McAllister, and you listen good. I own seventy percent of my mother's property, and all of her personal possessions. Why she would sell you an interest in her home is beyond me, but thirty percent does not allow you to make the rules here. I plan to do that, but I don't wish to be unreasonable. I am prepared to buy out your share and let you be on your way. My mother may have needed you, but I assure you I do not."

Slade began to laugh. The deep rumbling sound filled the room and vibrated along her spine. He leaned casually against the desk, legs crossed at the ankles and arms folded across his chest.

Anger at his apparent disregard sprang up hot and sharp inside Amanda. How dare he laugh at her? He might be as handsome as sin with his dark wavy hair and rugged good looks, but he was also rude and insolent, and the sooner he was gone, the better. It was clear that they would never get on.

"Now see here, Mister McAllister."

"No, Miss Jefferson," he interrupted, "*you* see here. I don't think you know what kind of house this is. Someone has played you for a fool."

"Excuse me, Slade." The sultry sound of a woman's voice behind her caused Amanda to spin around and stare in shocked silence at a beautiful Spanish-looking woman in the doorway. She wore a black corset, black silk stockings, black shoes with very high heels, and a robe that was almost transparent. Her smile was wide and friendly.

"Are you the new girl from Baton Rouge?" She asked Amanda.

If one more person asked her that question, Amanda was sure she would scream. Before she could answer, Slade did.

"No, she definitely is not. Miss Jefferson, I would like to introduce you to Rose Alvarez." His gaze shifted from one woman to the other. Laughter still lurked just behind his eyes.

"Rose, I would like you to meet Amanda Jefferson, Anna Marie's daughter."

"Oh, God!" Rose clutched her robe closed with both hands.

"My sentiments exactly, Rose," Slade responded.

Amanda could tell from his expression that Slade was having a hard time keeping a straight face.

She looked from the half-dressed girl to the smirking man and back again. Realization dawned slowly. Oh, Lord! The image of the heart-shaped door knocker flashed across her mind. She swallowed her surprise, trying to keep it off her face. When she raised her gaze to McAllister's, her resolve stiffened. She wanted to smack the amused expression off his handsome face.

Well, she wasn't about to let him have the last laugh. By heaven, this was her house, whatever kind it was, and she'd be damned if she was going to allow him to make a fool of her and ruin her cover.

Extending her hand to the young woman, she said, "I'm very pleased to meet you, Rose. Do you suppose you could show me to my room? It would seem that Mister McAllister is so busy laughing out of both sides of his mouth that he hasn't the time."

"I'd be happy to, Miss Jefferson." Rose spared Slade a quick look before leading Amanda into the hall. "Your mother's rooms are upstairs. I'm afraid they are the only empty ones. Will they do?"

Amanda felt a moment's discomfort at the thought, but merely nodded and followed Rose's shapely figure up the wide front stairs. Rose stopped before a closed door.

"Thank you, Rose. I think I'd like to go in alone."

Amanda opened the door, then stopped in the doorway. She turned back to ask, "Do you suppose someone could bring my trunk over from the stage office?"

"Of course, Miss Jefferson. I'll see to it."

"And, Rose, please tell Mister McAllister that I will want to inspect the business records in the morning. Say, ten o'clock." As an afterthought, she asked, "Will the house be awake by that time?"

"The girls may not be up by then, but Cook always is, and Slade is an early riser."

Amanda couldn't help asking, "You said 'girls.' How many are there?"

"Four, counting me. Our rooms are along the other hall." In an apparent effort to offer comfort, Rose continued, "Really, Miss Jefferson, this is a nice place. We never have any trouble with the customers. Sampson sees to that. The men who come here act like gentlemen and they treat us like ladies."

"Yes, well, I'm pleased to hear it. Would you tell the other girls that I will speak with them tomorrow also—and call me Amanda, won't you? I think, under the circumstances, we can dispense with formality."

That was the understatement of the year, maybe the decade, Amanda decided as she stepped into the room and closed the door. If her head didn't hurt so much, and her heart wasn't racing so madly, and her knees didn't feel so weak, she might just find this whole situation ludicrous.

Lord, what a muddle! She didn't know how she was going to handle this latest development. She owned a . . . Heavens! She wasn't even sure what word applied here. A bordello, or a house of ill repute, or something. Her face flamed at the thoughts those words brought forth.

Well, it didn't matter what it was called. She certainly could not take part in the kind of activity that transpired in a place like this. No wonder the men in town had treated her so strangely. They thought she was a. . . . Oh, my goodness!

She had to find a suitable way out of this dilemma and get on with her work. This wasn't at all the cover she'd envisioned for herself. She managed a smile at the thought.

But questions niggled at her mind. Why hadn't Robert Commings informed her of her mother's profession? As her deceased father's partner and lifelong friend, he must have known. Why in the world would he have withheld that information? It didn't make any sense at all not to have told her. Since he hadn't wanted her to come, he could have used the fact to discourage her. She might have had second thoughts if he had—although she still would have come.

Tomorrow, she would write Washington and try to get some answers to her questions. That decided, she took a deep, steadying breath and felt a little better.

Amanda stifled a nervous giggle and glanced about her mother's sitting room. She'd told Robert once that as a woman she could go places and talk to people her male counterparts never could. That was certainly proving the case.

# 2

*Amanda entered the nearly* dark room hesitantly. The daylight beyond the window was almost gone. She found a tin of matches and lit the lamp on a table. Its light cast a rosy glow over her mother's possessions—things belonging to a woman she hardly remembered.

It was a beautiful room. A settee and two wing chairs upholstered in sea green velvet dominated the space. Small tables of rich, dark wood held ornate oil lamps. The walls were covered with a flocked cream-colored paper, and the drapes matched the upholstery. A green and cream floral carpet covered the middle of the floor.

A writing desk against the far wall caught her attention. It seemed familiar. She ran her hand across the polished wood, touched the inkwell and pen, and fingered the monogram on the heavy vellum writing paper. Tears stung her eyes. She remembered this. Anger surged up from deep within her, so strong it hurt, and she hated herself for weeping over a woman who hadn't loved her enough to keep her.

"You could have written me, Mother."

Her whispered words seemed to vibrate in the quiet room. As her fingers traced the monogram absently, a sense of having done the same thing before swept over her. Hurriedly picking up the lamp, she fled into the bedroom.

A canopy bed draped in cream silk was centered between two windows. Its matching coverlet was accented by small green pillows. The drapes and carpet matched those in the sitting room. A large dressing table with a huge mirror and an upholstered bench stood against one wall, an ornately carved armoire against the other.

The room was a breathtaking combination of color, fabric, and rich wood, blended with grace and good taste. She had been prepared to hate this place, but she couldn't quite bring forth that emotion. A shiver of disquiet ran along her spine.

After placing the lamp on the dressing table, she sat down wearily on the bench and stared at herself in the mirror. She spoke softly to her image.

"Your mother was a prostitute, and there's not one thing you can do about that except accept it. But why would she choose a life like that?"

The image in the mirror didn't have an answer.

Amanda removed her hat and pulled the pins from her hair. It fell in waves that reached the middle of her back. The lamplight turned her auburn tresses to flame and brought out the gold flecks in her wide green eyes. She picked up her mother's brush and slowly drew it through her hair.

As she watched her image through a film of tears, it changed. A woman with auburn hair and green eyes stood behind a little girl, running a silver-backed brush through the child's long red-gold curls.

"Mama." Amanda's whispered word dispelled the vision, leaving her shaken. "Oh, God!"

She covered her mouth with both hands to stifle the cry that rose unbidden from the depths of her soul. "No! Leave me alone. I don't want to remember. I just want to find the man who killed my father, and go home."

Outside the wind gusted. On shaky legs Amanda made her way across the room to peer out. A jagged streak of lightning lit up the dark sky, followed by the rumble of thunder.

A knock on the door gave her such a start that she jumped like a scared cat. Reentering the sitting room, she paused to light another lamp. "Who is it, please?"

"McAllister. I've brought your luggage up."

Amanda groaned silently. She felt emotionally drained and physically exhausted, and in no mood for another encounter with McAllister. The man had the ability to rub her the wrong way.

She opened the door and allowed him to enter, wishing that someone else was delivering her trunk. "Put it at the foot of the bed, please."

Slade moved past her and placed it where she indicated, then stood in her bedroom doorway observing her.

"I think we've gotten off on the wrong foot, Miss Jefferson," he said, then crossed the room and made himself at home on the settee.

Amanda turned to face him, one small fist planted on each hip. "I can't imagine what would give you that impression, Mister McAllister." He raised an eyebrow at that remark, but didn't interrupt as she continued. "You were quite right in assuming that I hadn't been informed as to the nature of my mother's business. I will admit that I am a bit shocked, but you will find that I am a very adaptable person, Mister McAllister. I'm sure after I have time to think this through, we can work everything out to my satisfaction. Rose did tell you I would inspect the books in the morning, didn't she?"

Slade smiled in a way she was sure was meant to be charming. She would have to be careful not to fall into that trap, she decided.

"Rose told me, but you needn't trouble yourself. I can assure you everything is in order, and you probably couldn't make heads or tails of the records anyway."

Amanda bit her lip to keep back the sharp retort that formed in her mind. He had to be the most arrogant man she'd ever met. She formed her response carefully.

"I can only guess at the kind of women you are used to dealing with, Mister McAllister. Let me assure you that I am as competent in business as the average male. I ran my father's office for the past year without difficulty."

She allowed her gaze to slide slowly over the long, well-proportioned body lounging on her settee in the same manner he had used to inspect her earlier. He was too darned handsome for her peace of mind.

"In the future, Mister McAllister, you will not make yourself at home in my rooms without first asking my permission."

Slade rose instantly, his scowl as fierce as the storm raging outside her windows.

"You've got to be the damnedest female it has ever been my misfortune to meet! Believe me, lady, I wouldn't be here if I didn't feel I owed it to your mother to help you clear up her business affairs." He went to the door and jerked it open. "You're about as friendly as a well full of rattlesnakes!" he sneered at her over his shoulder.

She addressed his back. "I didn't come here to make friends, Mister McAllister."

He turned, and the look he gave her would have frozen water. "That's a damned good thing, Miss Jefferson, because you sure as hell don't seem to have the knack for it!" The room vibrated with the sound of the door slamming shut behind him.

Outside Amanda's closed door, Slade pressed his hands against the wall and struggled to keep from going back inside and shaking some sense into that woman's pretty, arrogant head.

Which, he couldn't help having noticed, was even prettier when her hair was loose. Good God! He'd wanted to run his fingers through the long silky strands to see if it would feel as good as it looked. He must be crazy, or desperate, to even think such a thing, hc admonished himself.

Lord, but she had to be one of the most beautiful and obstinate women he'd ever met. A deadly combination if there ever was one.

Why, he wondered, did he react to her with such intensity? He couldn't allow her to become a problem. She was trouble, and he had enough of that already. He took a deep breath and exhaled slowly. Tomorrow he would show her the books to pacify her, and do whatever it took to get rid of her.

With her high-and-mighty airs, she surely wouldn't want to stay at the house for long, he figured. He was surprised that she was staying overnight. He would remind her to consider her reputation. That would put the fear of hell into Miss Prim and Proper, and an end to this foolishness.

Slade stood in the hall a moment longer, listening to the tinkling sounds of the piano and Rose's laughter drifting up from downstairs. Outside, the thunder still rumbled. He hoped, for the tenth time since the rain had begun, that the storm wouldn't keep Buck Emmerson from showing up tonight and that Buck would have the information about when the long-awaited shipment of guns would arrive.

He reached the stairway landing just as Mattie, the girl hired to help cook and clean, started up the stairs carrying a tray. "What's all that?"

"Miss Jefferson's dinner. Cook made it special." She smiled and winked a blue eye at Slade. "I volunteered to bring it up. I want to get a look at the new boss lady. Rose said she looks like her mother."

Slade decided to ignored that comment. "When you come back downstairs tell Cook to send up some hot water. I'm sure the 'boss lady,' as you so aptly put it, would like to wash up before going to bed."

He gave Mattie a playful pat on the bottom as she passed him. He was truly fond of the girl, in a fatherly way. "Then you'd better get yourself to the parlor before Roger Bennet finds himself another girl."

At the mention of Roger's name, a radiant smile lit Mattie's pixie face. "I'm not worried about that. He said I couldn't get rid of him with a stick. Slade, I've got to be the luckiest girl in the whole world."

"I'll go tell him you said that," Slade teased. "Then maybe he'll forgive you for being late."

Mattie laughed from the top of the stairs, then disappeared down the hall.

Smiling to himself, Slade continued on his way. He was happy for Mattie; she didn't belong in this kind of place. The young rancher Roger Bennet was a fine man. He seemed to understand that she was working here only because she didn't have any other choice.

Another knock on Amanda's door caused her to abandon the search through her trunk for a nightgown. She sighed in exasperation. "Who is it?"

"I'm Mattie, Miss Jefferson. Cook sent you some supper."

The word "supper" made Amanda's stomach grumble. Her last meal, at the stage stop before Three Wells, had been awful, and that had been hours ago. Opening the door, she admitted a very pretty, petite, blue-eyed blond who didn't look a day over sixteen. This young girl *couldn't* be a prostitute, Amanda thought in horror.

"Are you one of the girls here?"

Amanda asked the question even though she wasn't sure she wanted the answer.

"Yes, ma'am, but I don't work with the customers. I help cook and clean, and sometimes I play the piano. "I won't be working here much longer, though. Roger Bennet and I are getting married in three weeks. He has a small ranch south of town."

The girl's face mirrored her happiness. Amanda

sighed in relief. "That's wonderful. Where is the wedding to take place?" The girl seemed a bit uncomfortable with that question.

"Here, in the parlor." Mattie hastened to add, "Slade gave us permission. You don't mind, do you?"

"Of course not. Why would I mind?" On the contrary, Amanda said to herself, it would be a breath of clean air. "I love weddings. Is there anything I can do to help?"

Mattie's eyes lit up, and her words tumbled out. "Do you sew? The girls and I are trying to make my dress, and we aren't doing very well. I wanted a white one—you know, like brides wear at church weddings. It's silly, I know, but I've got it all cut out." Her eyes were dark with exasperation. "I'm having an awful time trying to put it together."

Amanda took the tray from the agitated girl's hands and placed it safely on a nearby table. "I guess you're in luck then, Mattie. The Sisters at the convent school I attended stressed domestic studies as well as academic ones. Sewing is something I do very well. I'll be happy to help you with your dress." She smiled. "Now would you mind if I go ahead and eat? I'm starving."

"Goodness no, I'm sorry," Mattie apologized. When she reached the door she turned to ask, "Were you planning on becoming a nun?" There was disbelief in her voice, as though the idea was too absurd to be true.

"No, Mattie, I wasn't," Amanda reassured her without going into details. "I just went to school there."

"Well, I couldn't imagine anyone as pretty as you being a nun." As though embarrassed at being so outspoken, Mattie hurried from the room, closing the door softly behind her.

It was nearly ten when Amanda tugged her nightgown over her head and turned back the covers of the large canopied bed. She felt full and clean and oh so sleepy. Slipping beneath the coverlet, she burrowed into the bed's warmth.

In the morning she would have to thank the cook for the excellent meal and McAllister for sending up the hot water. How he could have known how badly she wanted it, she didn't know.

She felt a moment's discomfort as she contemplated sleeping in her mother's bed. She couldn't help but wonder how many men had shared it with her. Lord, Amanda, she chided herself, a bed is a bed. Stop acting like a child! You have bigger problems to solve.

Amanda blew out the lamp on the bedside table, snuggled beneath the covers, and willed her body to relax. Her headache had disappeared. The faint sounds of the music from downstairs and the soft patter of rain on the roof were soothing.

As her mind drifted on the edge of sleep, she decided that sleeping in her mother's bed was a little like being held in her mother's arms . . . warm and safe.

Now where had that feeling come from?

In the dim light of early morning, Amanda quietly descended the back stairs to the kitchen. The room was big, comfortably warm, and smelled of coffee, fresh baked bread, and something else she couldn't quite identify.

The remembered aroma of cookies baking and a feeling of security flooded her at the same moment. A face from the past floated across her mind. Her eyes sought out the stoop-shouldered Negro woman at the stove and her breath caught in anticipation.

"Granny!" The word came unbidden from the depths of Amanda's memory.

The old colored woman looked surprised, then opened her arm, and Amanda rushed into them with a feeling of coming home in her heart.

"Oh, Granny!" she murmured against the woman's shoulder.

Her mind raced. She'd spent the first five years of her life in this house. She knew that because her father had told her so, but he hadn't told her about Granny. Now she remembered her. How many other memories would this house hold for her?

She held the old woman tight for a long moment, then stepped back to peer into the wrinkled face. Granny was all smiles.

"Mercy sakes, child, I didn't think you would remember me. Lord, but you're a sight for these old eyes. I never thought to see you again this side of heaven."

Amanda stepped back and allowed the woman to inspect her. Granny's eyes were bright with pleasure.

"You've grown into a mighty fine-looking woman. Your mama would be proud if she could see you." Tears welled in Granny's eyes, and she wiped them away with the corner of her white apron. "I declare, I'm turning into a watering can." She sniffed. "Come sit at the table and I'll fix you some breakfast."

Amanda sipped a cup of steaming coffee as she watched the old woman flutter about the kitchen. A plate of ham, eggs, and biscuits was soon placed before her.

"Now you eat that all, child. You're a mite too

skinny for my liking. Why, a brisk wind would likely blow you away. We got to put some meat on those bones of yours."

Amanda smiled, remembering that the sheriff had used nearly the same phrase yesterday.

Reaching across the table, she took Granny's work-roughened hand. "I want to thank you for the dinner you sent up last night. After the horrid food at the stage stops, it was just what I needed."

Granny settled into the chair across the table. "No need to thank me, child. I been dishing up meals in this kitchen for near twenty years now. I'm just glad you liked it."

A frown turned down the corners of Granny's mouth. "When I think of you coming all the way to Texas by yourself, it scares me near spitless. Why, there's outlaws and Indians and all kinds of disreputable men just waiting to pounce on a pretty little thing like you. I can't believe your papa would allow you to travel all this way alone."

Amanda shook her head sadly. "He didn't, Granny. Papa died three months ago."

"Oh, dear." Granny patted Amanda's hand. "I'm sorry, child. I didn't like the man, but he was your father, and losing him and your mama so close together has got to be a strain. And I declare, you do look a bit tuckered to me. Why don't you go back to your room and rest a while longer?"

"No." Amanda carried her empty plate to the sink, then moved to the stove to refill her cup. "I'm fine. Do you know if Mister McAllister is up?"

"Of course he is. He's always the first one down. You'll find him in the library."

Amanda was accustomed to meeting problems head-on. She believed in the motto "Confront and overcome." Carrying her cup, she went in search of McAllister.

She had been contemplating what to do with the house ever since she'd opened her eyes this morning. She considered herself an open-minded, progressive woman. The fact that she worked in her father's business had already set her apart from what society considered proper for a young lady. That didn't bother her one bit, but being the owner and operator of a brothel was going too far. She could not in good conscience accept an inheritance secured in such a manner, but she needed to remain here long enough to complete her investigation. How was she going to accomplish one without becoming a party to the other?

She found McAllister behind the desk where she'd seen him yesterday, a set of account books spread out before him. He glanced up when she entered and motioned her to the chair beside the desk.

"These are the records you wanted to see, Miss Jefferson. You'll find that I have taken out my thirty percent of the profits and placed your seventy in the bank. You need only contact them to have the funds made available to you."

Amanda set her cup on the desk and took a seat in the chair beside it. She took her time scanning the books. It appeared to be a lucrative operation. The girls each received a wage, plus a percentage of the profits. Profit sharing was a progressive idea and a point in her mother's favor. The percentage was taken out for them as an expense, before the seventy-thirty split was made. She could find nothing in the accounts that seemed out of line.

"The accounts appear to be in order, Mister McAllister, but I will need to study them at length later to better familiarize myself with the operation of the house."

McAllister picked up the account books without comment, then placed them in the top desk drawer and locked it. Amanda couldn't help but notice the "I told you so" expression on his face, and her temper sparked.

"I would like a key to the desk, please." She extended her hand, palm up.

It was a test of wills, and they both knew it. The seconds ticked away as she waited, fully expecting him not to comply. To her surprise, he carefully placed the key in her palm.

"Whatever you say, Boss Lady." His lazy grin was back.

"Does that mean you're willing to sell your share of the house to me?"

His smile faded. "No. It means that while you're here I'll abide by Anna Marie's wishes. You really don't intend to stay here, do you? I'm sure you'll find the hotel more to your liking, if for no other reason than saving your reputation."

Thinking back to yesterday, Amanda couldn't help the small smile that turned up the corners of her mouth.

"I think, Mister McAllister, that if the attitude of the men I met yesterday is any indication of that of the townspeople, the damage is already done. No respectable boardinghouse would have me, and I don't like living in hotels even if they would.

"My father allowed me to be my own person, and I've never been one to worry overmuch about what other people think of me. I don't intend to start now. I am not sure yet what I intend to do with the house, but I assure you that you will be the first to know when I do."

Slade whistled. "Well, I'll be damned. I believe I can see a little of Anna Marie in you after all." His dark, penetrating stare was disconcerting. "Still, I've got to tell you I think you're making a big mistake. The townsfolk would understand if you explained that you didn't know what kind of place this is."

"Your concern for my reputation is touching, but unnecessary. I want you to prepare a schedule for me so I can better understand the routine here. I need to know what time the house opens and closes, what kinds of liquor and food you serve, and any entertainment provided. You may include any other information you deem pertinent. It is my intention to leave the management of the house in your hands until I make a decision about what to do with it, if that meets with your approval."

Slade nodded. She went on. "I must make one thing perfectly clear: I am not for sale. I don't know how these things are handled, but I would like that made clear to the clients so when I come downstairs this evening there will not be any misunderstandings."

Slade returned her steady gaze. His mouth twisted in a wry grin. "I never thought you were. Well, maybe I did for a few minutes, when I thought you were from Baton Rouge."

His smile was wide, and remembering the encounter, Amanda warmed.

"What do you expect me to do? Take out an advertisement in the paper telling all and sundry that you're in residence, and state the restrictions? Hell, lady, you don't know what you're asking." His dark gaze swept over her in that assessing manner of his. "That would be like putting food in front of a starving man and telling him not to eat."

"Don't be absurd. I have every confidence that you will handle the matter discreetly."

"I suppose I can, but your mother would have a fit if she knew you were planning on living here. When I had Anna Marie's lawyer inform you of the inheritance, I was sure you would have a lawyer take care of the matter for you."

Amanda had known this arrangement wasn't going to meet with his approval, but she also knew this place should be an absolute well of information. She needed to move about freely. She wasn't about to stay upstairs and take a chance on missing an opportunity that might provide information about the gun shipment.

The papers she'd found in her father's files confirmed that Three Wells was the town where the money and guns her father had died for was to change hands. Somehow, she and the Hawk had to stop the guns from reaching California. The Knights of the Golden Circle wanted to make California a separate country, and were planning to supply guns to the South if it left the Union. Washington wasn't happy about either possibility.

Amanda's thoughts returned to Slade. "Nevertheless, this is my home for as long as I choose to stay, be that a day, a week, or indefinitely, Mister McAllister. And while I think of it, are you expecting a new girl? One from Baton Rouge?"

A smile spread across Slade's handsome face, and

mischief danced in his bottomless brown eyes. Amanda's heart skipped a beat.

"I am. Yesterday I thought she was here, but she won't arrive until tomorrow. I picked up a letter from her when I was at the stage office getting your trunk." The smile disappeared, and he added grudgingly, "I'm sorry about yesterday."

Amanda had decided in the early hours of this morning, as she'd lain awake contemplating her multitude of problems, to make some kind of peace with McAllister. It would not serve her purpose to be at odds with him. Discord would only impede her work. She graced him with a smile.

"So am I. Since you weren't expecting me, I suppose I shouldn't have taken exception at being mistaken for someone else. However, I will expect you, in the future, to treat all ladies, no matter their profession, with equal courtesy."

She extended her hand, and he shook it. She wasn't at all prepared for the sensations that swept through her body at his touch.

"I can live with that," he responded, releasing her hand.

"Good. I want to thank you for sending up the hot water last night. I appreciate your thoughtfulness."

"You're welcome."

He favored her with that heart-stopping smile of his. She quickly changed the subject.

"I met a young girl last night named Mattie," Amanda began. "She said she was household help."

"She is, but not for long. She's getting married in three weeks."

"I know. We talked about it yesterday. I offered to help with the sewing of her dress."

"That was kind of you." McAllister seemed genuinely pleased. "The sooner she's married the better. She doesn't belong here."

"I certainly agree with that. So why is she?"

"It's a sad story. Mattie and her father arrived in town six months ago on the stage. He was very sick. He died the next day—from a heart attack, the doc said."

"The poor thing," Amanda murmured. "Didn't she have family somewhere?"

"None, and apparently very little money. She went to every business in town, but they either didn't have work for her or were unwilling to hire a young, single girl. I was in the saloon the day she asked about work there. The owner was more than willing to use her. I brought her here and put her to work with Granny. We really did need another girl, but your mother and I talked it over and decided to keep her in the kitchen. Your mother wired a friend in Baton Rouge, and he's sending out a girl with more experience."

His concern for Mattie was touching, and it soothed Amanda's heart a little to know her mother had shared that concern.

She rose from her chair and picked up her cup from the desk. "I'm glad to hear that my mother didn't force young, unsuspecting girls into becoming prostitutes." Her words were sharp and edged with anger.

Slade came up slowly from his chair to glower down at her. "You've no right to pass judgment on someone you don't know."

Amanda's anger was fueled by years of resentment and hurt. Her voice rose. "I know she was an unmarried woman with a baby, and that she ran a brothel. Neither of those are what I'd call sterling character references."

She saw the sudden flash of anger in Slade's eyes. It sent a chill along her spine. He grabbed her arm and pushed her back into the vacant chair so quickly she didn't even have time to react.

"Now you listen to me, you little fool. I'm only going to explain this once, and only because I don't want to hear you slander your mother again. She and I talked at great length during her illness. She needed a friend, and I'm a good listener.

"When she arrived in this town she was down to her last few dollars. She had you and Granny to feed and house as well as herself. The decent folks here wouldn't give her the time of day. So she served drinks and sang in the saloon." Slade stopped and took a breath for effect. "She did not go upstairs with the customers.

"One night, shortly after she went to work there, the owner of this house tried to talk her into changing her mind about that. She kept saying no. Finally, he offered her a deal on the cut of the cards. If she got the high card, she would get the house and he would get nothing. If he won, he would give her a hundred dollars and she would give him what he wanted."

Amanda shook her head in disbelief. "Why would a sane man make such a stupid bargain?"

Slade smiled—at her lack of sophistication, she supposed.

"Sometimes, Amanda, men become obsessed with getting what they want." His dark, compelling eyes flashed with inner fire. "Sometimes it clouds their judgment." He smiled again. "Then of course, he didn't think he would lose. When he did, being a man of honor, supposedly—and maybe because twenty or so men were witnesses to the wager—he wrote out a bill of sale and turned over the key.

"Needless to say, the saloonkeeper wasn't too happy when your mother left, taking two of his girls with her." His expression was solemn. "Sometimes, Amanda, you do what you have to do, and the sooner you learn that lesson, the better."

"I don't need instruction from you, Mister McAllister," she snapped.

McAllister scowled. "I think you do. Is your life so unblemished that you think you can judge others? I doubt it. What would you do if you found yourself in your mother's situation? Or in Mattie's?"

Damnation! She had done it again. Why did she allow the man to get to her? Since he wasn't going to sell out to her, she mused with as much reason as she could muster at the moment, she had best learn to tolerate his company, and she might as well start right now.

Amanda forced a smile. "You've every right to your opinion, of course." Her voice was so sweet, she could hardly stand the sound of it. "In the future I will endeavor to keep my thoughts on this subject to myself."

Slade settled back in his chair, looking confused by her change of attitude.

"I'll see that you have all the information you requested before dinner."

"Thank you, I'll see you then." Amanda felt his eyes bore into her back as she left the room.

Returning to the kitchen, Amanda left her cup, then climbed the back stairs to her room. She retrieved her bonnet and shawl from her trunk, donned them, and picked up her reticule. The small clock on the bedside table read ten of ten. There was plenty of time to get to the stage office and back before lunch.

Slade sat behind his desk, contemplating his Amanda problem. This was no meek miss, but a determined woman. He'd paid particular attention to her eyes during their encounter, and he'd seen her check her anger and put on a cool front in an attempt to smooth out the tension between them. He had the feeling there was more to Miss Amanda than she wanted him to know.

A devilish glint lit his eyes. He could hardly wait to see what she would wear down to the parlor this evening. He chuckled out loud at the picture his mind conjured up of a dress with a neckline so high it fastened up under her chin.

# 3

*Amanda strolled slowly* along the uneven board sidewalk, trying hard not to remember her reaction to McAllister's touch. It had been strange and exciting. His smile, when it gleamed in his dark, brown eyes and he was intent on being charming, could have a devastating effect on the senses. She would have to be very careful. It would not be wise to become enamored of the man.

To turn her thoughts away from the disturbing McAllister, she stopped to peer into the store windows along the street, making a conscious decision to enjoy the morning. It was bright with sunshine, but still cool enough to be pleasant. A welcome gift left by last night's rainstorm, she supposed.

Three Wells was much larger than she'd thought yesterday. The main street was three blocks long, with two cross streets. She saw a hotel, a newspaper office, a general store, the sheriff's office, and the stage stop. There was even a dress and hat shop. It was one of the many towns along the Great Southern Overland Mail Route that owed its life to the stage company.

No one spoke to her as she made her way through town. Two women in black dresses with matching bonnets went so far as to cross the street to avoid passing close to her. She remembered the way the men she'd met yesterday had treated her. How had her mother endured this kind of rejection? Slade's words came back to her: "You do what you have to do."

Lost in thought, she failed to see Samuel Griffin step from the saloon to block her path, and nearly walked into him. Placing a hand on her arm, he stopped her.

"If I'd a-knowed yesterday that you was a fancy piece, girlie, we coulda done some business on the stage. We coulda got to know each other real good."

The image those words brought to mind made Amanda shiver with disgust. Shoving his arm away, she tried to step around him, but he wouldn't allow her to pass.

"Move out of my way, Mister Griffin. I have business elsewhere."

His good-natured grin vanished. "Bitch!" he snapped. "You think you're too good for the likes of me, don't you. Just 'cause you live at the house and make more money than the saloon girls don't make you better. A whore is a whore, girlie."

Amanda gasped at the insult.

Griffin's arm captured her waist and he pulled her hard against him. He smelled of sweat and horse and God only knew what else.

Amanda groped blindly in her reticule for the derringer she carried there. Her hand closed around the small gun just as his foul, wet mouth found hers. She gagged, and tried not to be sick as she pressed the barrel hard against his groin.

His reaction was instant. Jerking back, he locked his gaze on the gun in her hand, which was pointed at the source of his intent.

Amanda concentrated on holding her hand steady; she couldn't let him know how frightened she really was. He eyed her warily.

"Now lookie here, girlie. You got no cause to pull a gun on me. I was just trying to make a deal with you. I got money, more than most of the men that come to the house—and I'm going to have a lot more real soon. You think about that and you might change your mind."

With great effort, Amanda managed to keep her voice steady. "I don't make deals, Mister Griffin. Now kindly step aside or you're going to have a hole in you. This little gun probably won't kill you, but a bullet where I'm aiming might very well change your life drastically."

A look of pure hate crossed Griffin's face. "All right, girlie. I'll move on, but you remember this: It don't set good with me to be snubbed by the likes of you. I always get what I want, one way or the other." He turned and stepped back into the saloon.

Amanda wiped at her mouth with a shaky hand, trying to rid herself of the taste of him. Relief washed over her, making her legs weak and trembly. Good Lord, she thought, what kind of town was this?

It was a good thing she was trained in the use of

firearms. She'd never had a reason to draw her gun before; she hoped never to have to do it again, but knew she could and would if necessary.

She wondered fleetingly if she should inform the sheriff about the incident. Probably not, she figured; he'd most likely laugh her right out of his office. Why should a lady associated with the house mind being approached by a prospective customer? She might as well get used to being treated in this horrid manner, she decided. It was part of her job.

Replacing the derringer in her reticule, she continued on toward the stage office. Loud voices and laughter came from behind the swinging doors of the saloon as she passed. The patrons were undoubtedly giving Griffin a hard time about being bested by a woman. She had made herself an enemy.

Adam Griswald was behind the counter at the stage office, and she smiled at him as if his change of attitude yesterday had never happened.

"Good morning. I'd like to mail a letter." She handed him the envelope addressed to Robert Commings.

"Sure thing, miss," he replied staring at her openly.

"I'm not the new girl from Baton Rouge, if that's what you're wondering," she said. If she was going to use the house as her cover, she figured, she might as well begin acting the part right here.

His smile broadened at the remark. "I know you're not. Slade got a letter from her late yesterday. She'll be here on the afternoon stage today."

"What about the Indian trouble?" Amanda interrupted. "I got the impression from the stage driver yesterday that the stage might not be running for a while."

"Well, miss," Griswald drawled, "You can't put much faith in what Shorty says. He's apt to get overly excited when it comes to the Comanche. Now, I'm not saying they're not a threat, 'cause they are. Thing is, Shorty almost lost his hair to a band of them a few years back. So he's kind of skittish when it comes to Indians. And then it also gives him a reason to whip up the horses now and again. He likes to show off his driving skills for the ladies when he can. It's true that the Comanche are riled up again because the Rangers have been ordered to round up what's left of them and put them on reservations, but that don't necessarily mean the stage won't be in. In fact it'll probably be a little early, 'cause Shorty is making the run again today."

"You mean that horrid ride yesterday was unnecessary?"

Griswald grinned.

"Well now, miss, I wouldn't go so far as to say that. A body never knows what the Comanche might be up to."

Griswald paused for breath and changed the subject. "I was thinking," he began, "that you look a lot like your mother. She was a real nice lady. Too bad you couldn't make it here in time for the funeral. Slade took care of the whole thing. I don't much like the man, but he done her up right."

Amanda's heart skipped a beat at the thought of her mother's funeral. "I didn't know. I'll have to thank him for that."

She handed him the letter to Robert, paid the postage, and left the office. Slade must have told Mister Griswald who she was, she reasoned, because he was a lot friendlier today. She wasn't sure what to make of that. Perhaps it was because he liked her mother.

Amanda glanced toward the saloon just in time to see Samuel Griffin ride away. He was headed west. She wondered where he was going and where all the money he said he had came from. The thought that he might somehow be connected to the gunrunners crossed her mind. Surely not, she decided, but she filed the idea in the back of her mind for future consideration.

Amanda searched the street for someone she might trust to leave a message for Mister Hawkins, her contact. She had originally intended to give it to Mr. Griswald herself, but she could see he was a nosy man, and it wouldn't do to let everyone know who sent it.

A young boy playing in the alley between two buildings looked promising. For a nickel, he agreed not only to take it inside, but if he was asked, to say that a man he didn't know had paid him to deliver it. She watched from across the street to be sure he completed the assignment.

Amanda arrived back at the house just as Granny called the girls to lunch. Leaving her shawl and bonnet on the hall table, she entered the kitchen. Slade was already there.

"Did you have a nice walk?" he inquired innocently. "Meet anyone interesting?"

He knew about Griffin; Amanda was sure of it. But how? Had he followed her?

"No," she replied, "not interesting; 'disgusting' would be a more appropriate word. Were you following me?"

"Now why would I do that? I just happened to arrive at the saloon shortly after you passed. I told Griffin to get out of town and stay out. I don't think you'll have any more trouble from him or any of the other men there, but if it frightens you to walk alone, take Sampson with you."

"I will not," Amanda sputtered. "I can take care of myself; I don't need a bodyguard."

That insufferable grin of Slade's was back. God give me strength, she prayed silently.

"I took care of Griffin without any help. I'm quite capable. I told you that before."

Slade made a sound of disgust. "We take care of our ladies here, Miss Jefferson. That includes you now. Either Sampson or I will escort you whenever you leave the house. You've made yourself an enemy," he warned. "A bad one, I hear. A back-shooter, from all accounts. So don't take any unnecessary chances."

Mattie and Rose entered the kitchen, followed by Granny and two other brightly dressed women, putting an end to the conversation.

"Amanda, I'd like you to meet Jeanne," Slade said.

Amanda extended her hand to a tall, willowy woman with green eyes and hair like midnight. "I'm happy to meet you, Jeanne."

"I'm glad to meet you, too, and we're sorry about your mother."

Her words were cordial, but her green eyes were cool and speculative. Amanda decided it might be wise to be wary of her

"Thank you, Jeanne," she said. "That is kind of you."

"And this lady"—Slade put an arm around the waist of a red-haired, blue-eyed older woman and gave her a squeeze—"is Wilma. She was with your mother a long time."

The woman's beauty had faded with the years, but enough remained to make her attractive. There was a brassy tone to her hair, and she was well rounded but not fat. Just pleasingly plump, Amanda decided.

Amanda shook her hand. "I'm glad to meet you, Wilma."

Wilma's smile was warm and friendly, her voice melodious. "Mercy, girl, but you're a vision. Your mama said you'd grow up to be a looker. Lordy, I wish she could see you." She hugged Amanda and whispered, "Who knows, girl—maybe she can."

Wilma released her and went on. "We were wondering what your plans for the house are."

Amanda realized she now controlled these women's source of income and that they were worried about their futures. Slade's words—"You do what you have to do"—came back to her. These seemed like nice ladies. She did not know what events had brought them here, and she had no right to cause them pain.

"I understand your concern," she responded. "When I reach a decision, we will all sit down together and discuss it. I promise I will endeavor to be supportive and fair. For now, Mister McAllister will continue to be in charge."

Amanda gestured toward the table. "Why don't we all sit down and eat, before whatever that is that smells so good gets cold."

After lunch Amanda returned to her room. She spent almost an hour deciding what dress she should wear later, then bathed and read the information Slade had given her at lunch.

One thing was clear immediately: This was a high-class operation. It was called simply The House, and the sign outside read A SOCIAL CLUB, FOR MEMBERS ONLY—all men, of course. The list of members was impressive, and the listed fees were, to her mind, excessive to say the least; but then, she supposed, you only get what you pay for.

When Mattie came at six to tell her supper was ready, Amanda declined. Her stomach had been doing flips all afternoon.

It had taken her two hours to dress and do her hair, and now that she was ready her feet didn't seem to want to move.

The derringer strapped to the outside of her right leg just below the knee felt strange beneath her skirt, but it was impossible to tell she was wearing it. Smoothing the skirt of her emerald green taffeta dress, she left her room. A last, quick glance in the hall mirror told her she was as ready now as she was ever going to be.

She stood at the top of the stairs, her heart pounding like a scared rabbit's. The sounds of a piano and male laughter floated up from below. Drawing a deep breath, Amanda took the first step. She'd read somewhere that the first one was always the hardest, but her next one didn't seem any easier. When she reached the landing, she could see into the entry hall. Slade was looking up at her.

It was too late to change her mind now. She wasn't about to let him see how scared she was and have him laugh at her again. And even more important, she had a job to do. She gathered all the courage and dignity she possessed and descended the remaining steps.

Slade watched Amanda's progress down the stairs in openmouthed admiration. The dress she wore definitely did not reach to her chin, he observed. Hell, it barely covered her breasts!

The neckline was just low enough to be seductive,

but not indecent. The bodice fit like a second skin, and only a ruffle over each shoulder held it up. The skirt was full and made of some shiny material that shimmered with each step she took. A sparkling emerald on a gold chain nestled between the swell of her uplifted breasts. It was the only time in Slade's life that he could remember being envious of an inanimate object.

The green of the dress was a perfect color to show off her creamy complexion. It caused her auburn hair to seem more red than brown and turned her eyes a deep forest green.

Amanda's hair was piled in a mass of curls atop her head, with little wisps about her face. Small emeralds studded her ears. God in heaven, he thought, she was beautiful.

She finally reached the hall and glided toward him, her head high and her bearing regal. "Jesus," he swore under his breath. She looked like a queen ready to hold court. He had a sudden, overwhelming urge to take her back upstairs and not share her company with the men in the parlor.

He pushed that thought from his mind, then managed to close his gaping mouth before she reached him.

"You look lovely, Amanda," was all he could think to say, and felt like a complete fool.

"Thank you, Slade. Have any guests arrived?"

"Yes, several," he answered. In an attempt to cover his schoolboy embarrassment, he continued. "The girl from Baton Rouge arrived this afternoon. Her name is Lily. She won't be coming down tonight, though. I didn't want to spoil your debut." Now he was rattling on like an idiot! He clamped his mouth shut and, offering her his arm, led her through the parlor doorway.

Every head turned, every eye seeming to study the vision in emerald green. The faces of the three men in the room, all leading citizens of Three Wells, held open admiration.

"Gentlemen," Slade addressed the assembly, "this is Miss Amanda Jefferson." He led her forward to make introductions.

The first man was John Anderson, the town's only doctor. He was portly, about fifty, and studious-looking. Slade watched as Amanda extended her hand and Anderson bowed over it.

"A pleasure, Miss Jefferson."

"And this is Frank Parker, Amanda. He owns the bank."

Amanda smiled warmly at Parker. "Hello, Mister Parker."

Slade suppressed the urge to drag Parker from the room. He was young for a banker, probably not more than forty. Parker's gray gaze was fixed on Amanda with such intensity that Slade thought he just might stare a hole right through her.

"And last, but not least, we have George Hadley. George operates the mercantile." George smile was his best feature, Slade decided. He used it continually, and for some perverse reason that eluded him at the moment, Slade realized it annoyed the hell out of him.

"I'm happy to meet you, Mister Hadley. Please, gentlemen, make yourselves at home. I didn't mean to interrupt."

Amanda released Slade's arm and took a seat in a wing chair near the sofa where she could observe the entire room. This was a lot like meeting her father's business associates when they came to call, and she was relieved to find that she felt quite comfortable.

Sampson, in his dignified black suit and string tie, was on duty just inside the door. Rose, Jeanne, and Wilma were also present. Rose and the doctor were deep in conversation near the fireplace. Jeanne, in a shimmering gown of red satin, sat at a table talking to the banker. Wilma, seated at the piano, began to play, filling the room with soft, soothing music.

Amanda was amazed at how normal and relaxed everyone seemed to be, like old friends enjoying an evening together. All her apprehensions faded away, and she smiled at George Hadley when he came to sit on the sofa.

"Are you planning to stay long, Miss Jefferson?"

"I'm not sure, Mister Hadley. It will depend on a number of things. I will have to wait and see."

Amanda knew Slade was hovering protectively behind her chair. She wouldn't get much information out of anyone with him leaning over her shoulder. His continued presence at her back was making her angry. She couldn't see him there, but George could. George excused himself and went to talk to Wilma.

Two hours later, Slade stood before the parlor window staring out into another stormy night. He was utterly disgusted with himself.

Why in God's name he felt he had to play the part of Amanda's protector was beyond his understanding. He'd made a damned fool of himself tonight.

A woman who carried a derringer and could face down a known killer didn't need his protection anyway.

All he had managed to do was make her furious. She had finally told him in no uncertain terms that she didn't need his assistance.

Just then, Amanda laughed at something Frank Parker said, and Slade felt compelled to turn and stare at her across the room. The lilting sound affected him strangely. A knot formed in his stomach, and his heart beat a little faster.

She was composed, regal, and beautiful, and deep in conversation with Parker. They could be talking over business matters, Slade reminded himself. There was the account at the bank that needed to be changed.

If Frank valued his hide, Slade thought, he had better be on his best behavior. Slade had informed the gentlemen over drinks this evening, before Amanda came down, that she was only here to settle her mother's estate.

He sighed, his gaze resting on the curve of her breast. That damnable green dress she was wearing must be the cause of his discomfort, he suddenly realized. It made a man's hands itch to touch the rounded swell of her bosom, just visible above the neckline.

Lord above! The woman must be a witch, Slade said to himself, because he'd been behaving like someone possessed ever since she'd floated down those damn stairs! That's when he'd begun to think of her not only as a beautiful, desirable woman, but as his responsibility. Why the hell that was he didn't know. He didn't owe the girl anything. It was out of character for him to get involved in other people's lives. Then again, her mother had touched a similar chord in him. He'd felt like a cad, worming his way into Anna Marie's life, but it had been necessary, and as it turned out, he had been able to help the lady in the last months of her life.

He had to admit it pricked his pride some to know that the beautiful Amanda didn't need his help, and it made him madder than hell that she was completely ignoring him, when he couldn't seem to keep his eyes off her.

His mind groped for an acceptable answer to his dilemma and hit upon a new idea. Maybe she wasn't the inexperienced baby he thought she was. Maybe she knew exactly what she was doing.

Making herself unavailable would have every man in this damn town following her around. He certainly was, and he should know better. Now this was something to think about. He knew how to deal with scheming women. It soothed his pride to think of her as conniving and deceitful.

It wouldn't be hard for him to find out just what made Miss Amanda tick. He could be very persuasive when he put his mind to it. He wanted a personal response from her, and at the first opportunity, he vowed, he would damned well get one.

A glance at the clock on the mantel told him that the evening was about over. He decided to give Amanda a free hand. If she wanted to take care of herself, he would let her.

Slade walked slowly across the room and out into the hall, then glanced back. Amanda was so deeply involved with Frank Parker that he didn't think she'd even noticed his grand exit. That sure took some of the starch out of his sails.

\*     \*     \*

The customers were gone, the lamps in the parlor were extinguished, the front door was locked, and Amanda was still too furious for bed. She stood in the entry hall trying to decide which she needed most, sleep or a showdown with the damnable Slade McAllister. McAllister won.

Amanda swept down the hall like a summer storm, her emerald green skirt billowing about her. The library door was open and she went in without knocking.

"Curse you, McAllister! What were you trying to do tonight? How can I get to know these people if you keep interfering?"

Slade looked up from the papers on his desk.

"Why do you want to, Amanda?"

Amanda thought fast. What answer did she have to that?

"Those men knew my mother. I was just being polite, and it's not any of your business."

"Now, Amanda, honey, don't get so upset. I just wanted to be sure you weren't getting in over your head. I was sure a refined lady like you would appreciate my concern."

He was mocking her, she could tell by the hint of a smile he was trying to suppress.

"Don't you laugh at me, you overgrown baboon! And don't call me 'honey'! I'm twenty-three years old and I can take care of myself, thank you."

Slade's eyebrows rose in mock surprise. "As old as that? Well then, I suppose the blush on your face when you realized Doc and Rose had gone upstairs was a sign of your experience. What are you, Amanda—The innocent babe you appear to be, or someone entirely different?"

Amanda was shaken by his question. There was no way he could have guessed her real reason for being here, she told herself. So why was he questioning her? Lord, but he was sharp. She would have to be very clever to stay even one step ahead of him.

"Ohhh!" she screeched, stomping her foot in exaggerated exasperation. "You make me so mad! You're trying to change the subject, and I won't allow it. You, you . . ." She couldn't think of a word vile enough and sputtered to a stop.

Slade was grinning from ear to ear. "Well, that's better, Amanda. I much prefer your anger to that icy exterior of yours. I was beginning to think I was losing my touch. I like you best when you're all fire."

He had closed the space between them before she could move. He had to be the fastest man alive.

His mouth, when it covered hers, was as hot as he accused her of being, and the heat took her breath away. The shock allowed her just an instant to enjoy the feel of his lips against hers, before she turned her face aside.

Well, she thought, she certainly had managed to get his mind off his questions and on to something else. Shoving her hands between them, she tried to push him away. She could not dislodge him, and that fueled her fury anew.

With his hand cradling the back of her head, he brought her mouth back to his. His arm around her waist brought her body in direct contact with the hard length of his.

The kiss was long and deep and when he finally allowed her to breathe again, she was gasping.

"Let me go!" she demanded.

The warm gust of his breath tickled her ear when he answered, "Now why would I want to do that, Amanda? Surely an experienced lady like you doesn't mind being kissed. Just relax and let yourself enjoy it."

At this moment, that was exactly what Amanda feared doing. It would be so easy to learn to like his kiss. It wasn't like any she'd ever experienced before—not that there had been very many. She had found in her adult years that women as educated and as forceful as she was scared off men like the plague.

"Come on, Amanda," he crooned. "Relax." He whispered the words softly against her throat as his hands began a conquest of her body, starting fires wherever they touched. He nibbled her earlobe before blazing a path along her cheek to her mouth. Her knees felt like wax melting in the heat he was creating within her.

The word "no" swirled in her mind, but never reached her lips. Her wildly beating heart drowned out any protest, her hands ceased to push and began to cling, her mouth opened to the gentle invasion of his tongue. Then she kissed him back with such intensity it frightened her.

"Amanda," Slade groaned against her mouth.

The sound of her name, uttered by a voice thick with passion, caused a surge of self-preservation to flow through her. A strangled cry escaped her as she fought him.

"Let me go! Please."

He released her, and she stumbled back a step, panting and shaken.

"Christ, Amanda." His breathing was ragged. "If you ever kiss me like that again, don't expect me to let you go." His dark eyes blazed. "Consider yourself warned."

She trembled—whether from the fear his words instilled in her or from her own body's reaction to his, she wasn't sure. Then she whirled around and ran from the room.

Amanda stared wide-eyed into the darkness, mulling over the events of the day. The bed beneath her was soft, but did not give her comfort. The blankets were warm, but did nothing to take the chill from her body. She was far too upset to sleep, not so much over McAllister's conduct as her own.

Damnation, she railed at herself, there was something about the man that caused her to lose her perspective and clouded her judgment. Something that made her body behave in strange and disturbing ways.

A shiver of pleasure shot through her at the remembered feel of his lips against hers, of his hard body pressed against her softer one. The feeling was so intense that it scared the life out of her.

Lord in heaven, what was the matter with her anyway? She could handle men like Griffin, who made her feel nothing but revulsion, and Frank Parker, who had charm and wit, and made her feel nothing at all.

But Slade McAllister was a horse of a different color, she realized. He didn't fit into any of her carefully arranged categories. In the future she would have to be very careful to avoid being alone with him. The two of them together were like oil and water—they just didn't mix.

With effort, she pushed McAllister from her mind and concentrated on Parker. She'd learned a great deal about the town and the people in it from him tonight. Once she'd gotten McAllister to retire to the other side of the room, Frank had spoken openly to her about many things.

When she'd steered the conversation around to the coming election, she found that he wasn't fond of Lincoln or his ideas about slavery. He also didn't sympathize with the faction in California that wanted statehood. An independent California, free to govern itself, was more to his liking.

That in itself wasn't so important, as many people held these same beliefs, but the fact that he had been so frank with her was. She had been right about using the house as a means of meeting people and gathering information. It was very possible that fate had dealt her a winning hand in placing her here. She sighed. Now, if fate would only rid her of McAllister, she would be eternally grateful.

She wiggled deeper into the covers, her body beginning to relax. Tomorrow she would meet with her contact to exchange information and make plans. There was comfort in organization and planning and knowing there was at least one person you could depend on. Robert had assured her the Hawk was that and more.

Snuggling even deeper into the warmth of the big canopied bed, she took that small comfort with her, giggling at the thought of strange bedfellows.


It was nearly six the next evening when Amanda entered the hotel lobby and took an inconspicuous seat near a corner window.

She arranged the skirt of her dove gray dress with nervous fingers, touched the red rose pinned to her lapel, then folded her gloved hands tightly in her lap to stop their fluttering.

She had helped Mattie work on her wedding dress most of the afternoon to pass the time and keep her mind distracted. The dress was progressing beautifully. She wished she had something to keep her nervous hands busy now.

The grandfather clock across the hotel lobby chimed the hour, and she looked up just as the fashionably dressed McAllister stepped into the room. Her anger flared. If the man was following her again, and interfered with her meeting with the Hawk, she was going to be tempted to shoot him.

He scanned the room and found her seated in the corner. His irritation was evident as he closed the distance between them.

"Damn it, Amanda! What are you doing here? I thought you were in your room resting."

"I was," she replied coolly. "I decided I needed a change of scene and came here for dinner. Is there a law against that?"

"I guess not," he answered as his angry gaze swept over her, around the room, and then back to her. It stopped to focus on the bright red rose fastened to her lapel as a way to identify herself to Hawkins. The expression in Slade's eyes changed from anger to surprise.

His hand moved slowly to undo the button of his tan coat, allowing it to fall open. The shiny silver buckle on his leather belt glinted in the light from the window behind her. The figure of a majestic hawk, its wings spread in flight, greeted her. It took a moment for its significance to register in her mind. When it did, she stifled a shocked gasp.

"Damnation!" She didn't realize she'd uttered the oath aloud until Slade spoke.

"My sentiments exactly, Miss Jefferson. I believe I'm your dinner partner this evening."

# 4

*Slade was the Hawk. Amanda's* mind reeled with the shock of it. He was the man she would have to work side by side with if she was to solve her father's murder and recover the guns. It was a hard pill to swallow.

Slade must have realized she was having difficulty digesting this latest turn of events. He stood glaring down at her, his displeasure evident in the set of his mouth and the ice in his eyes, but said nothing.

Reaching down, he tugged her to her feet and led her into the hotel dining room. They found seats in a secluded corner and waited in silence for someone to come take their order.

Slade's penetrating stare, Amanda couldn't help but notice, hadn't left her face since he'd seated her. His expression could only be described as grim.

Amanda felt like a butterfly pinned to a mat for inspection and display. She wasn't in the least bit hungry, but she ordered a chicken dinner when the waitress came. Slade asked for steak, rare. Amanda suspected he would probably rather devour her. The waitress smiled and left.

The ice in Slade's eyes turned to fire, and Amanda tensed, waiting for an explosion that didn't come. After several long moments Slade spoke. His words were calm and controlled. "I want an explanation from you, Miss Jefferson, if that's really who you are. I want the truth, and if I don't get it, I'm going to wring your pretty little neck. Do you understand me?"

The words were whispered, but they carried the weight of a brick building, and she feared it was about to fall on her. Her only recourse was to give as good as she got.

"I understand perfectly, Mister McAllister. I'm not any more pleased with this turn of events than you are, but I don't see that we have a choice in the matter. We're both here to do a job, and the sooner we get it done, the sooner we can part company."

The waitress returned with their food, and they were silent until she left.

Amanda could tell that Slade wasn't a happy man. She knew her cool, efficient manner infuriated him and that her impersonal, professional attitude was not what he wanted from her. He'd said he liked her best when she was all fire. She had no intention of giving in to her temper and giving him what he wanted. She wanted him to see her as a competent investigator.

"Well, I'm waiting, Miss Jefferson." He scowled at her. "Begin."

Amanda swallowed the lump in her throat. "In answer to your first question, I *am* Amanda Jefferson, and my mother was Anna Marie Dupree. It's just a coincidence that I happen to be working on this assignment. Receiving the letter about the inheritance provided an excellent opportunity for a believable cover. No one will suspect me of being an agent." She smiled slightly. "You didn't."

"Only because I was expecting a man." Slade bit off the words with undisguised animosity.

"And correctly. My father was to be your contact. He was murdered three months ago while working on this case. I worked undercover for him several times, mostly at social gatherings where a woman could see and overhear things and not be suspect. I'm not a hero or a patriot, Mister McAllister, but I do want to see my father's killer brought to justice. I hope I can aid the North's cause in the process."

She paused, but he said nothing, so she went on.

"It's imperative that the Knights in California not be supplied with enough guns to make war on Mexico, or to aid the South if it should be foolish enough to withdraw from the Union. Mister Lincoln is adamant in his views against slavery, and if he is elected this country is apt to bust wide open. California's gold would be invaluable to the North. We must keep California loyal at all costs. The Knights want to make it a country separate from the Union. We must not let that happen."

Amanda watched Slade cut up his steak and fork several pieces into his mouth. She could see his mind work as he chewed. He swallowed and picked up his coffee cup, looking at her over the rim.

"I'm sure you loved your father very much, Miss

Jefferson. And I suppose that I could even believe you would put your life at risk to solve his murder. But I don't believe that Mister Lincoln's people would send a woman to do this kind of job."

"That's an intelligent observation, Mister McAllister, and just what I want others to think."

Slade pondered that a moment. "You've admitted to me that there's more to this than patriotism, Miss Jefferson. The fact that you're here for revenge just might get us both killed."

"I think you're being a bit dramatic, Mister McAllister. I hope we both live a very long time, but in this line of work we must be prepared to take our chances. You're right: I do have personal reasons. But they won't interfere with my work. I would not have been sent here if that were the case."

"I realize you think you're a professional," Slade snapped, "and the people in Washington may think so, too, but revenge clouds a person's judgment. You are inexperienced. A few Washington parties don't count for much, to my way of thinking. If we are to work together, my life might depend on you. I think you owe me a better explanation."

Amanda's temper finally overcame her. "I don't owe you anything, Mister McAllister, and I have already given you my explanation. My father worked on this case for months. He was getting too close to someone, and he was killed because he knew too much. I am going to finish the job he started and avenge his death! You can work with me or not; suit yourself. But before this is finished, someone is going to pay for murdering my father."

Slade didn't doubt it for a minute, although he certainly wasn't going to tell her so. This cool, poised woman seemed capable of doing anything she set her mind to.

Under that soft-as-silk exterior of hers, she was made of steel. Still, this mission was dangerous, and it rankled him to realize that she didn't think she needed him. He scrutinized her beautiful face, remembering the feel of her in his arms. She was a whole lot of woman.

Slade glanced around the now crowded dining room. "I think we should finish this conversation in a more private place. Since we live together, we can continue this discussion when we get home." He added the last part just to get a reaction from her.

"Why do you constantly bait me, McAllister? Am I being tested, or do you just find working with a woman distasteful?"

Slade grinned. She'd fallen into his trap nicely.

"On the contrary, Miss Jefferson, I don't find you, or women in general, in any way distasteful. I do, however, like my women warm, and willing. What would it take to warm you up again, lady?"

Amanda's stomach fluttered. The smoldering heat in Slade's velvet brown eyes made her breath catch. She'd never in her life met such an attractive man, and she didn't know how to deal with him.

She couldn't help remembering the feel of his arms around her, and his mouth on hers. She had certainly been warm enough then. She felt a blush heat her cheeks and forced her mind clear of such unladylike thoughts.

"As you know, Mister McAllister, that isn't part of my assignment or my inclination. I suggest we finish here. I'm sure when we get back to the house, we will have guests to entertain."

"Well, I suggest you enjoy your dinner. This is the only time we will dine out. If we are to work together, I think it best to remain business associates and not get socially involved."

Amanda began to eat her food, with apparent relish. In reality, she had to force down each mouthful. Some things—like pride—were hard to swallow.

It was hours later when Amanda finally donned her nightdress and slid gratefully into bed. She and Slade had talked about the assignment for over two hours after the house had closed for the night. She was bone-weary, but too wide awake to sleep.

So Slade was a Texas Ranger. She'd heard all about them in Washington. A man named Austin had organized them in 1826. They were handpicked for bravery, marksmanship, and ability with horses. They never wore uniforms, but were provided a Colt .45, a saddle, and a rifle and, it was said, were grossly underpaid. At present most of them were involved in the removal of the Comanche Indians from Texas.

She couldn't help being a bit impressed, though she'd tried hard not to let it show. Slade had mentioned a Buck Emmerson, another Ranger, who was working with him. She would meet him as soon as he came to report.

Amanda shifted her pillows to a more comfortable position.

Something else Slade had said tonight disturbed her. Buck had reported a group of men camped west of town waiting for something or someone. He was trying to work his way into the group. She wondered if they were located in the direction Samuel Griffin had taken the other day. She would have to remember to mention him to Slade.

An image of Lily Langston's face floated across her mind. The girl from Baton Rouge had been in the parlor when she and Slade returned from dinner. Lily was lovely, with brown eyes, almost black hair, and a fair, smooth complexion. A Southern belle, if there ever was one, and so young. With the girl's image in her mind, Amanda finally drifted into sleep.

Lily was seated at the kitchen table the next morning, a cup in her hand, when Amanda entered looking for coffee and breakfast. Granny was absent.

"Good morning, Lily. Did you sleep well?"

"Very well, Miss Jefferson. And you?"

"Passably well, thank you. Please, call me Amanda. We're very informal here."

"Of course, Amanda."

Amanda saw Lily glance toward the door before she continued. "I'd like to speak to you in private, if I might?"

Amanda couldn't imagine what the woman had to say. Or why it couldn't be said here.

"If it's that important, certainly. Come up to my room after breakfast. No one will disturb us there."

Lily smiled. "Good. There's pancake batter in the bowl," she said, indicating a bowl on the worktable beside the stove. "Granny went out to speak to someone about wood for the stove. The wood box wasn't filled last night as it should have been. She's madder than a wet hen."

Amanda laughed aloud. "Well then, I'd best hurry and fix myself breakfast so we can get out of here before she comes back."

Half an hour later, Amanda allowed Lily to precede her into her sitting room and closed the door.

"Please sit down, Lily." Amanda waved a hand toward the settee.

Amanda took a seat in one of the wing chairs. She was curious to find out what the woman wanted.

"What can I do for you, Lily?"

Lily took an envelope from her dress pocket and extended it toward her without a word.

Amanda removed a note from the envelope and scanned it quickly. It was in the special code she and Robert used and contained key words to indicate that Lily was legitimate. It was signed by Robert Commings. Amanda looked the young woman over, then offered her hand. "It would seem Robert thinks I need additional help. Welcome aboard, Lily."

Lily laughed softly and shook the offered hand. "I don't think he thought you needed my help as much as my company. He seemed concerned that you would feel very out of place here."

Amanda sat back in her chair with a sigh. "I must admit that I did at first, but I've adjusted. I always do. Since you're here, though, I won't mind having a confidant. Are you really the girl from Baton Rouge?" She couldn't stop the laughter that bubbled out.

"No, but I've been there. I intercepted that young woman on her way here and made it worth her while to go elsewhere. Have you made contact with the Hawk?"

"Yes." Amanda thought for a minute. "I don't think we will tell him about you just yet. You might well be my ace in the hole here. It won't hurt to have an extra pair of eyes and ears."

Amanda was quiet for a moment, at a loss as to how to approach the subject of Lily's work. She decided it would be best to be direct. "Did Slade talk to you about the type of work you are expected to do here, Lily?"

Lily smiled broadly. "Yes. Don't worry about it. It was my way of earning a living before I went to work for Robert and your father. It's a good cover. Now tell me what you've learned."

Amanda spent the next hour filling Lily in on the men who came to the house, giving special attention to Parker. She told her about Griffin and the group of men camped west of town. She didn't tell her the Hawk's identity. The fewer people who knew that, the better. They agreed to meet each morning to exchange information.

After Lily left, Amanda sat contemplating the morning's events. She decided that she really did feel safer with Lily in residence. Robert knew her better than she knew herself. She would send Robert another letter, thanking him for the kindness.

An hour later a knock on Amanda's door caused her to look up from the book she was reading. "Who is it, please?"

"Slade, Amanda. May I come in?"

"It's open."

The door swung wide, and Slade stepped just inside and waited.

Amanda smiled to herself. He undoubtedly remembered her remark about not making himself at home without an invitation. She nodded toward a chair.

"Sit down, Slade."

"Are you sure? I don't want to get thrown out again."

She favored him with a smile. "Hush up, and sit down." Sobering, she asked, "Has something happened?"

"No. I'm going to walk to the cemetery. I thought you might like to see your mother's grave and the stone I had put on it."

Amanda's heart ceased to beat for several seconds. "Confront and overcome"; the words rang inside her head. Perhaps this was what was needed to put her mother to rest in her mind. And since Slade was evidently making the offer as a friendly gesture, it wouldn't hurt her cause to join him in the walk.

"It's all right if you don't want to. Anna Marie would understand."

"No, I would like to go. Do you visit there often?"

"I go once in a while. I really was fond of her, whether you believe me or not."

Amanda walked beside Slade, her hand in the crook of his arm, wishing with every step she took that she hadn't agreed to come. She was fast becoming a coward, and all because of a woman who hadn't loved her. Such foolishness, she thought.

The graveyard lay behind the church, about a mile from the house. Large pecan trees surrounded it. Shade and sunlight dappled the ground and the markers. Birds sang sweetly, filling the air with their music.

Slade led her to a back corner and stopped before a gray polished stone. The name and dates were neatly carved.

Warring emotions rose up inside Amanda: hurt, sadness, frustration, anger, love. She swallowed the lump in her throat. The love disturbed her the most. She'd fought that feeling for her mother so long, covering it with anger, that she was shaken by the strength of it. Tears filled her eyes. She rubbed them away with her fingers.

Slade watched Amanda closely as she fought the bat-

tle within herself. His heart twisted inside him. She'd
been such a little girl when Anna Marie sent her away.
Had she felt unwanted? Unloved? He was sure she had.

He remembered his own early years. The big house
full of laughing, fighting, noisy children and his loving
parents. How would he have felt in her place?

She looked so small, so fragile, so alone. He placed
a hand on her shoulder to offer comfort. She turned
toward him. He wrapped his arms about her and
pulled her against his chest.

"Go ahead and cry, Amanda. Get it all out." Slade's
hands stroked her back. "Your mother loved you,
Amanda. She told me so. She did what she thought
was best for you. Maybe she was wrong. She lived with
that doubt, died alone with it. You both suffered." He
held Amanda tight against him as she cried softly. He
pressed his cheek against her silky auburn hair. "Let it
go, love. Let the anger and pain go. She loved you."

Amanda pulled back to look up at him, her eyes
awash with tears.

"Thank you." The words were so softly spoken he
barely heard them. "Thank you for taking care of her,
and for the stone. And for holding me."

Slade felt tears well in his own eyes. Good God, he
wasn't going to allow himself to cry. Instead he did
the thing that seemed to come most naturally: He
kissed her. It was long and deep and immensely satisfying, and it left him a little breathless.

"You're welcome." He breathed the words against
her cheek. Taking her hand, he led her back the way
they had come. When they reached the house, he
turned her toward him. She hadn't said one word on
the walk back.

"Don't come down tonight if you don't feel like it."

"Don't worry about me. I'll be fine." Amanda rose on tiptoes to kiss his cheek, then fled up the stairs.

Two hours later Amanda lay on her bed, still trying to sort out her thoughts. Why had she suddenly fallen apart? Crying, and in front of Slade. Where was her pride? Oh, yes, she remembered: She'd swallowed it along with her dinner yesterday. Slade would be sure she wasn't capable of doing her job if she didn't pull herself together.

Amanda had to admit she did feel better about her mother, and she made a decision about what to do with her mother's money: She would send it to the Sisters, where it could be put to good use. If her mother really had believed she was doing what was best for her daughter, she would not object to her money being used to help other women and children.

Amanda supposed she owed Slade. He'd somehow known she needed to come to grips with her feelings about her mother, and she mentally thanked him again for having made the effort.

Still, she would have to explain herself to him, and try to win back his confidence. She would hate doing that, but she didn't want to owe him. She had learned in the course of her life that it was best to be completely self-sufficient. There was no reason to change now.

Amanda closed her eyes and tried to rest, but the memory of Slade's holding her assailed her. The feel of his mouth on hers returned with clarity. He had called her "love" at some point; she clearly remembered that. Damnation! She didn't need this distraction.

That evening when Amanda descended the stairs, the parlor was already a busy place. The banker was deep in conversation with the lovely Lily. The good doctor was visiting Rose again. That seemed a nightly occurrence. He should marry her, Amanda thought ruefully; it would certainly be cheaper. Ah, well. Hers not to reason why.

Sampson was on duty beside the door as usual. She smiled at him as she passed. He nodded a return greeting. The man seemed to be developing a big-brother type of affection for her. Yesterday he had offered to accompany her if and when she wanted to go out, probably because he had heard about her encounter with Griffin.

Slade had told Amanda that Sampson had been devoted to her mother and had been with her for years. Perhaps he had just transferred those feelings to her. She wasn't sure what to make of him.

Not finding Slade in attendance, Amanda headed for the library. The door was closed. She raised her hand to knock, just as it swung open. The man striding out nearly knocked her off her feet. He saved her from falling by putting his arms about her.

"Well, well," he chuckled against her ear. "Are you the new girl from—"

"I am not from Baton Rouge," Amanda informed him as she wiggled out of his embrace.

"Amanda, come in," Slade called. "Buck, come back and close the door."

So this was Buck Emmerson. Amanda looked the man over. He was tall and solidly built. He smiled at her, his gray eyes lighting up. His sun-streaked blond hair and a deeply tanned face attested to a lot of time spent out of doors. She liked him immediately.

"Sorry, miss, I didn't mean no harm," he drawled.

"Lord, but you're prettier than a newborn spotted pup. Slade's going to have his hands full trying to keep the men around here away from you." He held out a chair for her and bowed from the waist.

"Have a seat, miss," he said with a wink. Amanda couldn't help but laugh at his foolishness.

"Behave yourself, Buck," Slade commanded, then said to Amanda,

"Pay him no mind. He's always full of the devil, but he's a damn good man to have on your side in a fight. I thought you were resting in your room."

"I told you I'd be fine." Turning to Buck, she extended her hand. "Hello. I'm happy to meet you."

"Charmed, Miss Amanda," he drawled, bowing over her hand instead of shaking it. "Slade said we would be working together."

He tried to bring her hand to his lips, but she pulled it back, laughing at his shenanigans.

"Sit down, Buck," she instructed. "We have business to attend to."

An hour passed as they discussed Parker and Griffin. It was decided that Amanda should continue to keep an eye on Parker. She asked Buck to look into the Griffin matter, and he slipped discreetly out the back door.

Amanda turned to Slade, intending to explain her behavior at the cemetery, but the look in his eyes stopped her cold. His mouth was set in a thin line and anger radiated from him in waves.

"What the hell do you think you're doing?" he exploded. "I give the orders around here to my men. Not you. Is that understood?"

He loomed over her. When she didn't respond, he shouted, "Is that understood?"

Amanda took a deep, steadying breath. "Be quiet, Mister McAllister, before Sampson comes running in here to rescue me." She hoped her softly spoken words would manage to carry as much weight as his shouted ones. "I understood you perfectly. A deaf man could have heard you. Tell me this," she continued in a level, controlled voice, "would you have sent Buck to check out Griffin?"

"That's immaterial. What I would have done is not under discussion here."

Amanda stood, her hands on her hips, and stared at him. "But it's relevant, and you would have. I'm not going to fight with you over who has jurisdiction here. We should be working together. I'm sorry if I stepped on your male pride—I'll be careful not to bruise it again. Good night, Mister McAllister." Turning on her heel, she marched out of the room, the library door closing with only a soft click.

Slade struck the desktop with his fist, scattering papers in all directions. Damn the woman! She wasn't even emotional enough to slam the door. He flopped back into his desk chair and, with concentrated effort, tried to analyze his reactions.

Why did she always have to be right? Sending Buck to check on Griffin was exactly what he would have done if she hadn't suggested it first. That wasn't what made him angry. Damn it to hell, it had peeved him to watch her and Buck together. Amanda had laughed at Buck's silliness and acted like they were old friends.

She never took that attitude with him. She always shut him out. By God, he was damned tired of it, and he would tell her so.

Of course, why he felt compelled to do so immediately

was beyond his reasoning. But fury propelled Slade out of the room, down the hall, and up the stairs. Throwing Amanda's sitting room door open without knocking, he saw her standing just beyond the open bedroom door. She stared at him in wide-eyed astonishment.

She'd had time to remove her dress and slips and was wearing only a thin white camisole and pantalets, sheer stockings, and low-heeled shoes.

Her quick breaths caused the camisole to tighten across her chest, making her dark nipples clearly visible. The pantalets afforded him an excellent view of her hips and thighs. The silk of her stockings gave luster to her shapely legs.

He hadn't thought he'd find her nearly undressed. Hell, he hadn't thought at all. The sight made his heart thud painfully and his groin tighten. The fact that his body was nearly out of control made him angry. He hadn't allowed any woman this much power over him since Lydia. Christ, he wouldn't in his wildest imaginings have believed another woman could ever affect him that way.

As he started slowly across the room, Amanda regained her wits and grabbed the first thing at hand, a robe, and clutched it to her breasts. "Stop right there, McAllister, or I'll scream," she threatened.

"No."

That one word, and the gleam in his eyes, shocked the daylights out of her. With pounding heart, she backed against the bed. He was in front of her now, his hands reaching out for her.

"Don't do this, McAllister. You're still angry with me. I can see that. Don't do something you'll regret."

His hands closed around her upper arms.

"You think," she said, "that because I cried all over you today, I'm a weak, pliable woman." Her voice dropped to a whisper. "I'm not. Don't make me sorry I trusted you." She looked deeply into his dark brown eyes.

"Please," she added as a single tear slid down each cheek.

Slade's anger seemed to dissipate. The hands that roughly held her fell away.

"How is it," he asked softly, "that you can defeat me at every turn with just words? You have the power to twist my guts into knots. To make me lose my temper and my reason." He brushed the tears from her cheeks with his fingertips, then kissed each eyelid closed.

"My God, Amanda."

She felt the warm puff of his breath as he sighed the words against her cheek and shivered. His arms surrounded her; the heat from his body warmed her.

"This is the only way to keep from fighting with you," he whispered. "You respond to me when I kiss you, hold you, touch you. Your mind doesn't want to, but your body craves mine."

Amanda's heart raced as his hands massaged the back of her neck, rummaged through her hair, then ran the length of her spine, fitting her softness to his hardness.

Dear God, he was right, she thought: She didn't have the will to withstand him when he was this close. She wanted the feelings he ignited within her, wanted to be even closer, wanted him to make this ache inside her go away.

Her arms moved up and crossed behind his neck, and her hands slid into his hair. The robe she'd been clutching hung between them. He jerked it away, and a second later his mouth claimed hers. His tongue slipped inside to taste her, and she shuddered.

A discreet clearing of the throat brought them both back to reality.

Amanda opened her eyes and focused them on Sampson, framed in her doorway. His usually placid face was flushed, his jaw a little too firm.

"Excuse me, Miss Amanda. May I be of assistance?"

Amanda's mouth opened to answer, but no words came out.

"I can easily remove this annoyance," he continued. "You have only to say the word."

Slade spun around, shielding Amanda with his body. "You're not needed here, Sampson."

Sampson crossed his massive arms over his chest and ignored Slade. "I await your instructions, Miss Amanda."

Amanda's mind was clear now. She had to defuse this situation before someone got hurt. That someone would surely be Slade.

"Thank you, Sampson, but I won't require any assistance. Mister McAllister was just leaving." She gave Slade a little shove toward the door and directed her next words to his back. "Weren't you, Slade?"

Slade didn't look at her as he stalked across the room. Sampson moved aside to allow him to pass.

Amanda scooped up her robe and slipped it on as she followed Slade to the door. Placing a hand on Sampson's arm, she said, "Thank you, Sampson. I won't require anything further tonight. Please go to bed."

Sampson bowed formally and left the room, closing the door quietly. Amanda leaned her back against it for support. God in heaven, she didn't know whether to laugh or cry.

Across the hall Slade sat on the edge of his bed, a glass of whiskey in his unsteady hand. Every time he closed his eyes, he saw Sampson framed in Amanda's doorway. He wasn't really afraid of the man, but Sampson could intimidate a person. Lord, he thought, nobody in his right mind would want that man for an enemy. Slade liked the dignified old coot, but his protective attitude toward Amanda seemed to be growing. That might become a problem.

He took a fortifying gulp of the liquor and felt better. His Amanda problem seemed to grow in intensity daily. But how could he explain his actions to Sampson when he didn't understand them himself?

Stretching his tired body out on the bed, he sighed in frustration. He might not understand his feelings for Amanda, but he was damned well going to have to do a better job of controlling them.

# 5

Amanda's pale lavender gown swished about her ankles as she paced her sitting room, awaiting Lily's arrival. She probably wouldn't have anything of importance to report yet, but her visit would occupy Amanda's mind, which at the moment was behaving in a most contrary manner, by repeatedly returning to the previous night's events.

Truth to tell, she didn't relish the idea of facing either Sampson or Slade and was hiding in her room until this bout of cowardice passed.

After opening the door to Lily's knock, she offered the young woman a seat. "Well, Lily, how did your first night go?"

"Nothing very eventful to report, I'm afraid. I think Mister Parker found me attractive, and since he controls

most of the money in town something useful might
come from a friendship there."

"I thought much the same thing when I met him,"
Amanda agreed.

"Who was the nice-looking man you ran into in the
hall?" Lily asked. "I was leaving the parlor, and saw
him nearly knock you off your feet."

"A friend of Mister McAllister's. He was passing
through town and stopped to visit a few minutes."

Amanda didn't want to give away Buck's true identity any more than she did Slade's. What Lily didn't
know, she couldn't disclose. It wasn't that Amanda
didn't trust her; she just didn't know Lily's strengths
and weaknesses yet, and until she did, she would have
to be extra careful.

Lily excused herself moments later, and Amanda
returned to her pacing. Lord, but she hated idleness.
What she needed was something constructive to do.

Leaving her room, she descended the back stairs to
the kitchen and found Granny up to her elbows in
bread dough.

"May I help, Granny?"

"I'd love for you to, Missy. It would be like old times."

In a sudden flash of memory, Amanda recalled a
small girl standing on a kitchen chair beside the colored woman, pleading to be allowed to handle the
dough. A feeling of loss nearly swamped her.

"Yes, it would," she replied softly.

Tying an apron around her waist to protect her
dress, Amanda began to knead and shape the soft
dough. Within minutes there was flour not only on her
hands, her cheek, and the tip of her nose, but in her hair
as well.

She looked up from her work to find Granny laughing at her.

"You always did make a mess of this, girl. I'm glad to see growing up hasn't changed you much."

They placed the dough in pans and set them on the back of the cookstove to rise.

Amanda brushed the flour from her hands. It felt good to be a part of something as basic as making bread, to work and laugh with Granny, to remember the time long ago when she was happy here. She cut each of them a large chunk of apple pie left over from supper the previous night, while Granny poured two cups of coffee. Then they took seats at the kitchen table.

Amanda placed a hand over Granny's. "Thank you for letting me help."

Tears formed in the old woman's eyes. "It was like having my little girl back again. Land sakes, but I've missed you."

Granny wiped at her eyes with a corner of her apron, and with great effort struggled from her chair.

It occurred to Amanda then just how old Granny must be. She would lose her again in a few years. It made Amanda sad. The cost of her mother's decision to abandon her to the nuns was greater than Amanda had believed. And if she hadn't come West, she would not have even remembered Granny. The thought was too painful to dwell on.

Granny added wood to the stove in preparation for the baking, and Amanda noted the overflowing wood box.

"I see you've solved your wood problem. Did you give the boy a good talking to?"

Granny dug her fists into her hips. "I did, though I

can't say as I blame the boy much. Mister Parker offered him a dollar to deliver a message out of town. That's as much as we pay him for a week."

"It must have been important if he paid that kind of money," Amanda said, trying to hide her surprise. "Did the boy say who the message was for?"

"Not no one particular, just a bunch of men camped outside of town. I told the boy I understood his needing to make extra money, but to try and let me know when he wasn't going to be here."

Amanda's mind whirled. The banker might somehow be connected to the men waiting to take delivery of the guns. Did Buck or Slade know that?

She rushed from the kitchen to the library, and stopped a bit breathless before Slade's desk.

Slade looked up from the paper he was studying. He couldn't keep the look of amusement off his face. Amanda was a mess, an enchanting mess. Flour dusted her auburn hair, clung to her cheek and the tip of her nose. The print apron around her waist was covered with it.

"Have you been playing in the kitchen, Miss Amanda?" Slade asked, barely suppressing a laugh.

"Yes," she snapped. The infuriating man *would* have to comment on her disheveled state, she thought ruefully.

"I was helping Granny make bread. Now stop trying to be funny and listen. This might be important." She swiped at her face, trying to brush away the flour that was smeared there.

Slade chuckled, and she glared at him impatiently.

"Granny told me the boy who does the chores was late yesterday because he ran an errand for Frank Parker. It seems he took a message to the group of men Buck suspects are waiting for the guns. What do you make of that?"

The smile disappeared from Slade's face. "Well now, that is something to chew on." He was silent for a moment, then asked, "Do you ride, Amanda?"

"Of course I ride. Why?"

"Buck stays in a deserted cabin about three miles past the church. It's off the regular trail, so nobody goes there. I think we should talk to him about this. If he isn't there we can leave a message for him to contact us.

"It'll take me five minutes to saddle a couple of horses. Do you think you can get out of that flour and into something you can ride in by then?"

Amanda shot him an exasperated look. "Not funny, McAllister."

Five minutes later, dressed in a brown split riding skirt, tan shirtwaist, brown wide-brimmed hat, and soft leather boots, Amanda mounted the horse Slade had saddled for her.

Slade smiled approvingly at her as she rode beside him down the road that led to the church. She was thankful she'd had the sense to practice riding astride when she'd learned she would be coming West. She had received some odd looks from the stable hands then, but Slade's apparent appreciation of her ability to ride in this unladylike fashion made it worth it.

They rode swiftly past the church, then into a wooded area along a shallow, rock-strewn creek. Slade urged his horse into the water, and Amanda's followed. About a half mile downstream they exited the creek and continued on, following a faint path toward a line of low, rolling hills.

The horses picked their way carefully along the

narrow, rocky trail for about an hour before it curved behind one of the low hills to reveal a cabin tucked in a grove of trees. Slade halted his horse and Amanda brought her mount abreast of his.

"It looks deserted from here. Are you sure this is the place, Slade?"

"That's the way it's supposed to look, Amanda. Otherwise it wouldn't make a very good hiding place, now would it?"

Amanda noted the agitation in Slade's voice and decided not to press the issue.

As they rode closer, it did indeed appear as though no one was home. Reaching the edge of the trees, Slade slid from the saddle. "Stay here, Amanda. Buck should have seen us by now, and acknowledged us. He either isn't here or something is very wrong. I'm going to have a look around."

Amanda watched Slade move cautiously toward the cabin, pause outside to listen, then push open the door, which was slightly ajar, and disappear inside.

Slade took a quick look at the empty room. An overturned chair, a tin cup in a puddle of what looked like spilled coffee, and a trail of what appeared to be blood led to the door. He touched a drop and his finger came away rust-colored and sticky. "Damn!"

When Slade returned to Amanda, his face was lined with worry. "We've got trouble. You might as well get down and give the horse a rest while I check this out."

Slade moved away and Amanda dismounted. Deciding to have her own look around, she walked to the cabin. A quick glance inside told her Slade was right. Her heart hammered in her chest. Please God, don't let anything have happened to Buck, she prayed silently.

Going in search of Slade, she found him crouched beneath a tree examining hoofprints in the soft earth. She knelt beside him and he pointed to the prints.

"See, a horse and rider stopped here. The horse waited and the rider went in the direction of the cabin. And there—he indicated other prints—"the rider returned. These prints match the others. See, the heels of the boots make the same pattern, only these prints are deeper. He was carrying something heavy, and he put it on his horse. See how much deeper the hoofprints are here?"

"You think someone took Buck away, don't you."

"Looks like it, but I hope I'm wrong."

Slade walked in ever-widening circles among the trees, searching for other prints. A hoofprint and a broken branch gave him the rider's direction.

"You lead the horses, Amanda. I'll track on foot until we determine a trail."

They intermittently walked and rode. The trail was harder to follow once they left the soft ground beneath the trees and encountered the hard rocky earth of the plain. Every time they lost the trail Slade would dismount and walk in circles until he found it again. He was like a hound with his nose to the ground. He hadn't voiced his worries, but Amanda knew they were the same as hers: Buck was somewhere out there, probably hurt and bleeding. They were his only hope.

The afternoon sun was hot. Sweat trickled between Amanda's breasts and her bottom was saddle-sore, but she didn't voice her complaints. Slade was undoubtedly as tired and hungry as she.

They were nearing another line of low hills. Slade seemed doubly cautious now. It was as if he could sense something she couldn't.

The trail ended at the base of a hill strewn with boulders and brush. Slade dismounted and, holding up his arms, helped Amanda out of the saddle. He steadied her until she could stand alone.

"How are you doing?" he asked with a wary grin.

"I've been better," she admitted. "But I'll be fine. What do we do now?"

"We keep looking. You go that way along the base of the hill and I'll take this direction. If you find any kind of sign, anything you think out of the ordinary, call out. And be careful."

Amanda carefully inspected the ground and the rocky face of the hill for about a hundred yards. She almost missed seeing the low opening at the base of an outcropping of rock because it was obscured by brush.

"Slade, over here!"

"What is it?" he asked, a bit breathless from running to see what she might have discovered.

"I'm not sure. Look there." She indicated the dark opening behind the brush. On hands and knees, they peered into the dim, shallow cave. In the faint light Amanda saw what appeared to be a body.

"Oh, Slade," she whispered.

Slade crawled in and grasped the form, then pulled it out with him.

Amanda looked down at Buck and gasped in shock. There was blood on his clothes and face and in his hair. His eyes were closed, his hands and feet securely bound.

"Oh, my God! Is he dead?"

Slade felt Buck's neck for a pulse. "He's alive, but only God knows for how long."

Amanda let out the breath she'd been holding. As

Slade cut the ropes that bound Buck's feet and hands, Amanda examined his head for injuries. Several cuts, which had undoubtedly bled profusely, didn't appear to be dangerous. The numerous bumps, however, were a different story. He seemed to have been struck several times with something hard and blunt. Large swollen knots attested to that.

She helped Slade move Buck to the shade of the nearest tree, one of the few growing along the base of the hill. Then they laid him on a saddle blanket they'd hastily grabbed off her horse.

With water from her canteen and a piece of cloth torn from her chemise, Amanda bathed Buck's cuts and washed the blood from his face.

In order to obtain the needed cloth, she had turned her back to Slade when he went to care for the horses, slipped off her shirt, removed her chemise, and then struggled back into her shirt again. The thin, lacy scrap of cotton wasn't much, but it was all she had.

Folding another piece, she wet it and placed the compress on Buck's forehead, but didn't know what else to do. She watched as Slade finished unsaddling the horses and returned to her side.

"He needs a doctor, Slade, but I don't think we should move him. I don't know what else to do for him." She bit her bottom lip to stop its trembling, and her eyes sought his. "He can't die. Tell me what to do."

"You're right, he can't be moved. All we can do is keep him quiet, guard against shock, and wait. Head injuries are tricky." Slade checked Buck's body for broken bones and found none. "Get the other saddle blanket, Amanda. If he chills we can cover him with it."

Amanda ran to fetch it, glad for something to do.

The sun was sinking rapidly, and soon the night's chill would be upon them. Returning with the blanket, she asked Slade, "Do you think it's safe to make a fire?"

"I don't see why not. The Comanche haven't been sighted anywhere near here, and the person who did this certainly didn't stick around to get caught."

With a nod, Amanda silently agreed, then went in search of wood. When she had collected every twig and branch in sight and piled it beneath the tree where Buck lay, she cleared an area and made a circle with rocks to contain the fire. It would be close enough to Buck to provide some warmth. When the fire was burning brightly, she returned to sit next to Slade, who kept a silent watch beside his friend.

Amanda eyed the setting sun. It had turned the sky shades of purple and rose. It would be a beautiful sight to behold, she mused wistfully, if either she or Slade had the peace of mind to contemplate it. Instead she thought of the fast-approaching night and the chill it would bring.

She watched Slade tear off and moisten another scrap of her rapidly shrinking chemise and place it to Buck's lips.

A smile touched his mouth as he fingered a bit of lace that dangled from the cloth. His gaze went to her shirt-front. "It was kind of you to donate this. Thank you."

Amanda felt the heat of a blush rising to her cheeks, but she refused to acknowledge it. "What else can I do?" she asked, feeling the need to contribute something more than a flimsy bit of cloth to Buck's care.

"Nothing now, though you might try to rest while you can. It's going to get cold soon and we have only the blankets covering Buck." With his free arm, Slade pulled her close. "You'll be warmer here."

Amanda snuggled against his side and placed her head against his shoulder. She hadn't intended to sleep, but the rigors of the day had exhausted her, and the warmth of Slade's body and the security of his arm lulled her into peaceful slumber.

Amanda woke to the sound of Slade's voice calling her name as he gently shook her.

"What is it?" she asked, instantly alert.

"It's Buck—he's chilling. Build up the fire."

She hurried to do Slade's bidding as he tucked the blankets tighter around Buck's shaking body.

Amanda added wood to the fire, still wishing she could do more. Lord, she wondered, how could this dry, desertlike land be so hot in the daytime and so cold at night?

She watched Buck's body shake beneath the covers, and realized they had to do something to get him warm or he would surely die from shock. An idea formed in her mind.

"Slade." She touched his arm. "I have an idea."

Minutes later, with Buck sandwiched between them, their arms locked around his still shaking form, and the blanket edges tucked tightly beneath them, they warmed Buck with their body heat. Slowly—it seemed to Amanda to take forever—the chills subsided and Buck's breathing became normal.

Amanda relaxed a little then. The tension and fear had left her body drained. Slade's hand found hers, and he caressed its back with his fingers. "Sleep, Amanda," he whispered to her across Buck's chest. "It will be morning soon."

Amanda didn't think she could sleep, but she closed her eyes anyway and tried to relax.

Amanda was pulled from restless slumber by a sound she didn't immediately recognize—a kind of low, dry moaning.

Opening her eyes, she found that the sun had already crested the hills to the east and that it was god-awful hot beneath the blankets that covered her.

The moan came again, very close to her ear. Her sleep-fogged mind didn't seem to want to function. She turned her head to locate the sound and came face-to-face with Buck Emmerson, bringing yesterday's events back into sharp focus. Buck's gray eyes were full of pain and confusion.

"Amanda," he croaked. "I sure as hell wish I could remember how we got in this position." He tried to grin, but was defeated in the attempt by another groan of pain that twisted his mouth in a grimace.

"Oh, Buck!" she cried as she flung off the blankets and righted herself. "You're awake! Thank God."

She looked around for Slade. He was not in camp, and neither were the horses, but the saddles still lay on the ground beside the tree. He couldn't have gone far, she reasoned.

Returning her attention to Buck, she found his eyes closed again, and her heart plummeted.

"Buck, please open your eyes," she begged. Placing a hand to his forehead, she peered into his face.

He opened one eye.

"Amanda, sweet." His voice was a dry whisper. "I feel like I've been kicked in the head by my horse and the light hurts my eyes something fierce, but for you I'll try."

His other eye popped open, and Amanda's laughter echoed in the quiet morning air.

Slade, leading the two horses, broke through the brush.

"What the hell are you laughing about!" he exclaimed, breaking into a trot. He found Amanda wetting Buck's lips with a lacy scrap of cotton. Buck's tongue licked up the moisture.

"He's conscious, Slade."

Buck raised a hand to his head. "Amanda, sweet, don't shout. My head is killing me."

"All right," she whispered in his ear. "Now hush, and don't move around so much."

Slade was all smiles. "How long has he been awake?"

"Only a few minutes. He seems quite lucid. He knows who I am, and who he is, but he doesn't seem to remember how he got here. I was so excited about his being awake I didn't think to question him. Where have you been?"

"I woke early and went to have a look around. There's a tiny spring seeping out of the hillside a quarter of a mile to the west. I came back and got the horses. You were sleeping so soundly I didn't want to disturb you."

Slade squatted beside Amanda. "Glad to have you with us again, Buck. How do you feel?"

"Like hell," Buck complained. "Where am I?'

"About ten miles south of the cabin," Slade answered. "Do you remember what happened?"

Buck rubbed his head and squinted his eyes against the pain. "The last thing I remember is sitting at the table having a cup of coffee. It was early, just after daybreak. What happened?"

"Best we can figure, someone sneaked up on you and hit you on the head, probably with the butt of his gun, tied your hands and feet, and slung you across his horse. He stuffed you in a shallow cave out here where no one was ever likely to find you, and left you to die. You got any idea who hates you that much?"

"Plenty of people," Buck admitted with a hint of a grin, "but not around here. Hell, I don't know. My head hurts too much to think straight."

"Well, don't worry about it. Let's just concentrate on getting you out of here and back to someplace comfortable. Do you think you can sit up?"

With Amanda and Slade's help, he managed. Slade pushed a saddle behind him for support and Amanda placed a wet cloth across his eyes. They left him that way to rest a while.

Slade grabbed Amanda's arm and tugged her out of Buck's hearing. "We'll have to go slow. Buck's willing, but I don't think he can sit a horse yet." His hand slid down her arm to grasp her fingers. With his other hand, he pushed back her hair, tucking a loose strand behind her ear.

"I know you're tired and hungry. I'm going to scout around and see if I can scare us up something to eat. I'll try not to be gone too long."

Amanda watched Slade pick up his rifle and walk away with long-legged strides. Then she turned her attention to building up the fire.

When she checked on Buck, she found him sleeping. His body jerked slightly at the sound of rifle shots but he didn't wake.

A few minutes later Slade arrived with two rabbits, cleaned and ready to spit and hang over the fire.

The aroma from the roasting meat made Amanda's mouth water. When it was done, Slade offered her a piece and she ate it slowly, savoring each bite, then washed it down with a drink from her nearly empty canteen.

She braced her back against the tree, thankful for its meager shade now that the sun had warmed the cool morning air, and closed her eyes.

Lounging against his saddle, Slade closed his eyes too, allowing the image of Amanda—her clothes rumpled, her hair in disarray—to linger in his mind. Miss Amanda was turning out to be one hell of a woman. She hadn't swooned or gotten hysterical at the sight of Buck's blood. She'd behaved in a calm, efficient, and dependable manner. The word "beautiful" popped into his head. Yes, that too, he admitted to himself. And soft, so damned soft. Christ, why couldn't he stop remembering the feel of her in his arms, and the passion that had flared between them in her bedroom?

If Sampson hadn't interrupted them, he might have made a grievous error. Hell, no "might" about it. He would have allowed lust to rule not only his body, but his mind as well. Amanda wasn't a woman you could make love to and then walk away from. She would expect commitment, and rightly so. Only he couldn't give it.

He'd been that route before. A picture of Lydia, with her golden hair, blue eyes, and supple body, swam in his head. Lovely, lying Lydia. He had given her his love, his trust, and his name, only to be betrayed. Never again would he leave himself open to that kind of hurt.

The sounds of Amanda's movements chased the ghosts from Slade's mind. He lay, eyes closed, listening to her move about the camp, then to the quiet that told him she had left it. Probably to answer nature's call, he speculated with a small smile.

Moments later, when she hadn't returned, he sat up and looked around the camp. Damn fool woman. Just when he'd decided she was sensible, she had to do something stupid, like wander away from camp.

He eyed the ground where she'd been sitting. Her canteen was gone. Coming to his feet with a groan of disgust, he untied the horses. If he was going to follow her to the spring, he might as well water them again and save himself another trip.

"Fool woman," he muttered. Didn't she know this country was full of rattlesnakes and scorpions?"

Amanda knelt beside a shallow, rocky depression and filled her canteen. It was no more than a four-by-six-foot puddle, but its cool water was a godsend in this arid place. She drank from her cupped hand, then splashed her face.

Lord, but that felt good, she thought. Unbuttoning the top two buttons on her shirt, she scooped up another handful of water and splashed it on her neck, allowing it to trickle through her fingers and down between her breasts.

Amanda turned at the sound of breaking brush behind her to see Slade and the horses come crashing into the small clearing. The scowl on his face gave her pause. They hadn't had an argument in twenty-four hours. She had a gut feeling that the lull was about to end.

"Damn it, Amanda! Don't you have sense enough not to wander away from camp? Christ, woman, all

the animals for miles around come here for water, and
you don't even have a gun to protect yourself."

"As you can see"—she motioned with an arm at the
quiet surroundings—"I am perfectly safe. The only animal I've encountered was a rabbit trying to hide beneath
that bush. I'd hardly call that life-threatening."

Slade wasn't the least bit eager to tear his gaze
from Amanda's wet, half-open shirt to look at the
bush she was indicating, but he did anyway.

"I made plenty of noise getting here," she continued. "I'm sure the animals are as afraid of me as I am
of them."

She planted her hands on her hips and didn't try to
hide the exasperation in her voice. "You didn't need to
follow me."

She was, Slade decided, oblivious of the tantalizing
sight she presented.

"I didn't," he lied, attempting unsuccessfully to
keep his gaze from returning to her clinging shirt.
"The horses needed water." Even to himself his voice
sounded strained.

Realizing something was amiss, Amanda looked
down at her shirtfront and gasped, "Oh my!" She
whirled away from him, giving him her back.

His laughter made her angry and she had to resist
the urge to turn around and smack him. "Don't you
laugh at me, you despicable man! You should have
more manners than to disturb a lady at her bath."

"I don't recall ladies taking baths with their clothes
on. But it's an interesting idea. I hope it becomes
popular."

Slade teased her because he knew that if he began
to take seriously the tantalizing sight of her hardened

nipples beneath the almost transparent shirt, he'd do exactly what he'd promised himself he wouldn't.

As Amanda fled past him without another word, he resisted the urge to reach out for her. He watered the horses instead, then followed her.

She hurried along the path, acutely aware of his presence behind her as she trudged toward camp. Lord, he was a hateful man. She berated herself for having allowed her body to betray her. Gritting her teeth in frustration, she entered the camp, his mocking laughter still ringing in her ears.

# 6

"*Buck, what in the world* do you think you're doing?"

Thoughts of Slade vanished from Amanda's mind at the sight of Buck tottering about the camp. She rushed forward to steady him by putting her arm around his waist.

He grinned down at her. "If I'd known I'd get this kind of help, I'd have waited."

"You are an incorrigible flirt, Buck Emmerson. Now sit down before you fall down." Her tone of her voice left no room for argument.

Buck sat.

Amanda examined her shirtfront. It had dried enough not to be indecent.

"Just what did you think to accomplish by stumbling around the camp?"

"When I woke to find myself deserted, I thought to

get myself a piece of that leftover rabbit. It's no wonder I stumble—I'm weak from hunger."

The look Buck gave her was designed to gain her sympathy. She ignored it, but she did tear off a piece of the cold meat and hand it to him, hoping it wouldn't make him sick.

"Soup," she informed him, "would be better."

"Do you have any?"

"You know I don't."

"Then this will have to do." He took a small bite and chewed excessively, then favored her with another boyish smile. "I feel stronger already."

Slade led the horses into camp and hobbled them, then came to squat beside Buck. He watched intently as Buck took several small bites of rabbit. Amanda thought Slade probably had the same reservations about Buck's diet that she did.

"You seem to be a good deal better, my friend. There's still a lot of daylight left. Do you think you can ride? We could make the cabin by dark."

"I'm game if you two are. My mama always said I was hardheaded, so this little bump"—he winced as he fingered the back of his head—"shouldn't be a problem." He threw the rabbit bone away. "Where the devil did you both go to, anyway?"

Amanda's gaze caught Slade's, and she felt heat rise to her cheeks. Slade managed to look innocent.

Buck chuckled. "Never mind—I don't want to know."

Amanda turned away and began to gather their few possessions while Slade readied the horses.

The trip back to the cabin was uneventful, and Slade was grateful they had made it safely.

The sun was only an orange glimmer on the western

horizon when they entered the woods surrounding the rickety structure and stopped. Slade's arms ached from holding Buck in front of him atop the horse. He already regretted his decision to move him. Slade had had to give up the reins and allow Amanda to lead his horse, thereby freeing his hands to better support his half-conscious friend.

Amanda was speaking to him only when absolutely necessary. The encounter at the spring was evidently still as fresh in her mind—as it was in his.

"Would you have a look around and see if it's safe to use the cabin, Amanda?"

With a nod, she slid from her horse and moved away. "Be careful," he called softly after her as she disappeared through the trees.

Amanda approached the cabin cautiously, alert for signs of danger. Darkness was rapidly descending, throwing the clearing into shadow. Standing on tiptoes, she peered through the front window. The room was dark, quiet, and deserted.

As she turned away, she hit the solid wall of a man's chest and froze in fear. The black coat and white shirt seemed familiar, but she couldn't stop the scream that had worked its way up from her throat.

A large hand gently covered her mouth before she could utter a sound, and another grasped her arm. Her gaze slowly rose to the man's face. Sampson loomed above her, his countenance quite grim. She sagged against him in relief.

Setting her away from himself he asked, "Are you hurt, Miss Amanda?"

She finally found her voice, and stammered, "No . . . no . . . What are you doing here?"

His stony expression returned. "I might well ask you that question, miss. When you didn't return yesterday, we thought the worst. Cook is quite beside herself. I had the devil's own time finding this place, I might add. Where is McAllister? If you've come to harm, I'm going to break that man in half."

Amanda, having regained some of her shaken composure during his speech, quickly reassured him. "That won't be necessary—I'm fine. It's Buck Emmerson who's hurt." She headed for the woods. "Come on."

It was darker now within the stand of trees that sheltered Slade and Buck. "Slade? Slade, where are you?" Amanda called softly, not quite sure of her directions.

"Here, Amanda."

She followed the sound of Slade's voice, with Sampson close on her heels.

"I've brought help," she told Slade breathlessly when she reached his side, momentarily forgetting her vow never to speak to him again.

Slade could just barely make out Sampson's bulk in the near dark. "I don't know how you managed to find this place, Sampson, but I'm damned glad you did."

Amanda knew Slade couldn't see Sampson's face clearly, and that he might not be so "damned glad" if he could see the glower on it.

Slade went ahead of her into the cabin to light the lamp. Sampson carried Buck in, and she helped to get him settled on the narrow bed fastened to the back wall. Buck's face was ash gray and etched with pain. "Sorry to be such a nuisance," he mumbled before closing his eyes.

Suddenly, Slade was at Amanda's side. Sampson gave him a hard look and moved away.

Worry creased Slade's brow. "We can't put Buck back

on the horse in his condition. Damn it to hell! I wanted
to get him to The House under the cover of darkness."

Slade gave a tired sigh as he gazed down at Buck. "I
gave this situation considerable thought on the ride
here. We're going to have to keep Buck hidden.
Whoever did this thinks he's dead. We're going to
have to see that Buck does nothing to dispel that
notion until we find the person responsible." Slade
tucked the blankets tighter around his partner.

Amanda put a hand to Buck's brow. "No fever.
That's a good sign, I think, but he needs rest and
quiet. If we could only get him home, I'm sure Lily
will look after him. She and I have talked at length,
and I think she can be trusted to keep this a secret.
Being new, she has no steady customers. If anyone
should inquire about her, I will simply say she is indisposed. No gentleman would delve further than that."

"Miss Amanda," Sampson spoke up from the seat
he'd taken at the table. "It may be that I can assist you.
There's a buckboard and horses hidden behind the
cabin; that's how I got here. We could use it to trans-
port Mr. Emmerson to The House, if you think he
wouldn't suffer any further injury from the rough ride."

Amanda looked questioningly at Slade.

"I think that just might be the answer to my prayers,
Sampson. I'll help you bring it around," he said.

The expression in Sampson's eyes when his gaze
fell on Slade was hostile. "No thank you, Mister
McAllister. I can handle the job myself."

Slade watched in quiet contemplation as Sampson
left the room. Turning to Amanda, he asked, "What
the hell's the matter with him? He looks like he wants
my head on a platter."

Amanda tried hard to keep the amusement from her voice. "I believe he thinks that my honor may have been tarnished. After all, we did spend the night together." She smothered a giggle at Slade's look of amazement. "Shall I tell him we slept under the same blanket?"

Slade nearly exploded. "This is not a laughing matter, Amanda. And you keep your mouth shut about where we slept! I'll talk to the man. I'm sure he'll be reasonable."

Amanda would have liked more time to taunt Slade. He deserved to be made uncomfortable after his despicable behavior at the spring, she told herself, but the sound of the buckboard being brought to the door interrupted them.

Buck was carefully wrapped in a blanket and lifted into the wagon by Sampson. Amanda rode in the wagon with Buck cradling his head in her lap.

It was well past midnight when she crossed the dark kitchen and crept up the back stairs. She tapped lightly on Lily's door. She heard a muffled "Who's there?"

"It's Amanda, Lily," she answered softly.

A moment later the door opened. Lily peered at her in the faint light cast by the single sconce in the hall.

"My goodness, Amanda, where have you been? I've been worried sick." She stepped back, allowing Amanda to enter.

Amanda sighed. "It would take too long to explain, Lily. I'll tell you later. Right now I have a favor to ask."

Lily finished lighting the oil lamp on her bedside table and turned toward her. "I'll do whatever I can."

"Thank you. I knew you would. The man you saw

run into me outside the library has been hurt. Whoever did it believes he is dead. We need someplace to hide him, because we want the person responsible to continue to think that. I told Slade we could trust you."

Footsteps in the hall alerted them to the arrival of Buck supported by Slade and Sampson. They laid him on Lily's bed and she immediately began the task of removing his boots. Even in his weakened state, he managed to flirt.

"I must have died and gone to heaven," he mumbled. "You look like an angel."

Lily smiled down at him from the foot of the bed, his boots in her hand. "Thank you, sir," she countered. "I'll try to make your stay pleasant."

Sampson touched Amanda's arm. "You had best get some rest, Miss Amanda. I'm sure Miss Lily and I can take care of things here."

Amanda did indeed see the wisdom of that. She felt dead on her feet.

Slade steered her out of the room and closed the door behind them to shut away Sampson's frown. Amanda allowed him to guide her to her door, where he stopped and studied her face in the dim light.

She suspected there were dark smudges of fatigue beneath her eyes and that her hair was a mess. Slade brushed a strand of it from her cheek. His fingers lingered there for several seconds before he touched her mouth ever so lightly with his.

Amanda trembled beneath the soft persuasion of his mouth. It took all the will she possessed not to respond. She found she desperately wanted the kiss to go on, but Slade broke the contact.

"Thank you for helping Buck," he whispered. "Sleep well, Amanda."

Crossing the hall, he opened a door and stepped inside, closing it behind him.

It was only then Amanda realized that Slade McAllister's room was directly across from hers.


Amanda slept till noon of the following day and awakened feeling rested but still sore from the hours spent in the saddle and from sleeping on the ground. Her grumbling stomach reminded her that she was hungry, and a glance in the mirror above her dressing table informed her that she was much in need of a bath. She was certain a long hot soak in the claw-footed tub in the room off the kitchen would help to ease her aches.

Mattie and Granny were busy making apple pies when she entered the kitchen in search of lunch. Neither questioned her absence, so she supposed that either Slade or Sampson had explained it somehow. Both smiled in welcome.

"If you're hungry, child, there's chicken and dumplings simmering in the pot. And the coffee's hot. Help yourself."

Amanda filled her plate and cup and took a seat at the table. The dumplings were light enough to melt in her mouth, and the chicken was tender and delicious. Between bites she questioned Mattie on the progress of her wedding dress.

"Lily helped me yesterday. We got the lace sleeves set in and the lace and pearls sewn to the bodice. It looks so elegant, I can hardly wait till it's all together and I can try it on." Expectation lit her young face.

Amanda smiled at the girl's enthusiasm and assured

her that as soon as she could get a bath and they could finish the pies, she would be happy to help out.

"It will only take a couple hours to baste the skirt on for a fitting," she told Mattie.

"Oh, thank you!" Mattie exclaimed.

Granny smiled approvingly at Amanda. It was good to be home, Amanda thought. She felt content and safe for the first time in two days. Amanda was amazed at how quickly she had come to think of this unusual place as home.

Her father's house had never been that. His staff consisted of hired help who were always polite when she spent time there between school terms, and his work kept him away most of the time. It had been a safe place, a beautiful place . . . and a lonely place. It had never been her home.

The afternoon passed in a blur of activity.

The shimmering white dress, when Mattie finally got to slip it on, was lovely. Its long, lacy sleeves buttoned at the wrists, and the satin bodice, with its lace and pearl trim, clung to Mattie's small breasts like a caress.

Mattie's eyes grew round as she stood before the mirror, staring at her image. Amanda was afraid her young friend was going to cry.

"Oh, Amanda! It's so beautiful. How can I ever thank you enough for all your help? You've been so kind to me." Her voice caught and tears filled her blue eyes. "I wish Roger could see it."

"Hush." Amanda gave the girl an affectionate hug. "The dress is indeed lovely, but it's you that makes it beautiful. Now, hop out of it so we can finish the seams, and don't you dare sneak Roger up here for a peek at it. You know he isn't supposed to see it before the wedding. It's bad luck." She smiled at Mattie. "You'll take his breath away when you come down the stairs in this."

Amanda left Mattie's room two hours later, with eyestrain and fingertips that were sore from holding a needle too long, but also with a sense of satisfaction. The dress was nearly complete, and it felt good to watch it take shape beneath her hands.

The hall was deserted, and Amanda's mind went back to the night before, when she and Slade had said good night in the quiet of early dawn. The remembered brush of Slade's lips on hers caused a ripple of pleasure to course through her. The feeling both frightened and delighted her.

She had been kissed a few times by the men who'd escorted her to Washington parties, but none of those kisses had caused the wild sensations that plagued her body when Slade's lips touched hers.

She must try harder not to respond to him, she cautioned herself. He had warned her about where that would lead.

Pushing these disturbing thoughts from her mind, Amanda paused outside Lily's door. She wondered how Buck was progressing, and decided to inquire.

She tapped lightly on the door, then waited. There was a muffled reply, which she took for consent, and she opened the door.

Lily sat perched on the edge of a chair next to the bed, straightening her skirts. One of the buttons that ran in a row down the front of her bodice was undone. Her cheeks were flushed pink.

Buck's long, lean body was stretched out on the rumpled bed. A look that Amanda suspected was satisfaction adorned his face. He appeared, Amanda decided, very much improved.

Lily's blush deepened, and Buck had the presence of mind to look innocent. It didn't fool Amanda.

"Sorry," she murmured. "I thought you said to come in. I hope I didn't interrupt anything . . . urgent."

"Amanda, sweet." Buck smiled widely. "It's not anything that can't be brought up again later."

Amanda blushed at the comment, and Buck's amused laughter filled the room.

"I think if you're well enough for frivolity," Amanda said lightly, "you might be well enough to be moved to a room of your own."

"No!"

The word came simultaneously from Buck and Lily.

"Well." Amanda raised an eyebrow and smiled sweetly. "In that case, suit yourselves. I just stopped by to see if you're improving. Apparently you are."

"He's doing well enough," Lily assured her.

Amanda wasn't sure if Lily was speaking of his health. "Yes, well, I'm glad to hear that, I think." She left the room, closing the door quietly behind her.

Standing alone in the hall, Amanda suppressed a nervous giggle and wondered if she would ever get accustomed to the earthiness of this house and the people in it.

The sound of footsteps on the stairs brought her out of her contemplation. Slade came to a halt before her.

"How's Buck doing?"

"I believe he's back to normal."

Slade raised a hand to knock and Amanda caught it. "I don't think they wish to be disturbed." She couldn't stop the blush that warmed her cheeks.

"I see," Slade drawled. "Ah, Amanda," he teased. "A body might think you're not as worldly as you would have it appear."

Amanda remained silent, refusing to be drawn in. Slade moved closer.

"Are you, my little dove?" He whispered the last words against her ear and then slid a hand behind her neck to turn her head so his mouth had access to hers.

The kiss was long and deep, and she tried desperately not to respond as her world began to spin. She must not let him know to what extent his caresses affected her, she told herself.

Strange sensations spiraled inside her at the touch of his tongue against her lips. It traced the curve of her mouth, seeking entrance. She fought the overpowering urge to grant him access, but she was drowning in a sea of feelings so intense they seemed to take her will away.

Slade's voice penetrated the delicious fog that filled her mind. "Open your mouth, Amanda. Let me taste you."

His seductive plea triggered her already spinning senses, and her lips parted of their own accord.

His tongue darted in to search the warmth of her mouth. To tease and taunt until she could resist no longer and she allowed her tongue to duel with his.

A wildness swept through her; yearnings she didn't understand assailed her. Her body instinctively sought greater contact with his, and she arched against him.

Slade's arms encircled her, pressing her tightly to his long, hard length.

Amanda's arms wound about his neck; her hands delved into the silk of his hair. She was past coherent thought, lost in the feelings and sensations he invoked in her. Her breath came in short, almost painful, gasps.

"My sweet Amanda." Slade's words came out as a groan against her neck. "Now see what you made me do." His arms released her, but his body had her pinned against the wall.

Free of his mouth, Amanda's senses cleared enough to allow a small measure of reason to return. "You can't blame this on me. You started it. Now let me go."

Slade took a step back from her to peer into her upturned face. "I know, love." His voice held genuine regret. "I told you not to tempt me again, and you've been a good girl. But you're a fire in my blood, little dove.

"I promised myself I wouldn't kiss you again, that I would strive to be as professional as you are, that we would be just business associates. I seem to have regressed." Slade sighed and moved away, allowing Amanda her freedom.

"Never mind," he reassured her with a rueful laugh, "I'll attempt to control myself. But it would be so much easier if you didn't have such an adorable little mouth."

Amanda had always considered her mouth a trifle too wide to be considered pretty, so what was she to say to that? She hadn't the slightest idea, and kept silent as she tried to regain the rest of her composure.

She felt flushed and warm and confused under Slade's gaze. Why did her body continue to betray her like this? She was sure Slade was now very much aware that she wasn't indifferent to his kisses. Her chin came up in defiance. She met his gaze steadily, not allowing herself to flinch under his scrutiny.

A flare of compassion and understanding touched

Slade's eyes. "Don't fret, Amanda. If it's any consola-
tion to you, I'll tell you that I don't understand this
attraction either. Perhaps we will have time to explore
it further when our work here is done."

"Perhaps," she agreed softly. The word hung in the
air between them for several seconds, as a promise of
things to come.

"I was looking for you, before I was so pleasantly
sidetracked, to tell you that I've just spoken to a man
from town. He told me a body was found behind the
saloon this morning. He said the man's name was
Griffin."

"Samuel Griffin?" Amanda gasped.

"Yes, it would seem so. Come downstairs so we can
talk in private."

Amanda hesitated, glancing toward Lily's closed
door.

Slade seemed to read her thoughts, "Lily can take
care of herself, Amanda. She doesn't need you."

"But it was my idea to put Buck in there."

"And any ideas they've gotten since then are their
own. I'm sure Lily will take excellent care of him."
Slade grabbed her hand and pulled her along the hall.
"Now, come on."

# 7

*An hour later Amanda lay* sprawled on her bed, contemplating her next move. Slade didn't have much information on Griffin's death. Damnation! She swore at the silent room in exasperation. What was she going to do now that her most promising lead was dead?

She'd been so sure Griffin would lead her to the person masterminding the gunrunning here in Three Wells. Her father had been so close to uncovering the man's identity, maybe even knew it. Oh, Papa, if only you'd left us more information, she lamented silently.

Amanda sighed, flopped over onto her back, and stared at the canopy overhead. What part did Frank Parker play in all of this? Slade said he'd found nothing incriminating when he had him checked out. From her own conversations with Parker she knew his loyalties were with the South. But that by itself didn't make the man a thief and a murderer.

Still, Parker would bear watching. Tonight, if he came to the house she would seek him out. Since Buck was laid up, and Slade didn't seem inclined to check any futher on Parker, perhaps she could learn something that would tie him in.

Amanda dressed that evening with great care. Her gown was a shimmering blue satin, severe in cut and unadorned, and the only one left that she hadn't already worn downstairs. She hoped the style would flatter her slim body and make her look more attractive.

She coiled her hair atop her head to enhance the planes and angles of her face, giving her what she hoped was an innocent appeal. A gold locket on a thin chain was her only jewelry. Amanda did not consider herself a vain person, but she had worn this ensemble before and knew it suited her well.

It was dark outside when she descended the stairs. The parlor was occupied by Jeanne, in conversation with Doctor Anderson; Wilma, speaking with a new man Amanda didn't know; and, as luck would have it, Frank Parker, seated alone on the settee with a drink in his hand.

Sampson stood at his post inside the door. He greeted her formally.

"Good evening, Miss Amanda. I trust you had a good day."

"Very good, Sampson. Thank you," she replied, and moved past him to speak to Frank. "Good evening, Mister Parker." The smile she gave him was designed to melt ice.

He came to his feet and helped seat her, then returned to his place on the settee. "You look lovely, as always, Miss Jefferson. I missed seeing your beautiful face the past two nights. Sampson said you were indisposed. Nothing serious, I hope."

"Nothing to worry about, Mister Parker." She smiled sweetly. "I'm prone to headaches. They are a bother, and nothing seems to help except a bed and a dark room. I thank you for your concern."

Parker captured her hand. He brought it to his lips and kissed the palm. "If you would allow it, I would be happy to show you more than concern." He folded her fingers over the kiss and released her hand. "Think about it, please."

"I will," Amanda promised. Then she quickly glanced around the room to see if anyone had noticed the exchange.

Sampson's scowl assured her that he had. He made a move toward her, and she stopped him with a warning look and a tiny shake of her head. He remained where he was, but kept his attention focused on her.

Amanda continued to smile warmly at Frank. "It's too bad about Mister Griffin. I didn't like the man personally, but I didn't wish him dead. I suppose I could have identified him, had I been asked."

"No need for a lady to perform that unpleasant task, my dear. Don't disturb yourself about the man, Miss Jefferson. I've taken care of the matter."

Amanda thought the man protested too much, but let it pass.

"Griffin arrived on the same stage I did. I wonder what his business was here," she inquired carefully. "During our last conversation he told me he had a good deal of money and that he was going to get more. How do you suppose he intended to do that?"

Frank's eyes, which had been openly admiring her,

suddenly turned cold. He masked the look instantly, and if Amanda had not been studying him intently she would have missed it.

"He was probably just a lot of talk. Drifters usually are," he answered lightly.

"But I heard he had an account at your bank. It seems strange that a drifter would put his money in a bank."

The coldness returned to Frank's eyes momentarily and went away again just as quickly, but not before Amanda saw it. She was convinced that her questions were hitting a sensitive spot.

She had been so involved in her conversation with Frank that she'd failed to notice Slade's entrance. He frowned at her now from across the room.

Frank saw him also, and commented, "Your partner doesn't seem overly happy to find you in my company, Amanda. I wonder why that is."

Damn the man. McAllister was interfering with her work again. Between him and Sampson, she could hardly make a move without being observed.

"Don't let him disturb you, Mister Parker. He is a bit protective of me, but he is only my business partner."

Despite her reassurances, Frank excused himself and moved away to speak with Jeanne, and Amanda lost the opportunity to question him further.

She sighed in frustration and decided to call it a night. It was apparent that there was now nothing to be gained by her presence here, and no point in another confrontation with Slade. The man could be as stubborn as a mule.

Tension had gathered at the back of her neck and she felt the beginnings of a headache that would indeed require a dark room and a cold cloth. Perhaps after a good, long rest she would have another plan to put into action.

At some point during the long restless night, Amanda made a decision to take matters into her own hands. With Buck laid up, what other choice did she really have?

The sky was a dull gray when she slipped quietly out the kitchen door into the predawn chill. She was again dressed in her riding skirt and a tan shirt. Shivering, she wished she'd worn a jacket.

Making her way to the barn, Amanda quickly found the stall that housed the mare she'd ridden before.

"How you doing, pretty girl?" she crooned softly to the horse as she rubbed the mare's nose and scratched behind her ears before giving her the apple she'd picked up on her way through the kitchen.

Once the horse was saddled, Amanda led the mare around the house and out of sight before mounting. She skirted the town and then headed for the spot where the group of men Buck had been watching were camped. It wasn't hard to find. She heard horses nicker and smelled their campfire long before she was close enough to be discovered.

She tied the mare out of sight in a stand of pecan trees and silently approached the camp on foot, using the trees for cover. A small creek, its water murmuring pleasantly over a stony bottom, ran among them.

Lying facedown on the crest of a small rise, Amanda watched the camp come alive. Soon, five men were sitting around the campfire. The smell of coffee and food filled the air, reminding her that she had missed breakfast.

A sound on the road below drew Amanda's attention, and that of the camp. Frank Parker rode into the clearing and slid from the saddle. Snatches of the conversation taking place floated up to Amanda. "About noon . . . two wagons . . . be ready to ride . . . be back . . . money." Parker remounted and headed back the way he had come. The whole conversation had taken only minutes.

Amanda congratulated herself on her good luck— she was in the right place at the right time. She was sure the guns were being delivered today, and they would not have known if she hadn't taken the initiative. Wouldn't Slade be surprised with that news!

Amanda backed slowly off the rise and was about to turn when a large hand clamped over her mouth. An arm like a steel band encircled her chest, pinning her arms to her sides. She was pulled up, her back pressed against a solid chest. Her heart beat frantically, and fear coursed through her veins.

She squirmed and kicked. The heel of her boot struck a leg and she heard her captor grunt in pain. She bit at the hand covering her mouth, without effect. Her struggle was to no avail; a superior strength pushed her forward, away from the camp, along the bank of the creek, and into the trees where her horse was hidden. A raspy whisper near her ear cautioned her to be quiet.

Amanda didn't make a sound. She wasn't a complete fool—she knew it was far better to contend with one captor than with five. She was being held none too gently, but she wasn't really being hurt. And something about the man's body against which her own was molded seemed familiar.

Of course it was familiar, she suddenly realized. She'd been held against it before on several occasions. With renewed vigor, Amanda again began to struggle, managing to land a few well-placed kicks to the shins, and felt a small tingle of victory at the man's low cry of pain.

When they reached her mare, she was released and shoved toward her horse.

"Be quiet and get on," the voice commanded.

She spun around to face a very angry Slade McAllister.

"You silly little fool," he gritted out. "What are you trying to do, get yourself killed?"

Amanda could not remember ever being so angry. Well, perhaps she had been, once before—and that had been Slade's fault too. Words failed her as she tried to quell the need to retaliate. Finally she managed to sputter, "I am trying to do my job. What are you trying to do? Scare me to death?"

They glared at each other for a long moment.

"You can't handle these men, Amanda. I can. You can help, however. I want you to ride to the house. Tell Buck what's happening, and that I need him out here."

"But Buck's in hiding. Do you think it's safe now?"

"I don't know, but I need his help. We do what we have to do. I talked to him this morning, and we decided to chance it. If you really want to help me, Amanda, do as you're told."

Amanda knew Slade was right, but it galled her to have to admit it, so she didn't.

"All right, I'll send him out," Amanda finally said sharply as she swung into the saddle. This was not the time or place for a confrontation with McAllister.

Guiding her mare carefully through the trees, Amanda gained the road well away from the camp and urged her horse into a gallop. As she flew along the road toward home, she made herself a promise to get even with McAllister for his high-handed treatment of her, at a time and place of her choosing.

Thirty minutes later, Amanda knocked lightly on Lily's door.

"Who is it?"

"Amanda, Lily. May I come in?"

"Of course."

Amanda found Buck and Lily sitting cross-legged on the bed playing gin rummy. Buck grinned at her like a possum feasting on a pile of ripe persimmons, and wiggled his bare toes.

"Don't you two ever get out of bed?" Amanda asked without thinking, then wished she hadn't.

"Not if I can help it," Buck said with a wink.

Getting right to the problem at hand, Amanda filled them in on the events of the morning. Buck assured them both that he was fit enough to ride despite, as he termed it, one hell of a headache.

Amanda watched him pull on his socks and shove his feet into well-worn boots. She considered asking to ride with him, but decided against it. Even if she could talk Buck into it, Slade would just send her back. As soon as Buck closed the bedroom door, Amanda turned to Lily.

"Slade McAllister makes me so mad I could spit! There are five men out at that camp, so I know he and Buck could use some help. But will he trust me? No, of course not! I'm only a woman—what possible use could I be? Well, if he thinks I'm going to sit here and twiddle my thumbs, he's got another think coming. I'm at least going to keep an eye on them."

"You're not going anywhere without me," Lily informed her stubbornly. "If Buck needs help, I want to be there to give it."

"All right. Change into something you can ride in. I'm going to get a couple of rifles and ammunition from the gun case in the library and some food and water from the kitchen. Meet me in the barn as soon as you can."

The sun was high and hot by the time Amanda and Lily reached the stand of pecans beside the creek. Leaving the horses tied there, they crept up the rise to spy on the camp.

Two canvas-covered wagons now occupied a large portion of the clearing. As they watched, two men took their places on the wagon seats and the three remaining men mounted their horses and accompanied the wagons from the clearing onto the road.

"What are we going to do?" Lily whispered. "We can't just let them get away."

"I guess that's all we can do. Where is Slade anyway? The man's never around when you want him,"

Amanda wouldn't allow herself to ponder the possibility that something had happened to him.

She watched the wagons disappear down the road in a cloud of dust. There were times when being a woman was so frustrating. She couldn't just stand here and do nothing, she decided.

Her decision made, she turned to Lily. "Let's get to the horses. We can at least keep the wagons in sight until I can think what to do."

They collected their horses, then checked the camp and the surrounding area. There was no sign of Buck or Slade.

Amanda hadn't had any experience in trailing

anything, but common sense and self-preservation told
her to stay as far back as possible while still keeping the
wagons in sight. Three hours later, she realized they had
circled the town. From their vantage point a mile away,
she and Lily watched the wagons leave the road and disappear into a grove of oak trees in an area that seemed
familiar. Recognition came to Amanda in a rush.

"The cabin Buck used is in that stand of trees, Lily.
I'm sure this is the road Sampson took to get there by
buckboard. How can they know about it, and where
the devil are Buck and Slade?"

Amanda was nearly frantic with worry. She knew
Slade well enough to know he wouldn't abandon a job
of his own free will.

Had Frank Parker come back and caught them
snooping? She was torn between going in search of
Buck and Slade and staying to watch the guns. She
decided the latter was all she could really do; even
with Lily's help, they were no match for five armed
men. Lord, what a muddle, she thought.

"You stay with the horses, Lily, while I have a look
around. There's no sense in both of us being caught. If
I don't come back in an hour, you ride out of here and
get the sheriff."

"All right, I will. But you be careful."

Amanda worked her way through the trees and
brush until she could see the cabin. She dared not go
closer. The wagons were in the yard. The horses had
been unhitched. It looked as if the men planned to be
there for a while.

She was conscious of every sound around her—the
rustle of the breeze in the oaks, the scampering of a
small animal through the brush, and the pounding of her

heart in her ears as fear raced along her veins. What was she going to do? She wished fervently for the aggravating, but reassuring, presence of Slade McAllister.

It was disturbing to realize that in the short length of time she'd been here, she had come to depend on him.

McAllister, where are you? If you've gone and got yourself hurt, I'm going to wring your neck!

She pushed her hat back off her forehead and wiped her perspiring brow with the back of her hand. Lord, it was hot.

A man emerged from the cabin. He threw the contents of a coffeepot onto the ground and rinsed it with water from his canteen, then returned inside.

It looked like they were settling in. Amanda decided to go back to Lily so she wouldn't worry and to eat something while she had the chance. She had a feeling it was going to be a long night.

Lily was leaning against one of the towering oaks, her rifle cradled in the crook of her arm. Amanda called softly to her so as not to scare her.

"It's me, Lily."

"Thank goodness. I was about to go crazy with worry." Lily leaned the rifle against the tree and gave Amanda a hug. "I was so afraid you wouldn't make it back."

"Hello, ladies. Fancy meeting you here."

A voice from behind gave Amanda such a start she nearly screamed. The suppressed sound came out a squeak. She turned to find Samuel Griffin standing not ten feet away, his gun pointed at her chest. He didn't look the least bit dead.

Lily reached for her rifle, but was stopped by a rough command.

"I wouldn't do that if I were you. It would be a shame to have to put a hole in such a pretty little thing. I can think of a lot better uses for you."

While Griffin was momentarily occupied with Lily, Amanda used her fingertips to work her skirt up. She'd managed to retrieve the derringer strapped to her thigh just as Griffin's eyes shifted back to her.

"Oh, no you don't. Not this time. Toss that little peashooter on the ground or your friend is going to be a long time dead. That would be a real waste." A sneer twisted his mouth. "Then there would be just you for me and the five men at the cabin to share. I'm going to be first, and when I'm done with you there won't be much left for them to enjoy. We don't want to disappoint the boys, do we? Throw the gun on the ground. Now!"

# 8

Amanda did as she was told, reminding herself that she must not panic. She had to remain calm, and wait for Griffin to make a mistake. If she could keep him talking, perhaps she could delay their being taken to the cabin. Their chances were better here.

"You're supposed to be dead. Frank Parker identified your body."

"Did he?" Griffin smirked as he carefully picked up Amanda's little gun. "How convenient for me. No one will suspect a dead man of taking two women and a shipment of guns to California, will they. Frank can be very accommodating when he's paid enough for his services. That's more than I can say of you. You could have been nice to me when I asked you. Now it's too late." He directed a malicious smile at Amanda. "I told you I always get what I want."

A movement in the trees behind Griffin caught Amanda's attention. Her heart thudded in anticipation and fright. Was it Slade or Buck, or one of Griffin's men? Whoever it was moved like a shadow. She was sure Griffin was totally unaware that they were no longer alone.

Concentrating on keeping her face free of emotion, she tried to keep Griffin talking. She made herself smile at him.

"Yes, I remember you saying that. I should have paid more attention to you. It seems I've underestimated your abilities, Mister Griffin. Please, won't you put the gun away? It makes me nervous."

Griffin's grin was ugly. "Does it really? Well, that's just too damn bad. I seem to recall a gun in your hand, and where you had it pointed made me plenty nervous, too. I guess that makes us about even."

The shadow stepped from between the trees, and Sampson moved toward Griffin with the silent grace and agility of a mountain lion. Keeping her face passive as Sampson slowly closed the distance between them was the hardest thing Amanda had ever done.

Fighting the urge to look at Lily, Amanda said to Griffin, "Yes, I guess it does."

The butt of Sampson's gun struck Griffin behind the ear with a sickening thud. Amanda's hand flew to her mouth to stop the scream that rose in her throat. She heard a hiss of air as Lily let out the breath she'd been holding. Griffin crumpled to the ground in front of her.

"Miss Amanda, Miss Lily." Sampson dipped his head toward them in formal greeting. "You seem to have a knack for getting yourself into unpleasant situations."

Sampson bent and retrieved Griffin's gun, which

he tucked into his coat pocket. "Where is Mister McAllister?"

"I don't know, Sampson. Trying to find him is one of the reasons I'm here. Why are you here?"

Sampson seemed a bit put out by Amanda's question.

"To keep an eye on you, of course. I saw you and Miss Lily leaving. I couldn't allow the two of you to go gallivanting about the countryside unchaperoned. Really, Miss Amanda, you're going to have to be more careful."

It was a gentle reprimand, but Amanda detected a hint of anger beneath the softly spoken words.

Sampson nudged Griffin with the toe of a well-polished boot. "Who is this man? And why was he holding a gun on you?"

Amanda filled Sampson in on the events of the day as he bound and gagged Griffin. If he was surprised at her working for Lincoln's men, he didn't show it.

"As I see it, Miss Amanda, you must stop the men from leaving the cabin with the guns. If you would allow me to assist you, I think we can accomplish that without too much difficulty. This is how I suggest we proceed."

Sampson's plan placed Lily, with her rifle, to the left of the cabin, and Amanda, with her rifle, to the right. Sampson himself moved silently to a position near the shed that sheltered the horses.

Several long minutes passed before the cabin door opened and the man who had washed the coffeepot stepped out. He headed for the shed. Just as he reached it, Sampson's hand clapped over the man's mouth. The man was jerked off his feet and dragged out of sight. He hadn't uttered a sound.

Fifteen minutes later, another man emerged from the cabin and walked toward the shed. "Jess," he called out. "What the hell's taking you so long? Just 'cause you're losing your butt at poker don't mean you can hold up the game until your luck changes." He reached the shed. "Jess, damn it, answer me!"

His words were cut off by Sampson's hand, and he too was dragged away.

Two down and three to go, Amanda told herself, tasting fear as she waited and thinking it a wonder the men inside the cabin couldn't hear her heart thudding.

When the door opened again, the three remaining men stepped out, their guns drawn. Amanda waited until they moved away from the door, so they couldn't duck back inside, before she called out. "Throw your guns down—you're surrounded!" Her voice sounded strong and confident, but her knees were shaking.

"Sounds like a woman to me, boys," observed the tallest of the three men. Then, he had the audacity to laugh. "Now don't that beat all. I ain't surrendering my gun to no female. You want it, lady, you come and get it."

Sampson reinforced Amanda's order from his position near the shed. "You heard the lady, gentlemen. I suggest you do as you're told."

From her place of concealment, Lily fired a warning shot into the dirt in front of the tall man.

All three men made a dive for the nearest of the two wagons.

As Amanda debated her next move, Slade surprised her by moving stealthily behind the men crouched near the wagon. The gun in his hand glinted in the orange rays of the setting sun. He cocked the hammer of his six-gun. The sound vibrated in the early evening quiet.

"I suggest the three of you put your guns on the ground, careful-like, and turn around real slow. Like the lady said, you're surrounded."

The tall man, who seemed to be the leader, hesitated.

"Don't even think about it," Slade cautioned, his voice edged with steel.

The three men tossed down their guns.

Amanda had watched the scene unfold with mixed feelings. On the one hand, she had wanted the chance to take care of this on her own; to prove to herself and McAllister that she was competent. On the other, she had to admit that she had never been so glad to see anyone in her life. She felt shaky with relief. Gathering her composure about her, she marched toward the wagon, where Slade and Sampson were tying up the men.

"Where the devil have you been, McAllister? You're never around when I need you."

He flashed her a confident, cocky smile. "Looks to me like I made it just in time."

What answer did she have to that? He had. So she ignored his glib reply and dispatched Sampson and Lily to get Griffin and their horses. She silently leveled her rifle at the three prisoners while Slade finished tying the last man's hands.

She and Slade worked efficiently together. She had to admit they made a good team, even if he did constantly ruffle her feathers.

The first part of her assignment was done—the stolen guns had been recovered. The second half was yet to begin. And as much as she hated the idea, she was going to need Slade's help in getting the guns to Fort Worth for shipment north.

Amanda glanced over at Slade. His jaw was set and his eyes were determined as he tested the ropes that bound the outlaws' hands.

Her heart skipped a beat as she studied his unshaven cheek and the smooth, competent movements of his hands. She remembered the feel of those hands on her body.

Amanda forced the disturbing thoughts away. She was letting her feelings about McAllister confuse her usually clear mind. The man was arrogant and egotistical, but she could deal with that. What she couldn't deal with was the racing of her pulse when he was as close to her as he was now, or the way her heart hammered, or the fact that she forgot to breathe when he touched her.

How was she going to maintain her composure if she had to spend all those days and nights with him on the trip to Fort Worth? Amanda gritted her teeth in frustration. Her government wanted those guns delivered to Fort Worth, and deliver them she would, come hell or high water. No one could stop her—not even McAllister.

They deposited the bound men in the shed, tied their feet together, then headed toward the cabin. Halfway there Slade stopped and turned to her. His strong hands clamped about her upper arms as he frowned down at her.

"You're not hurt, are you?"

"I wasn't, but I will be if you break my arms. Let me go!" He loosened his grip, but didn't relinquish his hold.

Slade's voice was laced with exasperation when he spoke. "What the devil is the matter with you?"

Amanda glared back at him. "Nothing."

"That's a lie! Admit it, Amanda: Sometimes even you need a man's help. Christ, there's no crime in that. If you'd stayed at the house like I told you, I would have taken care of this whole mess."

Amanda wanted to strangle him. "Well, I chose not to take your advice, McAllister. I have a job to do, the same as you. Oh, never mind, you wouldn't understand. Anyway, I had the problem well in hand, thanks to Lily and Sampson."

"Did you?" Slade exploded. "Just what do you think you would have done if I hadn't shown up when I did?"

The lines around Slade's mouth were tight with suppressed anger. He released her arms and took a step away.

Holding back a satisfied smile over his loss of temper, Amanda crossed her arms over her chest. "I'd have managed. Is it so hard for you to believe that I might be competent enough to handle a situation like this? After all, I've had some training. And I did have Lily and Sampson's help."

Slade took a quick look around the clearing. "Where are they?"

As if he'd willed them there with his words, Sampson and Lily emerged from the trees, accompanied by Buck. Griffin was thrown across the horse Sampson was leading.

Buck grinned at Slade. "Looks like the ladies saved us a heap of work."

There was pride in Buck's voice, and Amanda silently thanked him.

"After we get these fellahs to the sheriff, I think I'm

going to take some time off." Buck slung an arm around Lily's shoulder. "We got some real serious talking to do."

Amanda turned to Buck. "Where have you and Slade been? I know you didn't follow the wagons, because we did."

"Well, heck, Amanda." Buck smiled that wickedly charming smile of his. "We overheard Parker telling those fellahs to bring the guns here, so we just rode over and waited on the other side of the trees. We thought we'd keep an eye on them till just before daylight and surprise them, get the guns, and be on our way. How were we to know you were going to get in the middle of this?"

Amanda rounded on Slade. "I thought you might be in trouble. I nearly worried myself crazy about you. And while you were sitting around resting I helped capture six dangerous men. You're the one who said I couldn't come with you because it was too dangerous."

Amanda ran out of breath and patience at the same time. Turning on her heel, she headed for the cabin. Slade stopped her with a hand on her arm.

"Amanda." He sounded patronizing. "I wasn't resting, I was watching the damn cabin. I was going to let you handle it, but when I saw you were in over your head, I came to your rescue. What more do you want from me?"

"Nothing." She jerked away and from the corner of her eye saw Sampson near the shed, where he reached up to lift Griffin from the horse.

Everything happened so fast Amanda didn't even have time to blink. Griffin's hands were free. The right one held a small revolver. Her derringer.

Sampson reached out to disarm Griffin, and the

gun roared to life. Sampson's big body straightened with the impact of the bullet. Blood spurted from the hole in his chest.

Another shot, close to Amanda, momentarily deafened her as Slade returned fire. Griffin screamed and pitched from the horse. He fell sprawled on the ground beside Sampson. The hole in the middle of his forehead hardly bled at all.

Amanda ran to Sampson's side without conscious thought. She reached for his hand. It was warm, and there was a pulse beat at the wrist. As she tore at his blood-soaked white shirt, she cried out, "Get me something for this!"

A petticoat was shoved into her hand. Her mind registered the fact that it came from Lily, but she didn't stop to thank her.

Folding it into a tight square, she pressed it to the wound as hard as she could. In minutes, her hand was stained red as Sampson's blood kept bubbling out.

Amanda was afraid she was going to be sick. No . . . No . . . She would not allow him to die. My fault . . . my fault . . . Her head felt light; the world around her began to tilt.

Hands dragged her up and shoved her toward the cabin. Amanda tottered as Lily helped her through the open door. Slade and Buck half-carried, half-dragged Sampson's limp body inside to the bed.

Slade stuck a poker into the hot coals left from making coffee. When the red-hot end glowed like Satan's eyes, he grabbed it up by the handle.

Lily lay across Sampson's legs while Buck applied his weight to the big man's shoulders. Still, Sampson's body cleared the bed with a jerk when Slade pushed the red-hot poker into the wound.

The sizzling sound and the smell of burned flesh were more than Amanda's rolling stomach could stand. Dashing out the door, she leaned weakly against the nearest tree and was sick.

Tears rolled down her cheeks; sobs shook her body. Sampson was going to die. Gentle, caring, politely funny Sampson would die, and it was her fault. "No . . . No . . . Please God, no," she said out loud.

Amanda beat her hands against the rough trunk of the oak but felt no pain, not even when she saw the blood dripping from her fingertips.

Arms enfolded her from behind and turned her. She pressed her face to Slade's chest and wrapped her arms around his waist.

"Hush, hush, Amanda," he soothed. His hands stroked her back. "If I'd had time to think, I wouldn't have allowed you to witness that. It was the only thing I could think of to stop the bleeding. I'm sorry."

The words were spoken softly against her hair. She felt a shiver run the length of Slade's body.

Slowly her sobs subsided and her body stopped shaking. Still, she held tight to the warm comfort he provided. She knew she had to return to the cabin and do what she could. Putting it off was cowardly, but she needed this moment. Finally, Amanda took a deep breath and stepped away from Slade.

"I have to go back inside. Lily or Buck might need my help, or a breath of fresh air." Her voice was still shaky, but determined.

"You don't have to, love. I'll do it. You stay here and rest as long as you need to."

"No! It's my fault." Anger spurted up in her. "I'm going in. He's my friend. We care about each other. I won't let him die without me."

She gulped back the tears that threatened to start again, squared her shoulders, and forced her feet to move. She didn't stop until she stood just inside the cabin's open doorway.

Sampson's face was pinched and white. She could hear his labored breathing from across the room. Lily sat beside the bed, Buck at the table. Amanda moved to Lily's side and placed a hand on her arm. "May I sit with him a while? Please."

Amanda sat through the long night holding Sampson's hand. Slade came to check on him. Lily hovered nearby. Buck was silent. Sampson clung to life. Then, in the gray dawn of early morning, just before the sun cleared the horizon, he died.

Amanda's mind told her his raspy breathing had stopped and that the pulse beneath her fingers had ceased. Still she held on, not wanting to let him go. Not willing to admit defeat.

Slowly she gained her feet, leaned over, and placed a good-bye kiss on his cheek. Tears dropped from her eyes and splashed the face that had become so dear to her. She brushed them away with her fingertips.

She felt Slade's arm at her waist, heard his voice floating around her. "Come away, love."

The room swirled like a carousel and colored lights swam before her eyes. Then for a few minutes everything turned as black as death.

For Amanda, the next few hours passed in a blur. The two wagons each now carried a body as well as their load of guns. Slade drove one, Buck the other.

The five gunrunners were tied to their saddles. Lily and Amanda rode behind them with their rifles pointed at the outlaws' backs.

It was a slow, silent, uneventful trip, and the noon sun was high and hot by the time they reached the barn behind the house.

Granny stood in the kitchen doorway with worried eyes.

Amanda slid from the saddle and went to her. "Come inside, Granny."

Something in the way Amanda looked, or in the sound of her voice, must have alerted Granny to trouble, because she turned and silently entered the kitchen. She took a seat at the table.

Amanda went to her knees in front of the old woman. Granny placed a work-roughened hand to Amanda's cheek. "What is it, girl?"

"It's Sampson. He was shot." Amanda's voice went weak and reedy. "He's dead, Granny."

Granny gasped. "Oh, Lord have mercy." Tears filled her brown eyes.

Amanda laid her head in the woman's lap. "I'm sorry, Granny. I know you were together a long time, and that he was your friend. It was my fault. He was out there because of me."

"That's foolish talk, girl. If Sampson was there, it was where he wanted to be. He was his own man."

"No, Granny. Griffin shot Sampson with my gun. I feel so bad, Granny. He cared about me, and it's my fault he died."

Granny patted Amanda's back gently. "Sampson would never blame you. He loved you, just like he loved your mother.

"Nothing ever came of that love, but it was there, and that was enough for them."

Amanda looked up to see a tear trickle down each of Granny's cheeks. Then she went to look out the window, giving Granny time to regain her composure.

A buckboard, with Buck on the seat, held the two covered bodies. Slade was mounted and armed with a rifle. The five prisoners were still on their horses. Lily stood beside the porch.

Amanda watched the group leave the yard and head for town, where the jail and the undertaker waited. She knew Slade would make all the proper arrangements for Sampson. A small smile touched her sad face as she remembered Slade's words about a woman's sometimes needing a man's help. This was one of those times.

Lily entered the kitchen through the back door. "The wagons and guns are in the barn, and Buck and Slade will take care of everything else. You look done in, Amanda. Let me heat you some water. You need a long soak, some food, and a lot of sleep."

"I think you have the right of it, Lily," Granny replied before Amanda could. "Only that applies to both of you. Now scoot on up to your rooms and I'll see to everything."

They wearily climbed the back stairs together and parted in the hall. Amanda closed her door and collapsed onto the sofa. She was tired beyond belief.

"Oh, Mama," she whispered to the empty room. "If it weren't for me, if Sampson hadn't followed to see to my safety, he would still be alive. I'm sorry, Mama, and I vow that if it's the last thing I do, I will see that all the people responsible are made to pay."

Amanda went to her trunk and removed a length of

black ribbon. Quietly she descended the front stairs and opened the heavy front door. She looped the ribbon through the brass heart and tied it there. Stepping back, she watched it flutter in the hot afternoon breeze. It was a sign to all who passed of a house mourning the loss of a loved one.

An hour later, bathed and fed, Amanda crawled into her bed. She didn't expect to be able to sleep.

Sometime later, she woke to the sounds of hushed voices floating along the hall. The girls were preparing for the evening ahead. She stared at the canopy above her.

She would dress and go down as usual. There was comfort to be gained from doing routine things, but more than that, it was what Sampson and her mother would want her to do.

Amanda put on the black dress she'd worn to her father's funeral, coiled her hair atop her head, and left the room.

Slade was in the library, his back to the door, placing the rifles she and Lily had used in the gun case. He turned, crossed the room, and extended his hand. She placed hers in his, and he seated her beside the desk and took his seat behind it.

"I've made all the arrangements, Amanda. At ten in the morning, the minister has agreed to hold a short service at the cemetery. Sampson had already purchased the lot next to your mother." His coffee brown eyes were filled with concern. "You don't mind that, do you?"

"Of course not. Why would you think I would?"

Slade raised an eyebrow. "I don't, so don't get in a huff. I was just checking."

Amanda knew she was being overly sensitive.

Perhaps it was guilt, or an accumulation of too many things happening too fast or both. She smoothed her black skirt with nervous fingers.

"I'm sorry, Slade. I must still be a bit tired. What did Sheriff Davis do with the gunrunners?"

"He locked them up and wired for a federal marshal to come get them. They won't be giving us any more trouble. He's still checking on Griffin. Parker is nowhere to be found. The sheriff seems to think he's hightailed it for parts unknown."

Slade pressed a hand to his forehead and then rubbed his eyes. "I had to tell Davis who and what I am. He knows you were out there, but I let him think it was by chance. I didn't see any reason to reveal your cover."

Slade was silent for a long moment. "You know what, Amanda? You were pretty damned terrific out at the cabin. You've got grit."

Amanda hadn't expected words of praise, and she didn't want them. It was her fault that Sampson was dead.

"If I had listened to you, Sampson would still be alive. I can't change what happened, so I will have to live with the regret. A person does what she has to."

"Don't punish yourself, Amanda. Things like this happen sometimes. You did a good job."

The look in Slade's eyes made Amanda's heart beat a little faster. She tried to ignore it.

"I promised Robert that if I recovered the weapons I would see to it that they were turned over to a man in Fort Worth. Does the fact that you think I did well mean you will help me deliver them?"

Slade's laughter filled the room. "You don't know

the meaning of the word quit, do you? I'll tell you what: You promise to smile at me at least once every day, starting now, and you've got a deal. What do you think about that?"

"I think that men make the strangest bargains, and that fatigue has probably fogged your brain, McAllister, but I'm going to hold you to the deal anyway."

# 9

*Amanda brushed back the* curtain at her bedroom window and looked down on the two black carriages waiting below to take her and the other ladies to the cemetery.

She tried to swallow the lump that had formed in her throat. It seemed to have been there for a very long time. Her chest hurt and her head ached. Why, God? she asked herself. Why do the people I love have to die? Papa . . . Sampson . . . It seemed so unnecessary, and so senseless.

Rage warred with grief, making her feel empty and weak. She pressed her hands against the cool window and felt the solid but fragile glass against her palms.

Life was like that glass: It could be shattered in an instant. But now wasn't the time to dwell on that. She could ponder later.

Letting the curtain slide back, she crossed the room and opened her bedroom door. The hall was empty. Voices floated up from the entry as she descended the stairs. The ladies and Slade waited below.

He met her at the bottom of the steps and took her arm. The ladies were dressed in their finest, if not the most sedate, gowns. Jeanne was tall and willowy in lemon yellow, and Lily seemed a bit fragile in pale pink. Wilma and Rose had donned two different shades of green. They were a covey of bright birds, dulled only by Mattie in demure gray.

Granny entered the hall through a rear door that led to the kitchen, a rose from her bush beside the back door in her hand.

"Child," she said as she approached Amanda, "will you take this to Sampson for me?" Granny held out the flower.

Amanda felt the sharp sting of tears, then anger, as she realized the old woman didn't plan to attend the graveside service. She understood the reason why, and she was not going to allow the color of Granny's skin to keep her from saying a last good-bye to Sampson.

"There is no need for that. You will come with us and do it yourself." She placed a hand on the woman's arm and tugged her forward.

Granny shook her head. "As much as I want to, I can't do that, Missy."

"I say you can. In fact I insist on it." Slade moved between them. Taking Amanda, then Granny, by the arm, he enforced Amanda's dictate and led the two of them to the waiting carriage. The entourage traveled the short distance to the cemetery in silence.

A wagon, its sides painted black, contained

Sampson's coffin. It was made of polished pecan, and Amanda marveled that Slade had been able to find one that large on such short notice. Money, she supposed, was the key.

The minister stood stiff and unsmiling beside the wagon. Two strangers in rough work clothes stood ready to help Slade, Buck, and the undertaker carry the cumbersome casket to the waiting grave.

The minister walked ahead, and Amanda, Granny, and the ladies trailed behind. None of the men who frequented The House had come to pay their final respects. But Amanda had not really expected that they would.

The coffin was lowered by ropes into the hole. The minister, solemn and disapproving, took his place at the head of the grave.

Amanda, surrounded by her bright birds, looked at him coolly. "You may proceed, Reverend Shockly."

She peered down at the top of the gleaming wood coffin and barely heard the words of the Twenty-third Psalm. Instead she let images of Sampson fill her mind.

The first time she'd seen him, as he'd filled the doorway of The House. His dignified presence as guard beside the parlor door. The way he looked the night he came to her bedroom to deter Slade's advances. The pale white of his face against the rough covers of the bed inside the cabin.

The minister's singsong voice intruded.

"Ashes to ashes, dust to dust."

Amanda glanced up. Granny, leaning heavily on Lily, left the grave site. Lily helped her into the small carriage and drove off toward the house.

Slade moved to Amanda's side. She met his gaze with tear-filled eyes and stood as stiff as steel. Her

*If* you have a passion for great historical romance, here's an offer you'll love...

# 3 FREE NOVELS

**SEE INSIDE.**

# *Introducing* The Timeless Romanc

Passion rising from the ashes of the Civil War...

Love blossoming against the harsh landscape of the primitive Australian outback...

Romance melting the cold walls of an 18th-century English castle —— and the heart of the handsome Earl who lives there...

Since the beginning of time, great love has held the power to change the course of history. And in HarperMonogram historical novels, you can experience that power again and again.

**Free introductory offer.** To introduce you to this exclusive new service, we'd like to send you the three newest HarperMonogram titles absolutely free. They're yours to keep without obligation, no matter what you decide.

**Free 10-day previews.** Enjoy automatic free delivery of three new titles each month — up to four weeks before they appear in bookstores. You're never obligated to keep a book you don't want, and you can return any book, for a full credit.

**Save up to 32% off** the publisher's price on any shipment you choose to keep.

Don't pass up this opportunity to enjoy great romance as you have never experienced before.

*Yes!* I want to join the Timeless Romance Reader Service. Please send me my 3 FREE HarperMonogram historical romances. Then each month send me 3 new historical romances to preview without obligation for 10 days. I'll pay the low subscription price of $4.00 for every book I choose to keep--a total savings of at least $2.00 each month--and home delivery is free! I understand that I may return any title within 10 days and receive a full credit. I may cancel this subscription at any time without obligation by simply writing "Canceled" on any invoice and mailing it to Timeless Romance. There is no minimum number of books to purchase.

NAME

ADDRESS

CITY                              STATE          ZIP

TELEPHONE

SIGNATURE

(If under 18, parent or guardian must sign. Program, price, terms, and conditions subject to cancellation and change. Orders subject to acceptance by HarperMonogram.)

stance conveyed a message stronger than words: *Don't touch me. I don't need you.*

It was a lie. Slade knew she needed comfort now more than ever. And he wanted to be the one to give it. That cool, controlled exterior of hers was going to do her damage, he feared. She couldn't keep all that emotion locked up without hurting herself.

The minister scooped up a handful of dry Texas dirt and dropped it onto the casket, then left.

Each of the teary-eyed ladies dropped a handful of dirt onto the coffin and then returned to the remaining carriage. Slade stood silently beside Amanda and watched Buck drive away toward the house.

Looking at her, he felt her pain. It wasn't just Sampson she mourned, though he doubted she knew it. She grieved for her lost childhood, for the countless times she'd needed her mother and had had to pretend she didn't, for the father she'd known for such a short time, and for herself. It must be hard to grow up with no one to love, he thought.

The sorrow in her eyes was unbearable for him. His head knew she might reject him, but the rest of him didn't give a damn. He needed to hold her as much as she needed to be held.

Slade pulled her stiff body into his embrace and held on. She struggled at first, but then by slow degrees her body began to soften. She leaned into him, accepted his strength, and finally allowed her head to rest against his chest.

He rocked her gently, murmuring soft words of comfort, taking his solace from the feel of her, and his ability, however slight, to ease her pain. Death was there in the polished box. Life was in the beat of her heart against his.

When she looked at him, her sea green eyes were shiny and wet. Slade felt his heart soften. Good God! he said to himself. She had such an effect on him.

"Come away, love," he pleaded softly.

She allowed him to lead her from the cemetery and along the road toward the house. Halfway there, Amanda stopped and stared in horror.

Black smoke was billowing up from behind the house. The buggies stood unattended beside the front gate.

Slade and Amanda rounded the corner of the house at a run.

Orange flames burst through the roof of the barn. Long red tongues of fire licked at the dry wood roof.

Buck was hauling buckets of water from the well and Wilma, Rose, and Jeanne were tossing water on the back of the house in an attempt to keep the fire from spreading to it.

"Get the women away from here, Buck," Slade ordered. "That damned ammunition will explode any minute."

Amanda picked up the bucket Jeanne dropped as she fled and headed for the well. Slade grasped her by the arm as she passed, almost pulling her off her feet.

"Damn it, Amanda. That means you too. Don't you have a brain? When those bullets in there start popping, we'll be as full of holes as a sieve."

He dragged her around the corner of the house, pushed her against the wall, and held her there.

"No!" She screamed and tried to wiggle away from him. "The house will burn, too, if we don't wet it down."

"Hold still! I'm not going to let you get yourself killed for a damned house. If it burns, I'll build you another one."

Amanda stilled under the bruising weight of Slade's body as he pressed her against the side of the house. The sound of the fire roared in her ears, but there were no exploding bullets. Slade leaned away and peered around the corner, and Amanda slipped under his arm to see, too. The barn was a red-hot inferno, fed by the exploding hay stored there and the dryness of the aged wood.

Amanda tugged on Slade's arm. "The wagons aren't in there."

Slade swore, using words that made Amanda's ears burn.

"But they must be. You left a guard." She realized then that the guard was missing also. "Oh, Slade. You don't suppose he's still in there?"

"I hope to God not."

Amanda's mind churned. Where was Granny? She raced for the back door and into the kitchen. It was empty. She burst through the door into the hall. Granny was sprawled on the hardwood floor. Mattie knelt beside her. Oh God, no! Not again, Amanda's mind screamed. She slid to the floor beside Mattie.

Blood smeared the back of the old woman's head. Fear knotted Amanda's stomach. When Granny groaned, Amanda felt a surge of relief course through her that left her weak.

"Get some water and towels from the kitchen, Mattie," she ordered. The girl ran to do her bidding while she cushioned Granny's head in her lap and prayed.


A few townspeople arrived to help Slade and Buck fight the blaze. Slade knew the act was not out of compassion, but out of fear that the fire might spread

to their properties. The barn was beyond saving, but a
bucket brigade was formed to wet down the house.

Three men climbed to the roof when sparks ignited
it to fight the small fires that started there. Others put
out the numerous small grass fires that started around
the barn.

An hour and a half later, the barn was a smoldering
pile of rubble, but the fire had been contained. Slade
thanked the men who had helped fight the blaze and
sent them back to their homes.

His face smoke-blackened, his clothing singed, Slade
observed the site with mixed emotions. It was clear to
him that whoever had taken the wagons had set the fire
as a means of slowing down pursuit. It had worked—
the time spent fighting the fire had given the thieves a
considerable head start. The good news was that there
hadn't been an explosion and that no serious damage
had been done to the house, or the town. Mattie had
reported the only injury: a bump on Granny's head.

Buck rounded the corner of the house. His face and
clothes were as black and tattered as Slade's. Worry
lined his face.

"I can't find Lily. No one has seen her since she and
Granny returned from the cemetery. Granny said she
went upstairs as soon as they got inside. She doesn't
remember anything after that. Everyone was so busy
with the fire and Granny that no one missed Lily until
now."

"Have you checked her room?"

"Amanda did that. She isn't there, and nothing
seems to be missing. I've searched everywhere." He
paused. "Parker's gone, the guns are gone, and Lily's
gone."

Slade didn't like the picture Buck was painting. "Don't jump to conclusions, Buck."

Buck swore and kicked at a piece of blackened wood. His cheerful disposition seemed to have disappeared with Lily. His voice was tight when he spoke again.

"I don't know about you, but I'm for hightailing it after the wagons. I'll lay money they headed west, and if I find Lily with Parker, there's going to be hell to pay. I'm leaving at first light. You going?"

Slade nodded and headed for the house. Amanda would insist on going, and this time he wasn't going to fight her. If he refused to allow it, she would only follow. He had learned his lesson: It was better to keep her in sight than to have her stumble into the middle of things. He found her in the kitchen tending Granny, who was protesting loudly.

"I'm fine, child." She pushed Amanda's hand away. "It will take more than a little bump on the head to slow down an old workhorse like me."

Amanda sighed and put down the wet cloth.

Granny motioned her away. "Now you run along upstairs, girl, and get out of them ruined clothes while I stir us up something to eat. Everything will be as fine as cats' hair by morning. A new day always makes things look better."

Amanda looked up and found Slade grinning at her from the doorway. He was a bigger mess than she was.

"What are you grinning at, McAllister? You look worse than I do."

"It's not that," he answered, striding forward. "Although I must say I've seen you looking better. I was just wishing I could handle you as well as Granny does."

"That's not likely to happen, McAllister."

"Don't I know it," he agreed. "That's why I came to tell you that Buck and I are heading after the wagons in the morning. I don't suppose you would consider not accompanying us?"

"You suppose right. What time do we leave?"

Early the next morning they took the trail out of Three Wells that led into west Texas. It was rough and barely traveled. The hot, dry trail ran through Comanche country, but it was the shortest route to the California border. Slade knew the men who took the guns would be aware of that.

He and Buck had traveled the trail before, and knew where the water holes were; otherwise he would never have consented to take Amanda. He knew from past experience that Amanda could hold her own with a gun and that she would not slow them down. Slade hoped they wouldn't have to chase the wagons all the way to California.

The morning's coolness had evaporated with the rising sun, which was high overhead now. Amanda was hot. Perspiration dampened her camisole and shirt. They'd been on the trail for hours. Her stomach grumbled, reminding her of how long it had been since she'd eaten Granny's tasty breakfast. The old woman had risen early to prepare it and pack the provisions they would need.

Amanda uncapped her canteen and let the lukewarm water trickle down her parched throat. It helped a little.

Slade was calling a stop every two hours to rest the horses. That gave her time to stretch her legs while he and Buck scouted the area ahead on foot for signs. It also allowed her a moment of privacy to take care of her own needs. She deeply appreciated Slade's concern and decorum.

A line of scrub oak ahead suggested another stopping place, probably a watering hole. Moments later, Amanda knew she had guessed right. The shady spot and small pool of water was a welcome sight.

She slid from her saddle and knelt beside the spring. Dipping her hands in the cool liquid, she splashed it on her face, filled her canteen, then drank from her cupped hand. After watering the horses, she tied them beneath an oak tree to allow them to graze on the sparse grass growing there.

Buck handed her a thick slice of ham and a chunk of Granny's delicious bread. He didn't smile or joke, and Amanda missed their easy banter. She hoped Lily could explain herself if they found her with Parker.

Amanda found a spot of shade against the trunk of one of the scraggly oaks and ate slowly, savoring every bite. She washed down her meal with fresh water from her canteen, then leaned back and closed her eyes. God, it felt good to be off the horse.

She heard Slade return from his scouting trip. He hunkered down beside her, and she opened her eyes.

"Find anything?"

"There are lots of tracks, both horses and wagons. Maybe they're the ones we're following; maybe not. One set is fairly fresh."

Slade rested silently beside her for a few minutes, then stood and offered her his hand. "Come on, lazy, we still have six hours of daylight left."

Amanda groaned, placed her small hand in his large callused one, and allowed him to pull her to her feet.

Six hours later, Amanda was sure she should have let him leave her beneath the tree. Her bottom was numb. The inside of her thighs were raw, and her hands, even though protected by leather gloves, were stiff and sore from holding the reins. She wasn't sure her legs would support her—that is, if she could get off her horse to stand on them. She couldn't even imagine being capable of dismounting.

Slade, realizing her predicament, slid from his saddle and approached her. He raised his arms and she slipped into them, allowing his body to absorb her weight.

"You all right?"

"Of course," she said, moving away from him. "I'll help Buck with supper."

Slade walked to a spot near the tree-lined creek he had chosen for their overnight camping spot. There would not be many places as nice as this, so they might as well be comfortable tonight. He unsaddled and watered the horses, then strung a picket line between two trees and left them to graze.

He scouted both sides of the shallow, rock-strewn creek for signs, and found the distinctive print of a repaired wagon wheel he was looking for. It was identical to the one he'd found at the noon stop. Another, not so distinctive set of wagon tracks gave proof of two heavily loaded wagons traveling together. He'd bet his last dollar they were the wagons carrying the guns.

Kneeling beside the creek, he scooped up handfuls of water to splash his face and rinse the dust from his hair. He shook his wet head to dispel the clinging water, dried his hands on his thighs, then headed back to camp.

A small fire blazed in a circle of rocks. The aroma of food and fresh-made coffee greeted him.

Amanda smiled at Slade from her seat on a flat rock. He looked clean and refreshed. His dark, wet hair glistened in the firelight. She felt decidedly dirty by comparison. She would remedy that after supper.

An hour later, Amanda retrieved her soap, towel, and clean camisole and drawers from her saddlebags and headed for the creek. Keeping the campfire in sight, she found a sheltered place and unbuttoned her shirt.

The sound of footsteps in the dry grass alerted her to Slade's approach. He appeared beside her out of the darkness.

"I dug this out of my pack." He extended a tin of salve toward her and grinned. "It will help soothe the places you hurt the most. You did well today. Tomorrow should be easier."

She held her hand out, and he placed the tin in her palm.

"Thank you. I hope so. Is that all you want?"

Moonlight, filtering through the branches of the sheltering oaks, lit his face. The silence stretched between them. She needed him to hold her. As if he'd heard her, he leaned toward her, and his hands found her waist under the open shirt.

She went to him willingly, allowing him to press her against him. Their mouths met and clung together. Some instinct told her to wind her arms around his neck and to stretch up on tiptoes to increase the pressure of her body against his.

Slade buried his face in the hollow of her neck. His tongue licked at the pulse that throbbed there, then moved down to explore her breasts above the camisole and the valley between them.

She heard him groan, heard his harsh indrawn

breath. His mouth came back to hers. The greedy kiss made her dizzy; the night appeared to spin around her. The touch of his probing tongue excited her. It seemed right to just keep on feeling and not think.

Amanda's mouth opened beneath Slade's, allowing him to explore it further. Her body felt so soft, so good, to him. He wanted to lose himself in her. Running his hands over her hips and then around to cup her bottom, he lifted her against himself. The feel of her body pressed to his was so unbearably sweet he could hardly stand it. He heard her moan of pleasure through a fog of feeling so intense it shook him to his very core.

Slade felt the tin of salve in her hand press against the back of his neck. God, oh God, what was he doing? he asked himself.

He let her slide down his body until her feet touched the ground. He heard her gasp for breath, felt the beat of her heart against his chest.

Had bringing the tin to her been for her comfort or an excuse to take advantage of her? He knew the answer, and he didn't like it one bit.

Her body was still pressed against him. He took a deep, cleansing breath and stepped back to look down into her passion-flushed face. Her eyes were closed, her mouth slightly swollen from his kisses. He kissed the tip of her nose and each eyelid.

Her eyes fluttered open. Confusion and desire dwelt in their smoldering green depths. Her arms slid from around his neck.

He pulled the edges of her shirt together.

"You'd best take your bath, pretty lady. Much more of this," he said hoarsely, kissing the palm of her free hand, "and I won't be able to let you go."

She stepped away from him and turned her back. Her breathing sounded raspy.

"I'm sure that would be best. I mean, getting on with my bath, of course." He turned to leave, but her soft voice stopped him. "Slade."

"Yes." He didn't turn around.

"Sometimes, when we are in danger or under stress, you call me 'love.' Why is that?"

What did she want from him? A declaration of some kind? He couldn't give one, but felt that perhaps he did owe her an explanation.

"I didn't realize I did that. I'll try to be more careful."

"I didn't ask you to stop." She sounded annoyed. "I asked why."

Slade stood very still, watching the moonlight shimmer on the water, listening to the murmur of the creek flowing over stone.

"I suppose," he began slowly, "that I might be confusing you with someone else. She wasn't anything like you—in fact, the very opposite. You're small and compact, she was tall and willowy. I remember, she seemed to float across a room rather than walk. I was so taken with her beauty I failed to see her faults." He tried hard not to let the bitterness he felt come through in his words.

"She was self-centered and demanding. Her world revolved around her clothes, her comfort, and her entertainment."

He took a quick breath and hurried on, determined to tell it all. "I came home from an assignment early. Eager to hold her, to bed her. Lord, she was good in bed, and that's where I found her—but not alone. I wanted to kill them. The man would have been easy.

But I'm not sure, even today, if I could have put an end to Lydia's life. I didn't do either."

Amanda spoke from directly behind him, her hand soothing his back. He resisted the urge to turn around.

"She was your wife?"

"Yes."

"Where is she?"

"Gone."

Amanda said nothing, but Slade thought he discerned a note of pity on her face. It was the last thing he wanted. He wasn't sure what he did want, but it wasn't that.

He'd never told that story to anyone. Why had he felt he had to tell it to her? Maybe it was an attempt to put some distance between them. He needed that. He wanted her too much, was beginning to have feelings again that he had thought dead and buried.

He wasn't going to let any woman get as close to him as Lydia had. It hurt too much when things went wrong. He didn't need a woman in his life again, and if he found he needed some female company of a more temporary nature, he could always go to a place just like the one in Three Wells. Those kind of women he knew how to deal with.

He turned to Amanda. She was staring up at him, her face bathed in moonlight. Her lovely green eyes were lustrous and wet. Her throat, exposed by the open shirt, was a creamy white. Slade thought she was the most beautiful thing he'd ever seen.

He wanted to touch and taste her. To feel her body pressed against his.

But what he wanted he couldn't have. Slade turned from her. It was the hardest thing he had ever done.

# 10

When Amanda returned to camp the fire was banked and Buck was rolled up in his blanket. Slade was sitting atop his bedroll taking off his boots. She managed to calmly bid him a good night, even though her heart was beating double time.

Amanda crawled into her bedding and tried to seek peace in sleep. It was not to be. Her mind conjured up as erotic a scene as her twenty-three-year-old virgin's mind was capable of. Her pulse pounded as she remembered the feel of Slade's mouth on hers. She grew warm and breathless thinking about his hard muscular body.

A convent and a girls school hadn't prepared her for Slade's assault on her senses. Her escorts to Washington parties and government functions had been friends of her father or occasionally the son of one. The few times she'd been kissed were pleasant enough, but unexciting.

What was there about Slade McAllister that affected her so? He was handsome, but beauty is only skin-deep, or so the nuns had continually told her. She didn't even like him most of the time, but there were moments, like the time he took her to visit her mother's grave, or when he comforted her at Sampson's funeral, that she felt drawn to him on a deeper level. Then, it almost seemed like their souls touched. It was scary as hell. The nuns had spent a considerable amount of time warning her about "sins of the flesh." Was that what these feelings were?

Amanda blushed, remembering that Slade had been the one to call a halt to their lovemaking. She certainly hadn't been in any condition to do so.

His restraint was admirable, she supposed. A shiver ran through her that had nothing to do with the cool night air. What must he think of her?

He has a wife, she suddenly thought disconcertedly. Where was she now? Had he divorced her? He hadn't said so.

Amanda slept fitfully, and was already wide awake when the gray fingers of dawn came stealing over the low hills to the east. For a few moments she listened to the sounds the men made as they went about their morning routines. She was still tired and her head ached from lack of sleep. Reluctantly, she slid from her blankets and approached the fire.

Buck favored her with a smile for the first time in two days and handed her a cup of coffee. She wrapped her hands around the cup to warm them.

Taking her share of the breakfast Buck had prepared

to the rock she'd used as a seat the night before, she sat on the ground and used the rock as her table. A shiny object, half buried in the dirt at the base of the rock, caught her eye. After brushing the dirt off, she picked it up. A silver button lay in the palm of her hand. Amanda glanced up to find Slade, plate in hand, standing beside her.

"What's that?"

He squatted beside her and plucked the button from her hand. The touch of his fingertips against her palm sent small, shivery sensations racing up her arm.

"Only a button. It appears quite new," she managed to say without sounding breathless. He turned the button over to examine the other side and ran his thumb across the delicately embossed front.

"I believe I've seen one like this before. Buck, come look at this." Slade held the button out in the palm of his hand.

"Where did you get that?" Buck growled.

"Amanda found it beside the rock. It's off the dress Lily was wearing the day of the fire, isn't it?"

"Yes. I helped her button it up." Buck's face was grim. "If those bastards have hurt her, they're as good as dead." He scooped the button from Slade's hand and slipped it into his vest pocket. "I'll see she gets it back," he said, leaving.

Amanda's gaze met Slade's. "Do you always remember what women wear, right down to their buttons?"

"Not usually, but I remember these because they look like silver, and I wondered how a girl in Lily's line of work could afford them if they were. Other times, other things catch my eye, and I retain those memories, too." Slade's wicked grin was back.

"Such as?" she inquired innocently, before realizing she had fallen into another of his traps.

Slade's grin widened.

Amanda felt heat rise to her face.

"I remember you have a blue ribbon lacing your camisole closed, and how your mouth looks after I've kissed you senseless."

Amanda scooted away from him. She was very aware of another kind of heat he was creating in her. "Hush," she hissed at him. "Buck will hear you. And for your information I have never been kissed senseless in my life, Mister McAllister."

Slade stood and offered Amanda his hand. She felt reckless as she placed her hand in his. It felt as warm as she did.

"You could have fooled me, Boss Lady."

"You're impossible, McAllister." She pulled her hand from his, determined to get back to the business at hand.

"Now, about the button," Amanda said, a bit more breathlessly than she would have liked. "If it's Lily's, did she lose it or leave it, hoping we would follow and find it?"

"I can't say yet. We'll inspect all the campsites closely. I've already found wagon tracks at yesterday's noon stop and at this site that match. The tracks are deep, indicating a heavy load. If you team that up with the button, I'd say we're on the right trail. Let's mount up. Time's a-wasting."

They carefully checked each watering hole and campsite they came to, and each time they found nothing. Amanda's heart ached for Buck. He seemed torn between believing Lily had been taken and despairing

that she'd gone willingly. If they could just find something more, she thought, anything that would indicate
it was really Lily leaving a trail for them to follow,
they would know she wanted to be found and Buck
would be reassured.

The late-afternoon heat was stifling, the air humid.
Slade scanned the sky. Gray clouds, their fat, billowy
bottoms filled with rain, had formed on the western
horizon. He searched his mind, trying to remember
the exact location of the next available shelter that
would also provide water. He thought there was a
small spring at the base of an outcropping of rock
with a ledge overhang about a mile or so ahead.

Slade moved his horse alongside Buck's. "I'm going
to take a quick look around. I think there is a campsite just ahead that will keep us out of the weather."
His mouth twisted in a wry grin. "Of course every
Comanche in the country knows about it."

Buck nodded in understanding. "You want me to
go check it?"

"No, I'll do it. You keep a sharp eye out. We don't
need any surprises."

Amanda, riding close enough to hear the exchange,
watched Slade ride away. She shivered despite the
heat. There were so many dangers here—Indians and
outlaws and snakes and God only knew what.

Buck either sensed her concern or saw it was written on her face. He dropped back to ride beside her.

"Don't worry about him," he said. "It's a rough,
tough land, but he's a hard man. He's had to be."

Amanda's eyes met Buck's. "Why?"

"Guilt and hurt mostly, I think," he said, then
added. "He needs someone." Buck paused a moment,

as if trying to decide how to proceed. "I need to know if you're applying for the job. You can tell me to shut my mouth and I will, but I got to tell you, if you're not a sticking kind of woman, leave him alone. He don't need any more pain."

Amanda thought that over a minute. She wasn't sure what her relationship with Slade was, but she knew she didn't want to hurt him.

"What makes you think he's interested in me or me in him?"

"I'm not blind. I see the way he looks at you when you don't know it. And you look at him the same way. Just now you were afraid for him. He trailed you to the creek last night. That's none of my business either, but this is the first time in a long time he's shown that kind of interest in a woman."

"Is that because of what his wife did?"

"He told you about her?"

"A little."

Buck seemed relieved. "Well, if that don't beat all. He doesn't ever talk about her."

"He didn't tell me much. What do you know about her?"

"Not much. I think I've said more than I have a right to already."

Buck spurred his horse and moved away from her before she could ask any more questions, and she knew the subject was closed. Buck and Slade cared about each other like brothers. A tiny pain pierced her heart. No one had ever cared about her that deeply. A friendship like theirs was special. It saddened her that she'd never had a special friend.

Slade was lifting his saddle off his horse when she

and Buck arrived at the campsite. He'd already built a
small fire and gathered extra dry wood, placing it
under the ledge to keep it from getting wet. Amanda
slid from her mare and, while the men took care of the
horses, fixed a quick meal.

It began to rain while they ate. Thunder rumbled
and echoed off the low hills. Lightning flashed. She
scooted back under the overhang to finish her dinner.
Slade and Buck quickly joined her there.

"We made it just in time," Slade observed.

"Yes," Buck replied, gazing out into the gathering
darkness. "I hope Lily's not getting wet."

Amanda's gaze met Slade's as she offered, "I'm sure
she's fine. She's probably under one of the wagons."

Whatever image her words conjured up for Buck, it
must have been distressing. He uttered a string of
cusswords as he left the shelter of the overhang.

"Buck, come back! You'll get soaked."

"Leave him alone," Slade growled.

Amanda sighed. "I'm sorry."

"Me too." Slade sounded resigned. "He'll be fine as
soon as we find Lily. A man in love does strange
things sometimes."

"Are you speaking from personal experience?" As
soon as the words left her mouth, Amanda wished
them back.

"Curiosity killed the cat, Amanda. Don't push me."

She knew he'd never hurt her. It wasn't a threat,
just words he'd used to avoid her question. "All right."

They finished their meal in silence, watching the
rain ease up and finally stop.

Amanda washed the plates and made her bed. She
lay down on her stomach and watched Slade from

beneath her lowered lashes as he spread his blankets. Because of the limited space beneath their stone roof, their bedding nearly touched. He sat and took off his boots, not speaking.

"Confront and overcome." Amanda's mind whispered her motto, then added, You will never know if you don't ask.

"Are you angry with me, Slade?"

"I don't think so."

Amanda smiled, "Good, I'm glad." She closed her eyes. "Good night, Slade."

"Good night, Amanda."

Slade lay quietly with his eyes closed, listening to the rain and the night sounds, and was still awake when Buck came back. He heard him put on dry clothes and go to bed, but didn't speak, because there weren't any words to comfort his friend.

He listened then to the regular sound of Amanda's breathing. She was so close, he could reach out and touch her. He wanted to. His Amanda problem wasn't going away. In fact, she was driving him crazy, and he didn't think she even knew it. What the hell was he going to do about her? The woman was still a pain in the neck. The problem was, he was beginning to like the pain.

A smile touched his lips. It crossed his mind to wonder how much experience the lady had with men. Not very much, he guessed. But she certainly hadn't rejected his advances.

She was so sweet to touch and taste. Slade groaned inwardly at the memory. When the assignment was done, she would be leaving. All he had to do was stay away from her a little longer. Perhaps she needn't be a threat to his well-ordered life after all.

*        *        *

Early the next afternoon, Amanda was checking the bushy edges of an abandoned campsite for any sign from Lily. A spot of color near a fallen tree caught her eye. She scrambled over the log and plucked a scrap of pink cotton from its hiding place.

Buck, who was checking the ground near a stump, glanced up. She held out the piece of cloth. "It's from the dress Lily was wearing, isn't it?"

Buck took it from her and ran his fingers over the smooth material. "It's hers." He smiled, relief evident in his expression. "She wants to be found."

Amanda watched him head for the stream, where Slade was watering the horses.

They rode hard all afternoon. A feeling of urgency kept them moving until it was almost too dark to see. When they finally camped, Amanda was almost too tired to eat, but she consumed what she could, then crawled beneath her blankets. Her body ached from head to toe. Lord, she thought, she would give anything for a big tub of hot, scented water to soak her battered body in.

They were on the trail the next morning before the sun cleared the horizon. By midmorning the sun was gone, replaced by a gray, overcast sky. At noon they ate beef jerky washed down with water, using an old oak tree as shelter from the drizzle. Slade found the distinctive prints of the wagon wheels in the soft earth when he watered the horses. They were getting close.

Two hours later the sound of rifle fire in the distance alerted them to danger. Slade ordered them to dismount and tie the horses. Rifle in hand, Amanda followed the two men as they climbed to the top of a low ridge.

Below them and across a narrow valley stood the two wagons, filled with guns. They were under attack by a small band of Indians. Lying flat on her belly, Amanda watched as the whooping Indians made a sweep down the valley toward the wagons. She counted eleven, and each was armed with a rifle. Several carried bows and arrows slung across their backs.

She looked over at Buck's face and knew they had the same thought: Lily was down there.

"Stay here and keep down, Amanda," Slade whispered. "Buck and I have the advantage of surprise. We will slip down close and try to catch them in a cross fire."

The words "I will not" were on the tip of her tongue, but she swallowed them. This was no time to be assertive. Someone had to guard the horses. If this was where she was needed, this was where she would stay. But where were all those Texas Rangers who were supposed to be rounding up the Indians?

Slade motioned to Buck to follow, and Amanda watched as they crawled away, using the low-growing brush as cover.

The Indians reached the end of the valley and turned back to make another pass at their prey. Their bloodcurdling war cries gave her goose bumps. Sporadic rifle shots from the wagons indicated that at least two people were returning fire.

It seemed to take an agonizingly long time for Slade and Buck to travel the short distance to the valley floor. Amanda caught sight of Slade just as the Comanche began another sweep.

She felt detached from the action before her, as though she were the audience at some kind of macabre play. As the Comanche galloped past the wagons, one screamed and clutched at his chest, then slid sideways off his horse. The rest rushed on toward the end of the valley and began the swing to reverse their course.

Amanda tensed knowing that any second now Slade and Buck would open fire. Even so, she couldn't stop her body's jerk of surprise at the sound of the first shots.

Two Indians screamed and pitched from their horses. The surprised Comanche wheeled away in retreat as more shots were fired. Another Indian hit the ground. Another slumped forward, clinging to his horse's neck, as the Comanche sped away out of range.

A thin film of perspiration beaded on Amanda's brow. Her heart thumped inside her chest. She clutched her rifle tighter. An eerie quiet enveloped the tiny valley battlefield as the combatants regrouped. When the Comanche came again, their war whoops were tinged with rage, but their charge was tempered with caution. Once past the wagons, they slowed their horses, preparing to make their turn out of the range of the new enemy.

Slade must have known that would be the plan, because he and Buck had changed positions also. The Indians scattered and quickly headed back down the valley as rifle fire spat at them from close range. Two more fell, and their riderless horses sped away with the remaining Comanche.

As the scene played out before Amanda in slow motion, two mounted men topped the rise at the end of the valley and opened fire on the Comanche. One Indian toppled from his horse, and the remaining three took the only option open to them: They swung toward Amanda, urging their mounts up the rise at breakneck speed.

Her only thought was to defend her assigned position. Raising her rifle, she took careful aim as the three Comanche bore down on her. Her first shot hit its mark. The Indian was close enough for her to see the surprised look on his face as her bullet dug into his chest. How he managed to remain in the saddle was a wonder to her. As his horse galloped by she pulled the trigger again, but the shot went wide.

Suddenly, her gun was wrenched from her hand by the second Comanche who flew past. The force of the gun's being ripped away spun Amanda around, but she managed to keep her legs under her. Then hands grabbed from behind and dragged her up onto a horse. Her screams pierced the late-afternoon quiet as she fought the strong arm of the Comanche brave who held her. Pain exploded in her head when he hit her, then gave way to blackness.

Slade swore, sighted along the barrel of his Winchester, and squeezed off a shot. It was a futile effort, and he knew it—the Comanche were already out of range.

Amanda's screams still rang in his ears. Impotent rage twisted his gut as he watched the three braves, one leading the way, one holding Amanda across his lap, and one clinging to the neck of his horse, disappear over the crest of the ridge.

"Bastards, damn cowardly bastards!" Slade resisted the urge to sprint up the bushy slope in pursuit. Why in blue blazes hadn't she tried to conceal herself? "Stubborn, stupid, bullheaded female." He was still swearing as he and Buck raced across the valley floor to the wagons.

Ranger Captain Ed Whitman and his deputy reached

the wagons at the same time Buck and Slade did. Buck
was out of the saddle and at Lily's side in a flash.

Lily was holding a gun on Frank Parker. He was
bleeding from a shoulder wound. Another body was
sprawled, facedown, near one of the wagons.

"Damned good to see you, Captain," Slade said to
his longtime friend.

"You too, Slade. Looks like you got a mite of trouble."

"More than I want. Those bastards took my girl. I
need your horse and some food and a favor."

"Anything you need, you can have," Whitman replied.

Slade watched Buck dismounted and take the gun
from Lily's shaking hand. He passed it to Ranger
Hank James.

"Are you all right, pretty lady?" Buck inquired of Lily.

Her lower lip trembled as she gave him a shaky
smile. "I am now that you're here. Oh, Buck, those
Indians have Amanda."

Buck pulled her to him. "We're going after her. Try
not to worry—we'll get her back."

Despite the audience, Buck gave Lily a quick kiss,
and Slade smiled.

"See if you can rustle up a grub sack for Slade and
me, will you, Lily?"

Hank James grinned down at Buck from the back of
his horse. Slade tensed. There was no love lost between
Buck and Hank.

Hank inclined his head in Lily's direction. "That's a
fine-looking lady."

"She sure is, and she's mine." Buck's hand moved to
rest on the butt of his six-shooter. "You get my meaning?"

Hank's laugh held no humor. "Don't get in an
uproar, old man. I was just making an observation."

Buck gave the younger man a black look. "See that's all you do." Turning away, he went to help Lily get their supplies ready.

It took Slade all of five minutes to outline the events leading up to today for Captain Whitman. But he regretted the loss of every second.

"So you see, Captain, I've got to hightail it after Amanda. I'd consider it a favor if you could see your way clear to getting the prisoner and wagons back to Three Wells for me."

"I think we can handle that. What about the girl?" He glanced in Lily's direction.

"She wasn't in on the gun business. She and Buck are good friends. He'd take it kindly if you'd see she gets to Three Wells safely." Slade changed the subject. "If you and Hank would step down off your horses, we'd appreciate the loan of them. You'll find ours tied in the draw the other side of the ridge, if the Comanche didn't get them. We've got to move quick or we'll lose Amanda's trail."

Minutes later, Slade and Buck reached the crest of the hill. Slade's heart lurched at the sight of Amanda's hat caught on the low branch of a scrub oak. He grabbed it as he flew past on the borrowed mount.


Amanda fought her way up from the depths of oblivion. The sounds of an argument in a language she didn't comprehend pierced her foggy consciousness. The voices were loud. She tried to raise her hand to her throbbing head and discovered that her wrists were bound behind her back. The ground beneath her was hard and damp.

She opened her eyes. Two Indians squatted near a small fire. Both wore buckskin pants and vests. Another Indian in similar dress lay sprawled a short distance away. The events of the afternoon soon returned to her.

Fear churned in her stomach and made her nauseous. Were those two by the fire arguing over what to do with her? Would they kill her to avenge the one she had shot?

She glanced again at the Indian on the ground. She was sure he was dead.

One of the braves stood and moved toward her. Would he kill her now? Amanda took a deep steadying breath and tried to slow her wildly beating pulse. If she was going to die, it wouldn't be lying in the dirt.

She rolled onto her back and struggled into a sitting position just as the Indian reached her side. He squatted before her.

He wasn't carrying a gun and his knife was still in the sheath he wore at his waist. A beaded leather band around his head held two white feathers that stuck straight up in back. His thick black hair was parted in the middle and held in place by the headband. His black eyes glinted in the light of the full moon as he appraised her steadily.

Amanda forced her gaze to meet his without flinching. Dignity might be all she had left. She would try to hold on to it as long as possible.

"What do you want with me?" she asked. His expression didn't alter at her question. It appeared he didn't understand English any better than she did Comanche.

She held her body stiff as he reached behind her to check the rope that bound her wrist, then rocked back on his heels to peer at her face.

When his fingertips probed her sore and swollen cheek, she suppressed a shudder, but she couldn't keep her head from jerking away from his exploring hand. He let it fall to his side.

Perhaps he didn't mean to hurt her, she thought. His eyes weren't friendly, but neither did they appear hostile.

She licked her dry lips. "Water. May I please have some water?" Her tongue came out to wet her parched lips again.

The Indian rose and went back to the fire. Amanda scooted backward to rest her back against a small scrub oak. What now?

She was apparently safe for the moment. Perhaps they didn't intend to kill her. They might be planning to ransom her. That was a thought. Or maybe they made slaves of their captives. She'd heard that some Indian tribes did that. It might be better to die now than have that as her fate.

Panic threatened to overcome her. She fought it. Slade would come. He would find her. She had to believe that. He was good at tracking, she knew that. She closed her eyes, retrieving his face from her memory.

The touch of a hand on her arm caused her eyes to pop open. She just managed to stifle the scream that rose in her throat. Two Feathers—her mind gave him that name—was leaning over her, a canteen in his hand.

He hunkered down beside her and put it to her lips. Water sloshed down her throat, ran along her chin, and splashed onto her shirt. She swallowed several mouthfuls before he took the canteen away. She met

his gaze. He seemed almost compassionate. Perhaps
he understood more than she thought.

"Thank you." Again he showed no sign of having
heard her.

He returned to the fire, and he and the other Indian
spoke in loud, angry voices. It seemed to Amanda that
Loud Mouth—she now thought of him by that name—
was very upset with Two Feathers for having given her
water. At one point in the conversation, he drew his
hand across his throat in a cutting motion, and Amanda
could almost feel his blade against her throat.

Two Feathers didn't seem particularly bothered by
Loud Mouth's ranting. He wrapped himself in a blanket and lay down beside the fire. For long, fearful minutes, Amanda waited to see if Loud Mouth would
carry out the deed his words conveyed. When he too
rolled up in a blanket, she gave a sigh of relief.

She relaxed a fraction and experimentally worked
her jaws. Pain radiated along the right cheekbone. She
hoped it wasn't broken. Drawing her knees up to her
chin, she tried to gain some warmth from her own
body. How could the days be so hot and the nights so
cold? She wished she had a blanket. She wished she
knew what time it was. God, she wished she'd never
left Washington.

No, that wasn't true. She mustn't allow herself to
become despondent, she resolved. Slade would come
for her—if not tonight, then tomorrow. She needed to
get some sleep if she could. She wouldn't be of any
use if she was too tired to stand.

After dozing—for how long, she couldn't tell—
Amanda was jerked awake as she was roughly hauled
to her feet by Loud Mouth. Her first thought was that

he had decided to wait for her to fall asleep before making good his threat to cut her throat. But he only shoved her toward the dead Indian's horse and boosted her onto its back.

She glanced around the deserted clearing and wondered what they'd done with the body. Loud Mouth untied her hands, and the blood rushed painfully into her fingers. He thrust the reins at her. She managed to hold on to them even though she couldn't feel them. They headed east. Two Feathers rode in front of her, Loud Mouth behind. The rising sun blinded her and made her head hurt.

The horse beneath her had no saddle, and she had to grip its sides with her knees to keep her seat. Slowly the numbness left her hands. Hours later, it reappear in her feet, legs, and bottom. The sun was high now.

Did Indians never stop to rest or eat, she wondered. Her empty stomach was beginning to grumble and she was thirsty again. She pushed her sweat-dampened hair off her forehead and realized she'd lost her hat, she couldn't remember when or where.

Two Feathers slowed his horse, allowing her to ride beside him. He extended the canteen and she drank deeply. When she returned it, he passed her a long piece of beef jerky. It was hard and tough, but the chewing process eased her stomach and the smoky flavor was pleasant enough.

The sun had set long before her captors called a halt for the day. She slid from her horse and staggered a few steps before collapsing. The Indians seemed to realize she was in no condition to flee, and let her be. Amanda was thankful for small favors. Every inch of her body hurt. She couldn't remember ever being this exhausted.

While the two braves saw to the horses, she squatted behind a fat bush to relieve her aching bladder. Two Feathers' dark eyes followed her return to her original spot. His face was void of expression, but she knew he knew exactly what she'd been about. She couldn't stop the blush that stained her cheeks, but she didn't flinch under his scrutiny. Dignity was all she had, and she wouldn't allow him to take it from her. For some reason she thought he understood that.

Later, Two Feathers brought her food and water. She thanked him and he left her. He returned when she was done and tied her hands again, this time in front, and her feet as well.

He crouched before her and peered into her face with dark, unreadable eyes for a long moment. Slowly, he removed his blanket from his shoulders and wrapped it around her body. With a nod of approval, he returned to the fire.

Loud Mouth's voice was raised in anger again. Yet she had the sudden thought that of the two braves, Two Feathers might be the bigger threat. His small acts of kindness, no matter how much she appreciated them, worried her.

Slade, her mind cried, where are you?

# 11

Slade was crouched in the brush not a hundred yards away, his eyes fixed on the three people in the circle of light cast by the small campfire. His heart drummed with relief when he realized Amanda was alive and at least reasonable well.

It worried him that the Comanche didn't seem overly concerned about discovery. Their fire burned brightly and their voices were loud. He understood a few of the words that reached him. They seemed to be arguing about Amanda.

He had stationed Buck on the other side of the camp to wait for a signal from him to attack. Slade planned to be sure the braves were sleeping before making that move.

Amanda was jerked from sleep by unfamiliar sounds. A grunt, a muffled curse, and labored breathing startled her. Her first, sleep-fogged thought was that it was the two Comanche, and that once Loud Mouth killed Two

Feathers it would be her turn. Then the pale light from the moon illuminated Slade, not Loud Mouth, locked in combat with Two Feathers. Slade's knife flashed in the moonlight.

Flinging aside her blanket, she lurched to her feet, forgetting for the moment that they were tied. Her forward momentum brought her crashing down against Slade's back.

Slade grunted in surprise. His attention was diverted from his opponent for a second, and Two Feathers took the opportunity to roll away from him and sprint toward the brush.

Slade spun around on his knees, knife in hand, to fend off his new attacker. He recognized Amanda in time to halt the blade just inches from her chest.

"Jesus Christ!" Fear knotted his gut. He'd damn near stabbed her. Placing his hands on her arms, he shook her roughly. "What the hell do you think you're doing?"

Amanda's body shook with a mixture of fear and relief. "I—I couldn't let you kill him," she stammered. "He was kind—kind to me."

"Kind!" Slade exploded. "Hell, you don't know what you're saying. Comanche aren't kind, Amanda. They're bloodthirsty savages." He felt like he'd been kicked in the stomach. "God, if I wasn't so glad to see you, I'd throttle you."

Amanda collapsed into Slade's arms, allowing him to hold her quaking form tight against his body.

She clung to that solid, safe haven as he looked around for signs of Two Feathers. Slade was her anchor in this sea of uncertainty. His warmth seeped slowly into her cold body.

Buck's voice intruded. "If you two are about done, I

think it might be wise to decide what to do with this."
He indicated Two Feathers, whom he was holding captive at gunpoint. "And then get the hell out of here."

Amanda smiled up at him. "Oh, Buck, it's good to see you, too."

"You're right, Buck," Slade agreed as he began the task of untying the knotted rope from around Amanda's wrists and ankles. "We ought to shoot him like you did the other one and leave him for the buzzards to chew on."

Amanda peered around and saw the body of Loud Mouth sprawled facedown at the edge of the small clearing. She shuddered. "No! You can't; I won't let you. I told you—I owe him."

"Damn it, Amanda, be reasonable!"

"I'm always reasonable," she shot back at Slade. "You're the one who acts like a stubborn jackass all the time."

"Is she your woman?" The question came from Two Feathers. His voice was low and guttural, his English hesitant.

Amanda's mouth fell open in surprise. "You speak English!"

Two Feathers chose not to respond to her. His eyes were fixed on Slade. "I buy."

"You're in no position to do anything," Slade replied. "Besides, we don't sell our women."

"Too bad." Two Feathers' voice held genuine regret. "She would make fine wife, have many strong sons. You lucky man."

"Yes," Slade agreed grudgingly.

Amanda gasped in outrage. She would not stand by and be bartered over by two stupid men.

"Don't you two discuss me as if I weren't even here. I will decide whose wife I'll be, and it won't be either of you. And how many children I have is my business, not yours." She crossed her arms over her chest and glared at them both.

Two Feathers cocked his head to one side and observed Amanda intently, then spoke to Slade. "The she-cat chatters like a squirrel. Maybe you not so lucky man." A tiny smile twitched at the corner of his mouth. "I buy anyway."

Slade looked from the tall, sleek, dignified Indian to the bedraggled Amanda. "No." Slade's voice was firm, but he grinned.

Two Feathers inclined his head at Slade, then turned and took a step toward the brush.

The hammer on Buck's Colt clicked as he cocked it. Two Feathers stopped but didn't turn around. Amanda's eyes begged Slade not to allow Buck to shoot.

Slade sighed and shook his head in disbelief at his own stupidity. "Let him go."

Two Feathers walked out of the clearing and disappeared.

Buck lowered the gun. "That was a damned fool thing to do!"

"Probably," Slade agreed, already regretting his decision. "Follow him and be sure he doesn't double back on us. Amanda and I will head for Three Wells. Catch up if you can."

Buck nodded and left them.

Amanda watched Slade drag the limp form of Loud Mouth into the brush. He returned and kicked dirt over the coals of the smoldering fire.

Leading their horses, they moved on foot across the

moonlit, brush-covered terrain until they reached a path of sorts. Then they mounted. Slade seemed to know where they were and where they were going; Amanda didn't know or care. She was weary to the bone, but she managed to stay in the saddle.

When they'd put several miles between them and the Indian camp, Slade called a halt beneath a scrub oak. "We can rest here for a few minutes," he said, sliding easily from the saddle.

Amanda's exhausted mind failed to comprehend his order, but his hand on her arm brought her to a halt. She swayed groggily. Her head was spinning. She nearly toppled from the saddle.

Slade caught her and hoisted her into his arms. "Damn it, Amanda, why didn't you say something?"

"I didn't want to slow you down," she mumbled, "Do you know you start half your sentences when you speak to me with 'Damn it, Amanda'?" Her voice was faint, her head drooped back over his arm, and her eyes were closed.

Slade swore, then laid her down near the base of a tree. He knelt beside her and brushed a wayward wisp of hair off her cheek. Only Amamda, he mused, would think to reprimand him for cussing at a time like this. "I was so afraid for you," he whispered. If she heard him, she didn't answer.

Slade hobbled the horses, got a blanket and canteen from his saddlebags, and returned to Amanda. He took her hands in his and examined her rope-burned wrists, then wet his handkerchief and gently cleaned her dirt-smeared face. One cheek was bruised and swollen.

Amanda's eyes opened slowly. "I knew you'd find me," she whispered huskily.

"They didn't hurt you, did they?"

Amanda struggled up and leaned back against the oak. "No. Not the way you mean." She shuddered at the thought of what her fate might have been if Slade hadn't come.

Slade helped her drink from the canteen, then wrapped the blanket around her shoulders. "Rest a while. I think we are far enough from the camp now." Amanda closed her eyes, grateful for the respite.

The short rest restored her flagging strength somewhat. So when Slade helped her into the saddle again, she squared her shoulders and smiled at him, determined to put on a good front.

Slade led the way, allowing the horses to pick their own path across the rocky terrain. A faint tinge of gray was beginning to light the eastern sky when he called the next halt in the shelter of a draw. He helped Amanda dismount, and then hobbled the animals. Returning with the canteen, food, and blankets, he offered Amanda jerky and water. "It's not much," he apologized.

"It will do nicely," she assured him. She chewed the jerky thoroughly, savoring its smoky flavor, and drank deeply from the canteen.

Slade cleared a spot of brush at the base of a boulder and they made themselves as comfortable as they could, then finished their meal. When they were done, he pulled Amanda against his side and drew their blankets around them both, sealing out the cool predawn air.

She wrapped her arms around his waist, laid her head against his chest, and listened to the comforting beat of his heart beneath her ear. She felt safe and warm and cared for.

Heaven help her: She was beginning, she suddenly realized, to depend upon and care deeply for this man. That wasn't a wise thing to do, she was sure, but could she stop it? Did she want to? Her eyes slowly drooped closed, and she sighed. She was too tired to think about it. For now she was content to sleep within the circle of his arms.

Slade felt her relax against him and allowed his chin to rest against her silky hair as he pondered the fate that had placed her in his care.

He had not wanted, had not sought, any female involvement since his wife's death. He had not wanted to even think about the events in that period of his life. Now, with Amanda's warm body pressed against his, he was amazed to find he was not only attracted to her, but that his feelings went much deeper. He cursed himself for being twice the fool.

Leaning back against the boulder, he shifted to allow Amanda to rest more comfortably on his chest. The terror he'd felt when the Comanche took her from him rose again like bile in his throat.

He'd ridden like a man possessed in pursuit of her. His arms tightened involuntarily around her beneath the blankets. He shut his eyes and relished the feel of her. "Amanda. . . . Amanda," he whispered into her hair. "What am I going to do about you?"


Buck watched from his place of concealment as the Comanche he'd been following met with six other braves. There was much waving of hands and loud arguing. It was evident that the one he'd been following was a person of some importance and that he didn't seem inclined to lead the small band back to pursue his lost captive.

After a few minutes of argument, the small group rode away to the south. Buck waited quietly for some time to be sure they didn't change their minds, then turned his mount and headed back the way he'd come, setting a fast pace toward Three Wells and Lily.

Amanda came awake slowly, her mind still drugged with fatigue. Fear was the first emotion to surface, and in response she fought against the arms that held her. Slade's voice finally penetrated her foggy mind.

"Easy, love—you're safe," he crooned. "I'd like to let you sleep longer, but I'm not sure how long we will be safe here. We need to move on."

Slade's head was bent close to hers. The warmth of his breath as he spoke sent pleasant shivers along her spine. She was reluctant to give up the comfort and security his nearness provided. Finally, she capitulated with a groan and moved away from him.

She felt hot and sticky and a little unwell. Picking up the canteen, she drank deeply, then offered it to Slade. He took it, recapped it, and stood. Offering her his hand, he pulled her to her feet. A pain behind her right knee caused her to wince.

"What's the matter?" he asked. He steadied her as she bent and pushed up the hem of her split skirt to examine the spot. Slade knelt to examine it also.

"I see the problem," he informed her. "The back of your knee is red and hot to the touch. There's a small festered spot with a tiny thorn embedded in it. Just hold still a second and I'll have it out."

Grasping the thorn between the nails of his middle finger and thumb, he pulled it out. "That ought to take care of it," he assured her. His hand lingered a moment on her calf.

Amanda put her full weight on the leg, and it didn't hurt nearly as much. "Thank you."

She brushed her skirt down as she tried not to think about the way his fingers had felt on the soft sensitive skin of her leg.

"How long will it take us to reach Three Wells?" she asked, turning her thoughts to a new subject and safer ground.

"About three days, if we don't run into any trouble."

"By trouble, do you mean more Comanche?"

"Could be. Those two back there weren't trying to hide. They either didn't think they were being followed or they were waiting for friendly company. There's plenty of Comanche movement right now because they're riled up about being forced onto reservations. I can't say I blame them. If it was me being forced to give up my home, I'd be mad as hell too."

"I thought you called them bloodthirsty savages."

"I did. I didn't say they didn't have reason."

A new thought popped into Amanda's head. "Oh, Slade, I've been so preoccupied with my problems I didn't think to ask about Lily and the guns."

"Lily is fine," he assured her. "The two men that came to our aid were Texas Rangers who were trailing that particular group of Comanche. They agreed to take Lily and the guns to Three Wells while Buck and I came to find you. They should be waiting for us when we get there."

"What about Parker?"

"He was wounded, but not badly. We can question him when we get back. The other man, the one I hired to guard the barn, was killed. He was either in cahoots with Parker before I hired him or Parker somehow got him to go along. That's one of the questions I want answered."

"Are you sure Lily wasn't hurt?"

"Well, I didn't talk to her, but Buck did and he seemed reassured." Slade grinned. "In fact, he was downright cheerful. I suspect he and Lily came to an understanding of some kind. Come on." He tugged on her hand. "The sooner we get moving, the sooner we'll get to Three Wells."

The hot noon sun beat down on them, causing heat waves to dance across the rocky terrain in front of Amanda. Lord, but she was hot. She tucked a strand of sweat-damp hair behind her ear, thankful for the return of her lost hat.

She allowed her mind to linger on Slade a moment. He was considerate, even if he was a little overbearing sometimes. He was also strong, protective, and caring, and he was just as dedicated to his job as she was to hers. She smiled. When he wasn't being stubborn, they even worked well together.

She was going to miss him when this assignment was over. That revelation was disturbing. He had managed to penetrate the protective shell she'd spent years building. And she was very much afraid that she was never going to be the same again.

The plain was behind them now, and they urged their horses up a steep incline. Amanda's gaze was fixed on Slade's broad back. She followed him blindly, trusting him to lead her to safety. They paused at the crest of the hill to survey the valley below.

A narrow river wound its way along the valley floor. The band of green growth along the edges were a welcome change from the brown, brush-covered area they had just crossed. A cabin and corrals built at a bend in the stream should have been a welcome sight. It wasn't. A cloud of smoke, and the smell of burning wood, hung in the hot, still air. The cabin was a pile of burned rubble and the corral fences had been pulled down.

Amanda's stomach knotted with dread. "Oh, Slade."

"I think we had best go take a look, Amanda. There might be someone left who could use our help."

In silence, they descended the hill and crossed the valley. Proceeding with caution, they approached the cabin. A dark-haired woman lay in the middle of the yard. Her skirts were bunched about her waist and blood smeared her thighs. Her torn bodice revealed pale, lifeless skin. Amanda covered her mouth with her hand to stifle a scream.

"Wait here, Amanda," Slade commanded. "There's no need for you to see this."

Slade dismounted and went to the woman, rearranged her clothing, and checked for a pulse. There was none. At the side of the cabin he found a man, about the same age as the woman. His sightless eyes stared up at the blazing sun. The front of his shirt was stiff with dried blood.

Slade made a circuit of the cabin, found nothing more, and returned to Amanda. She dismounted and stood beside her horse.

"Did the Comanche do this," she asked.

"I don't know. It could have been them, or Mexican bandits from across the border. Hell, it could have been anyone. If I can find a shovel, we'll stop long enough to bury them. You take the horses and tie them in the shade. I'm going to see what I can find."

Amanda took care of the horses and then went in search of Slade. She found him behind the cabin, near the edge of the clearing. He'd found a shovel and was digging in the sandy earth.

She sank to the ground and hugged her knees. "Why do people do this to one another? It's so senseless."

"I don't know." Slade leaned on the shovel. "I suppose it's because someone has something the other wants, or maybe because the white man hates the Indian, and vice versa. Or maybe it's because some people are just plain evil."

He started to dig again, and tossed a shovel of dirt away with more than a little force. "Damned if I can figure it out, but that's the way it is."

Slade dug in silence for a while, then said, "Will you see if you can find some rocks to lay over the graves when we're done? That will help keep the animals from digging it up."

Amanda went to look for stones. Her search took her along the wooded edge of the clearing to a spot where stones taken from the yard during clearing had been placed. A rather large pile near a brush-covered mound would provide all they needed.

After several trips between the pile and the grave site, she was breathing heavily and sweat beaded her brow. She felt somewhat weak and nauseous, and a bit light-headed.

Taking a seat on a large, flat rock, she tried to get her racing pulse to slow down. What the devil was the matter with her, anyway?

A faint mewing sound reached her ear, and she

cocked her head to listen. There it was again. It sounded like some small creature, either hurt or in pain. What a pitiful sound, she thought.

Amanda investigated the mound near the pile of stones and found that the brush had been piled loosely on top of it to conceal a small cellar of some kind. A board, held in place by several large stones, covered the opening. The faint cries came again from behind the board, and Amanda's heart thudded with anticipation and fright.

"Slade!" Amanda screamed. "Slade, come here. Hurry."

# 12

*Slade threw down the shovel* he was using to fill in the graves and sprinted across the clearing to Amanda's side.

"Are you hurt?" He grabbed her arm. "You're not snake-bit, are you?"

"Shhh." She put a finger to her lips. "Listen."

"Damn it, Amanda, you just scared the hell out of me! What's the matter with you?"

She pointed toward the wooden door of the cellar. "Be quiet and listen. I heard sounds coming from in there."

The faint cry came again. Slade hurriedly moved the several stones that were being used to keep the door closed and pulled it open. Just enough light filtered into the dark interior to see the crude ladder that gave access to the floor below. Slade backed through

the opening, allowing his feet to search out the rungs
of the ladder. Seconds later he was standing on the
floor, his head and shoulders level with the opening.
He squinted into the darkness, but could make out
nothing. Digging in his pocket, he found his tin of
matches and struck one on the rough metal box.

The flame illuminated a six-by-six-foot room. A few
potatoes and turnips lined one wall. Two half-filled
sacks leaned against the other. A wooden cradle sat in
the middle of the floor, and the weak cries were coming from the wrapped bundle inside. "God Almighty."
The match sputtered out, burning his fingertips.

"What is it, Slade?"

"Trouble," he answered. He bent and searched the
darkness with his hands until he touched wood. Picking
up the cradle, he turned and passed it through the
opening to Amanda.

Amanda placed the cradle on the ground and knelt
beside it. "Oh, my goodness!"

A tiny face, red and pinched from hours of crying,
was visible above a small pink patchwork quilt. The
baby's bright blue eyes blinked rapidly, trying to adjust
to the sunlight after the darkness of the cellar. Wisps of
dark hair framed its small face.

Slade scrambled out of the hole and stood peering
down at the tightly wrapped bundle in the handmade,
intricately carved cradle.

A thin wail, interrupted by little hiccuping sounds,
came from the infant. Slade placed a shaky hand on
Amanda's shoulder. "What are we going to do with it?"

Amanda tipped her head back to look up at him.
"Why, take care of her, of course."

"Her."

"I suppose," she answered hesitantly. "The blanket's pink."

Amanda tried to focus her eyes on Slade's face, but couldn't quite see him clearly.

"Slade . . ." There was a ringing in her ears and her head was spinning. The world was slipping away beneath a black cloud that was slowly swallowing her. She reached for his hand as she tried to get to her feet. "Slade, I don't feel very well."

He took her hand to help her up. When she was halfway to her feet, her legs crumpled beneath her. He caught her as she slid to the ground.

"What the hell," Slade exclaimed. He lay her limp form next to the cradle and knelt beside her. "Amanda!" He placed a hand to her forehead. It was hot, way too hot. She was burning with fever.

He rubbed her wrists and patted her cheeks. Panic fought with concern inside him. This was the worst mess he'd ever been in. What was he supposed to do for an unconscious woman and a screaming baby? He remembered the look on Amanda's upturned face moments earlier. She had answered that question for him already: Take care of them, of course.

His eyes scanned the devastated homestead and came to rest on the only shelter left standing, a small three-sided shed that hadn't been damaged by the fire. He had checked it earlier. It still held some hay and a little feed for the horses the corral had once contained. It would have to do.

He scooped up Amanda's limp form and carried her to the shed. Laying her on the soft hay, he peered at her flushed face. He would have to do something soon to break her fever.

He left Amanda just long enough to fetch the baby and hurry back. The poor little thing barely had the strength to cry, and most of the other sounds she made were pitiful. Slade felt a stab of sympathy unlike anything he'd ever experienced. How long had the baby been in the cellar? She needed to be fed, but how, and with what?

After quickly hobbling the horses and retrieving his pack and canteen, he knelt beside Amanda and bathed her face with a wet cloth. Damn, he'd known she was exhausted, but she never complained. How was he to know she was sick. Did fatigue and exposure make a person run a fever? Could she be in shock? That thought scared the hell out of him—people died from shock. He unbuttoned her shirt partway and placed his hand over her heart. To his relief, it was beating steadily. She moaned and her eyes fluttered open.

"Slade, water . . . please."

"I'm here, love." He grabbed the canteen and, supporting her head with his hand, brought it to her lips. She took a small sip.

"I'm sorry to be such a bother. I'm so tired . . . hot too. Why is it so hot?"

"Hush, Amanda." He wiped her face and neck with the damp cloth. "You have a fever. Lie back and rest. You'll be fine."

"No, I have to help with the baby. How is she?"

"The baby's fine. I'm taking care of everything."

He soothed her with words that held more conviction than he felt, and her eyes drooped closed. Her breathing was rapid and shallow.

Reluctantly, he turned his attention back to the baby. Using his finger, he placed drops of water in the child's mouth. The baby sucked hungrily on the finger each time Slade placed it there. It was amazing, Slade marveled; there was so much power in that tiny little mouth. It was a time-consuming method, but after a while the baby quieted and Slade was elated—although, just for a moment. Water, he knew, wouldn't keep the baby alive for long. He had to think of something else to feed it.

While Amanda and the baby were quiet, he returned to the cellar and checked the available food. One of the bags contained cornmeal, the other salt. Nothing to feed a hungry baby. Good God, what was he going to do?

He searched the saddlebags for anything he might use as food for the infant. At the very bottom he found a small oilcloth packet containing sugar. His heart leapt at the discovery.

Dissolved in water, it would at least have some food value, and he didn't see how it could be harmful to the infant. He dumped a small amount into his tin cup and added water so he would be ready when the child woke.

He returned to Amanda and placed a hand to her forehead. She felt hotter than the last time he'd checked her. If only he knew what was wrong with her, perhaps he could help. He removed her boots and loosened the waist of her skirt to make her more comfortable. It was then he remembered the thorn he'd removed from her leg. He turned her on her side to examine the spot.

Damn! The area was swollen and red. Heat radiated from the spot. He probed it carefully with the tips of his fingers. A small, hard core had formed where the thorn had been embedded. Pus oozed from the center. Lord! If he hadn't gotten the entire thorn

out it could cause this abscess, he knew, and if it was
a mesquite thorn it could cause blood poisoning.

Slade quickly built a small fire outside the shed. He
retrieved the pot from the burned-out cabin, emptied
his canteen into it, and added a small handful of salt.
He would use hot, wet salt pack on the leg to pull the
infection out. He wasn't sure it would work, but it was
all he could think of.

He held his knife in the flames for a moment, then
moved back to Amanda's side. He waited for the blade
to cool before pressing the tip to the inflamed center of
the wound. Pus spurted from the small incision.
Placing a finger on each side of the spot, he exerted a
gentle pressure. More fluid came out. Amanda moaned
and tried to jerk her leg away.

"Easy, love. I'm almost done."

She didn't respond, but her body stilled. He pressed
again, and the small dark end of the thorn surfaced.
After removing it, he soaked two squares of cloth in
the hot saltwater. He used one to clean the wound; the
other he folded and placed over it.

He sat down then, between Amanda and the cradle,
and tried to organize his thoughts. The sun was sinking.
It would be dark soon. God, he was tired, he reflected;
this had to be the longest day of his life, and it wasn't
over, not by a long shot.

He glanced down at the tiny form in the cradle, so
small and helpless. His heart hardened with hate for
the animals—he wouldn't call them men—who had
deprived the innocent child of her parents.

God surely didn't intend for this baby to die, Slade
reasoned, or He wouldn't have led them to her. His
mother had always said that God works in miraculous

ways. Slade was sure he needed a miracle, or something close to it, if he was to get through this night. It had been a long time since he'd prayed. He wasn't sure he remembered how.

He closed his eyes. "God, I don't know if You're listening, but if You are, I could sure use some help down here. I'm in way over my head. Please, show me what to do." Slade opened his eyes and watched the sun set in a blaze of orange.

The baby stirred and began to cry. Slade folded back the pink quilt and slid a hesitant hand under the small bundle, intending to pick it up. He encountered a very wet bottom.

Removing the squirming infant from her wet bed, he placed her on the hay. A search of the cradle turned up several squares of rolled flannel stuffed at one end. Picking them up, he discovered a glass bottle with a nipple. Slade breathed a sigh of relief. "Thank you, God."

He spread the wet bedding out to dry, then filled the bottle with sugar water and set it aside. Returning to the child, he stared down at her.

Where did a man start?

He hiked up the child's gown and tried to decide how a person with hands as large as his was supposed to work on anything that small. He fumbled with the pin that held the folded triangle of flannel in place. The baby's short, chubby legs pumped and the little bottom wiggled as he removed the soiled napkin and tried to replace it with a clean one.

"Be still, little girl, or I'll never get this done."

The pin slipped, stabbing his finger, and he swallowed back a cussword. "I don't want to hurt you, baby, so be still." He finally got the pin fastened. "Now see, that wasn't so bad."

He wanted to remove the wet gown, but there wasn't anything to replace it with. He placed another dry napkin between the baby's skin and gown and laid her back on the hay.

It was fully dark now, the only light coming from the campfire and the pale crescent moon. He picked up the bottle and then the baby and placed the nipple to the child's lips. The little mouth latched onto it and sucked hungrily. Slade smiled as he watched the mouth work, amazed anew that anything so tiny could have such strength. The liquid disappeared from the bottle rapidly.

"Take it easy, little girl, or you'll make yourself sick."

He put the empty bottle aside. What was he supposed to do now? He sat the baby upright, supporting her tiny head with his large hand. A burp issued from the small mouth.

"Well, that should make you feel better." He wrapped the baby in her almost dry quilt and laid her on the hay. He gazed smugly down at her. There really wasn't much to this baby business, he decided.

He turned his attention to Amanda and replaced the now cold salt pack with a hot one. Her skin was so hot it scared him. He started to pick up the canteen and remembered that it was empty.

After retrieving a bucket he'd seen earlier near the burned cabin, he made his way by moonlight to the stream. It was undoubtedly spring-fed, he figured, because it was icy cold.

Amanda was delirious with fever by the time Slade returned. In desperation, he removed her clothing and bathed her in the icy water. He tried not to think

about the beautifully formed body beneath his hands.
It was a damned hard thing to do.

She could feel the hands that tended her. They must
be her mother's hands, she thought, because they were so
gentle. Her mind wandered. She was a child in the convent again, and she cried for her mother. She screamed
at the Sisters and railed against their strict rules.

Amanda moaned and thrashed about on the straw.
Slade tried to soothe her with soft words and gentle
touches. But nothing he did seemed to work. Finally,
he scooped her up, held her hot body against his, and
rocked her like a baby. She quieted, and he bathed her
again. He repeated the process over and over through
the long night. Just before dawn, her fever broke.

Slade would have wept with relief if he'd had the
time. He didn't. He bathed the sweat from her skin
and covered her with the remaining blanket. He was
so tired he could barely move, but his heart soared:
She was going to be all right.

The baby cried. He changed and fed her, folded the
dry quilt and put it back in the cradle, then placed the
baby on it.

Sliding to the ground, he leaned his back against the
side of the shed. He'd never been this exhausted in his
entire life, but he'd never felt this satisfied with a night's
work, either. Dawn was breaking in a display of lavender and pink. A new day was beginning. He lay down
between Amanda and the cradle and closed his eyes.

It seemed like only moments before the baby's cries
woke him. "Oh no," he groaned. "Please, not yet."

He rubbed the sleep from his eyes with the back of
his hand and sat up. Reaching out, he laid a hand on
Amanda's forehead. She still had a fever, but nothing

like the night before. She moved restlessly beneath the blanket and it slipped down, revealing the tops of her breasts. He quickly tucked it back under her chin and turned away.

The baby was wet and screaming at the top of her lungs. He changed her and balanced her on his hip while he dissolved the last of the sugar in a cup of boiled water. He was going to have to think of something else to feed the hungry little girl if she was going to survive.

He balanced her in the crook of his arm and she sucked the bottle dry with her usual hearty appetite. His own stomach grumbled, and he realized he hadn't eaten anything in the last twenty-four hours. Potatoes and turnips were the only food choices, and he didn't like turnips.

He burped the baby and, for a long moment, cuddled the soft little body to his chest. A queer feeling twisted his gut: If his wife had been faithful, if his life had gone according to plan, he might have been holding his own daughter against his heart. He didn't want to think about that. He placed the baby in the cradle. A man couldn't live with regret as a constant companion.

It was time to get back to work. He went to the stream for another bucket of water and then washed and peeled about half the potatoes. He quartered them, put them in the pot, added water, and placed the pot over the fire to boil.

He checked Amanda's leg. The swelling was down, the redness not so vivid. The small incision he'd made appeared to be healing. She was sleeping peacefully.

When the potatoes were tender, he drained off enough of the water to fill the baby's bottle and one of their two tin cups.

He could only hope he wasn't harming the infant with this strange diet. Then he added half his remaining beef jerky to the pot so it could simmer with and flavor the potatoes.

He returned to the shed, sat down, and leaned his weary body against the wall. He rested, at the same time keeping a diligent watch over his charges. At about noon, the baby began to fuss again.

He changed the child and offered her the bottle. She screwed up her little face at the first taste and spit out the nipple.

"Come on, baby, be a good little girl and drink this," he pleaded. "I know it doesn't taste as good as sugar water, but it's all we have."

He tried again. She still didn't like it, but with patient effort, he got her to take half the bottle before she spit it out again.

"That's a good girl," he crooned. He patted her back and was rewarded with a healthy burp.

"What are you doing?"

Slade was so surprised by the sound of Amanda's voice he almost dropped the baby. He turned to find her sitting up, the blanket clutched to her chest.

"I'm feeding the baby. What did you think I was doing?"

"I thought you were hitting her on the back."

Slade grinned. "I see you don't know anything about babies, either. I was burping her. Would you like to see her?"

He displayed the infant proudly, pointing out her tiny fingers and little toes.

"She's really a very good baby. Why, she's hardly any trouble at all. And you should see her eat."

Amanda touched the crown of soft dark hair and ran a finger over her satiny cheek. "She's beautiful. What are you feeding her?"

"Potato water. I gave her sugar water first, but we're out of that." Slade placed the child in the cradle and turned back to Amanda. "How are you feeling?"

"A bit strange. Weak and a little dizzy." She clutched the blanket under her chin. "What have you done with my clothes?"

Slade picked up her shirt, skirt, and underwear and placed them on her blanket-covered lap.

"I didn't know what else to do, Amanda," Slade said in his own defense. "You were burning with fever. The thorn in your leg must have caused some kind of poisoning. I put salt packs on the wound to draw out the infection and bathed you in icy spring water to break the fever."

Amanda's mouth fell open. "All over!"

"Yes. All over. Now let's talk about something else. Are you hungry?"

He turned his back and busied himself at the pot. When he turned to face her again with a cup of broth in his hand, she was dressed. "Here, drink this. It will make you feel better."

He filled a tin plate with potatoes and meat and sat down beside her to eat. She placed a tentative hand on his arm.

"Slade."

He looked over at her. "What?"

"Thank you."

"For what."

Her eyes sought his. "For taking such good care of me, that's what. I'm sorry if I sounded ungrateful."

"You're welcome." He smiled widely. "It was my pleasure."

Amanda glanced away quickly, but not before Slade saw the pink flush on her cheeks.

Half an hour later, at the stream's edge, Slade finished the last of the baby's wash. His hands were blue and his arms were numb to the elbow from the icy water of the stream. Picking up the small pile of wet clothing, he headed back toward camp.

The afternoon was warm, the air humid. A few gray-tinged clouds scudded across an otherwise unbroken expanse of bright, blue sky. The skirt of green growth along the edge of the stream smelled faintly of flowers. Birds chirped in the trees. Slade breathed deeply, savoring the scent and sounds of the place. He could see why the couple had chosen this spot to settle.

He made a mental note to check with the nearest land office for the name of the baby's parents and to somehow have the title transferred to the baby's name. He would try to hold the land for her if he could. It was all that remained of her birthright.

He moved slowly along the path from the stream, enjoying the freedom from his nursing duties. But he knew he really should get back. Amanda wasn't well enough to tend a screaming baby. And the child certainly did have a strong pair of lungs, which she hadn't quit using for the past hour.

Slade was jerked back to full awareness by the sound of Amanda's earsplitting scream. He sprinted the rest of the distance and skidded to a halt before the shed.

Amanda was scrunched against the back wall, clutching the screaming baby to her chest. Two Feathers was bending over them.

Slade's chest was heaving from the run, and he had to drag air into his lungs before he could speak.

"If you've come for the woman, the answer's the same: You can't have her—she's mine!"

Two Feathers spun around at the sound of Slade's voice.

"Now back away from her and keep your hands where I can see them," Slade commanded. He breathed an inward sigh of relief as Two Feathers stepped away from Amanda.

Slade still held the wet wash in one numb hand, and the other was so stiff with cold he couldn't have fired his Colt even if he could have gotten it out of his holster. Two Feathers eyed the drippy wash Slade clutched and smiled faintly.

"I no come for woman," he said as he drew abreast of Slade.

"Well, good. At least we agree on something. What did you come for?"

"My braves find Mexican bandits camped one day from here. They have many horses—this brand." He indicated the homestead with a sweep of his arm. "People here my friend. I come see."

"What happened to the bandits and the horses?" Slade questioned.

"Them bad men." Two Feathers's countenance was grim. "Now, they dead men. My people have horses. We keep. Last time I here, woman big like melon. Is this papoose?" He pointed at the crying baby in Amanda's arms.

"I think so," Slade answered. "We found the child in the cellar. Do you know the name of the couple who lived here?"

"They called O'Shannon. What wrong with papoose?" Two Feathers asked, gesturing toward the crying baby.

Amanda was trying unsuccessfully to quiet the screaming child. "I think Slade may have made her sick. We have no milk, so he fed her potato water."

Two Feathers stepped back into the shed and held out his arms to take the baby. Amanda looked to Slade for consent. He nodded. Amanda handed the infant over and watched as Two Feathers examined the child. He placed a large hand on the baby's stomach. "Here trouble. Hard. Have bellyache."

"We don't know what to do for her," Amanda confessed.

Two Feathers looked at Slade. "You need help."

"That's the understatement of the year," Slade agreed.

Two Feathers handed the baby back to Amanda. "My woman medicine woman. I get root, we boil, fix papoose." His chest expanded with pride. "I have two sons and another soon."

"If you can help us, we would be grateful," Slade said, relief evident in his voice. One look over at Amanda told him she felt the very same way.

# 13

*Amanda watched Two Feathers* disappear into the brush in search of the root remedy. She shifted the crying baby to her other shoulder and patted her back gently.

"Hush, hush, little baby," she crooned softly. She tested the baby's tummy with her hand as the Indian had done. It was rock-hard. She rubbed it carefully, hoping the warmth of her hand might somehow soothe the child. It didn't seem to help. She had to raise her voice to be heard above the wail when she addressed Slade.

"Do you think he knows what to do for her?"

"We are going to have to hope so, since we don't."

"I guess so. You know, I think that man has the biggest ego I've ever encountered. He has two sons and another on the way, he said. And he wanted me to give him more. Do Comanches have harems?"

Slade grinned. "I don't think so, although I've heard some tribes do allow more than one wife. The usual fate of a white captive is that of a slave. To help the wife with the work and to be available if the brave should have need of her."

Amanda shivered at the picture Slade painted and cuddled the wailing baby closer. "I'm grateful to you for convincing Two Feathers that I'm already taken."

"You don't mind being my woman?"

Amanda thought Slade's voice lingered a moment too long on the words, "my woman."

She chose her own words carefully. "Not at all. You've been the perfect gentleman." Her eyes met his steady gaze. "I don't think there is any way I can ever repay you for the concern and care you have shown me. Just to say thank you doesn't seem to be quite enough."

A dark look crossed Slade's face. "Thank you is more than sufficient. After all, it's part of a Ranger's job to rescue damsels in distress."

Amanda sensed the chill in his tone. He turned and left her to spread the baby's wash on what was left of the corral fence.

What had she said to put him in such a temper? Why did they always seem to be at odds with one another? She sighed, leaned back against the wall of the shed, and closed her eyes.

Suddenly another question occurred to her: What were they going to do with the baby when they finally got back to Three Wells?

"Woman fix."

Amanda's eyes flew open at the sound of Two Feathers' voice. He deposited an armload of white roots at her feet.

"I find much. I take some to my woman. You keep rest."

Amanda eyed the tubers. They were clean, indicating that he had taken the time to wash them before bringing them in. That was a small kindness on his part, she was sure, and her momentary anger at his brusque tone evaporated.

"How?"

A trace of a smile touched his mouth. "Boil in water, give water to baby." He turned to Slade. "Your woman not know much."

Amanda was sure Two Feathers was making fun of her. In his own droll way, the man had a sense of humor.

"But she learns quickly," Slade countered with a straight face.

Amanda almost laughed at the subtle play between the two men. She hid her amusement as she handed Slade the fretting baby and began to brew the Indian remedy for colic.

Slade and Two Feathers sat in the shade of the shed and watched her work. They must have reached some sort of male understanding, Amanda decided, to which she wasn't privy. Their conversation was covered by the wail of the baby, but the two of them seemed as thick as thieves.

When the root tea had sufficiently cooled, Amanda filled the baby's bottle and retrieved the crying child from Slade. Then she made herself comfortable on a blanket in the shed and offered the baby the nipple. The baby sucked down half the bottle, burped largely, and promptly fell into an exhausted sleep.

Amanda placed her in her cradle and stepped from beneath the shed's roof in time to see Slade and Two

Feathers clasp hands. Apparently Two Feathers was leaving.

"I wish you long life, and many sons. Cubs from the she-cat will be strong," he said to Slade.

"We thank you for the wish and for being a good friend to the babe. Perhaps when she is grown," Slade added, "we will bring her to visit the camp of the Comanche and collect her share of the ponies from the herd that you are so kindly keeping for her."

Two Feathers actually smiled at that remark. "I will await your return" was his parting comment. Then he slipped silently away into the gathering twilight.

Slade returned to the small campfire and placed the pot containing what was left of the meat and potatoes over the coals to warm.

"Is he gone for good?" Amanda asked him.

"I think so. Is the baby sleeping?"

"Yes. I think she's better, but we need to get her to town. She needs milk and clothes and someone who knows how to take care of babies. I'm terrified of hurting her by doing something wrong."

Slade moved to sit beside Amanda and took her hand. "We're doing the best we can, Amanda. She's a lot better off than if we hadn't found her. But you're right: We do need to move on. How is your leg?"

"Lots better—it hardly hurts at all. I still feel a little weak, but a good night's sleep ought to fix that."

"Then, we will leave in the morning."

Amanda poked absently at the fire with a stick, sending a small shower of bright sparks into the darkening night. "What do you think happened to Buck?" she asked. "He should have caught up with us by now."

"Don't worry about him. He'll be waiting for us in Three Wells. Lily's there."

Slade touched the back of her hand, then began to move his fingers over it in a slow circular motion. She didn't think he even realized he was doing it. His touch caused her pulse to race and made it difficult for her to keep her mind on the conversation.

"Yes, I suppose he will be."

Amanda withdrew her hand from Slade's gentle grasp, dropped her stick into the fire, and went about filling their plates with the warmed-over food. She handed Slade one, thinking that eating would give him something else to do with his hands, and wondering why his touch caused her such distress.

They ate in silence as the night settled around them. The hum of insects and the calls of the night birds were the only sounds to break the quiet.

Amanda spoke softly, "It's really nice here, isn't it?"

"Yes, the baby's parents picked a fine spot. I'm going to see if I can hold it for her until she is old enough to decide what to do with it. Now that Two Feathers has given us the couple's name, that shouldn't be too difficult. The land office in Three Wells should have a record of the sale."

"Slade," Amanda began hesitantly. "I think we should give the baby a first name. "I don't like calling her 'baby' all the time, and since we are the ones who found her, I think her parents would understand."

"I think that's a fine idea, Amanda. What name did you have in mind?"

"I was thinking Faith might be appropriate. Her parents must have had a great deal of it to have put her in that cellar."

"Faith O'Shannon. It sounds good to me."

The newly named Faith chose that moment to intrude on their conversation. Her hungry howl floated on the quiet night air.

While Amanda quickly filled Faith's bottle with three parts potato water and one part colic tea in the hope that the new mixture would keep her from having another bellyache, Slade changed her wet napkin. He had more experience in that department than she did and he really didn't seem to mind.

Slade waited until Amanda settled herself beneath the shelter before handing Faith over. He took a seat close by and watched as the baby latched onto the nipple with her usual hearty appetite. He laughed aloud when she screwed up her face at the first taste.

"It's not sugar water, is it, Faith." His remark ended with a fond smile. The strange taste didn't deter her for long.

The light from the campfire cast a golden glow around Amanda and Faith. Slade's heart expanded with affection and pride as he gazed at the woman and child.

In that moment he realized he wanted Amanda to hold his child in just that same way someday. The sudden desire for a wife and a family of his own nearly took his breath away.

He watched Amanda place the sleeping baby in her cradle and rearrange her blanket on the hay in preparation for sleep. Then he went to tend the fire to give her a few private moments. When he returned, Amanda was stretched out on the blanket with her eyes closed. Her face was relaxed and serene and beautiful in sleep. It took all the willpower Slade possessed to keep from reaching down to run his hand along the curve of her cheek. Damn! he muttered to himself. Oh damn! Desire swirled within him, making his pulse race and his body hard.

Turning away, he spread his blanket next to hers and tried to settle down for the night. The sound of Amanda's breathing, deep and even, reached him. It was best for them both that she slept. He remembered the feel of her naked body beneath his hands as he'd cared for her during her bouts of fever, and the way he'd felt when he'd thought she might die would haunt him forever.

He needed time to think—not that he was capable of making any reasonable decision at this particular moment. His mind was in a muddle and his heart, which he usually guarded so carefully, was in danger of being stolen away by a green-eyed imp who didn't seem the least bit interested in settling down with him and raising his children.

How could she be? He had only just begun to contemplate the idea himself. He knew she was attracted to him physically by the way she responded to his touch. But did she love him?

He was going to get an answer to that question at the first opportunity, or when he got up the nerve, whichever came first. If she didn't, he was going to do his damnedest to see that she came around to his way of thinking. He was sure he could be quite lovable if he put his mind to it. With that decided, he closed his eyes.

The sun was shining on Amanda's face when she woke. She covered her eyes with her arm to block it out. Morning birds were singing their heads off and she could hear baby Faith gurgling happily at Slade's coaxing.

Amanda peeped at the two of them from beneath the cover of her arms. Slade was bouncing the baby on his knee and making stupid-looking faces that would have scared the daylights out of grown men. But Faith seemed to love it.

"What do you think you're doing?" Amanda asked as she scooted to a sitting position.

"Faith and I are playing while we wait for a certain lazy lady we know to wake up."

"Why didn't you wake me?

"Because it's early and we have a long ride ahead of us and you needed the extra sleep."

There was concern for her in his voice.

"I used the time to repack the saddlebags and fill the canteens. By then, Faith was awake, so I changed and fed her." He offered Amanda a drink from one of the canteens and a piece of beef jerky. "It's a poor excuse for breakfast, but it's better than nothing."

Amanda took the offering with a smile. "I'm not very hungry anyway."

Slade raised an eyebrow and gave her a wry smile. "I think the lady lies."

Ten minutes later, they were riding side by side along the stream that flowed out of the secluded valley. Faith was sleeping peacefully in a cradleboard strapped to Slade's back, the rocking gait of the horse having lulled her to sleep.

Apparently, Two Feathers had managed to find the time to make the flat, framed board used by Indians to carry infants, then left it in the shed for them to find. Slade had discovered the unique device while checking for any forgotten items just before their departure. Two Feathers, Amanda decided, was a good friend.

Faith's cradle, the only thing that had survived the fire, was tied behind Amanda's saddle.

Amanda glanced over at Slade. "How long will it take to get home?" She hoped the answer would be "soon."

"A day and a half if we make good time, two if we don't," Slade replied.

"Then I hope we make good time, because I can't wait to see everyone. It's funny—a short time ago, I would not have believed it possible that I could miss a place and its people so much." She paused, hunting for just the right words. "I think it's going to be very hard for me to go back to Washington and leave everyone here."

Slade grinned at her. "Including me?"

Amanda smiled back. "Yes, you too. But I wasn't going to say that. I didn't want you to get a swelled head."

"You know that I'm too modest for that, love," Slade teased.

Suddenly the light of amusement disappeared from his eyes. "Then why don't you stay?" he asked.

Slade's words hung between them. Amanda realized that their relationship had changed while they had been alone together. She had grown accustomed to relying on him for her care and protection, but she wasn't sure how she felt about the closeness that had developed between them.

"Stay. Stay and do what? You know I'm not comfortable about owning the house. It was only a cover for me to use while I looked for my father's killer. Now, I can't decide what to do with it. I've been searching my mind for a way to dispose of it without taking away the ladies' home or their source of income."

"I have a suggestion. Why don't you let the girls buy you out? I'm willing to turn over my share to them. I never intended to keep it from the beginning. As you say, it was a source of cover, and now there is no need for it. And I think that when we question the gunrunners, we will probably find out who masterminded this whole operation and you will find your killer. I've found in the years I've been a Ranger that there is no honor among thieves. They will give us the information we want in the hope of saving their own necks."

He paused. "With your father gone, what will you do in Washington? Do you have someone waiting for you to return?"

Amanda saw his jaw tighten as he waited for her answer. Her heart rate quickened. There might be more meaning in the question than was obvious, she knew.

"No, there's no one special, but my home and my half of Father's business is there. I can go back to work with Robert and make some kind of life for myself. But, you know, I think your idea about what to do with the house might be the answer to my problem. I will suggest it to Wilma at the first opportunity to see what she thinks. What will you do when your job here is over?"

Slade's countenance was solemn. "I believe I have some thinking to do along those lines. I've been wandering around with no sense of direction since my wife's death. I think perhaps it's time to take a good look at what I want to do with the rest of my life."

They rode in silence for a long time. So Slade's wife was dead. Amanda wondered if he would tell her about that if she asked, and if she should allow herself to be drawn deeper into his life.

She had long ago vowed not to marry or have children. Her own childhood had been her example of what "family" meant. Should she, like Slade, take some time to rethink the course her life was to take?

Slade hadn't actually asked her to stay, but he had posed the question, so he must have given it some thought, she figured.

She glanced at the sky. The sun was higher now and the warmth of the day increasing. Slade signaled a halt and they dismounted. Slade shrugged the cradleboard from his shoulders and placed Faith in the shade of a nearby tree before leading the horses to the stream to drink.

Amanda busied herself with the task of changing and feeding Faith. The baby cooed and snuggled against her breast, content to be cared for by her.

Amanda knew she was growing far too fond of the baby. If she allowed herself to love Faith, where would that leave her? After all, she reasoned, a single woman couldn't raise a child by herself.

Pain welled up in her heart. This, she suddenly realized, was how her mother must have felt.


The sun was setting in a blaze of purple and orange when Slade, Amanda, and a fussy Faith finally rode into the clearing where a line shack stood amid a grove of pecan trees.

Slade had remembered its existence late in the afternoon, and he and Amanda had decided that four walls and a roof was worth the extra two miles it took to reach it. Its two front windows stared blankly at them, like eyes in a gray, weathered face. Though it was empty and desolate, Amanda found the cabin a most welcome sight.

While Slade cared for the horses, Amanda and Faith explored the one-room haven. The bed was sturdy. Its tick mattress looked lumpy, but clean. The table and two chairs were wobbly, but serviceable. A small potbellied stove with a pipe through the wall evidently served as both cookstove and heat source. A shelf nailed to a side wall contained two cans of peaches, a tin of coffee beans, and a heavy layer of dust.

Amanda placed Faith in the middle of the bed and went back out to retrieve the saddlebags and bedrolls from beneath the tree where Slade had left them. After bringing them in she went to find twigs and branches to start a fire.

By the time Slade returned to the cabin, the coffee was brewing and Faith had been changed and fed a mixture of peach juice, water, and root remedy. She was happily staring at her own fists and making baby sounds on the bed.

Slade's hair was wet and his shirt clung to his broad chest. Evidently he had taken the time to wash in the creek, Amanda reasoned. His freshly groomed appearance only served to make her feel more rumpled and grubby.

"Will you keep an eye on Faith while I make a trip to the creek?"

"Sure, but you had best hurry. There isn't going to be a moon tonight, and it will be darker than a well's bottom in a few minutes." Slade sniffed the air appreciatively. "That coffee sure smells good." He went to the stove as she hurried out the door.

Amanda stripped to her camisole and drawers and quickly washed. The creek water was cold. It and the rapidly cooling night air gave her goose bumps. She shivered, but her discomfort was slight compared with the feeling of being clean. She decided to take the extra minutes required to wash her hair. The heat from the cabin's stove would dry it before bedtime.

When she returned and opened the cabin door, the warmth of the room enveloped her. She moved closer to the stove, hoping to dry her damp clothes.

Slade handed her a cup of steaming coffee. "Here, drink this. You're shivering like a leaf in a windstorm. You're apt to catch your death running around with all that wet hair. Go sit down."

Amanda took a seat at the table and accepted the blanket Slade placed around her shoulders. His light touch caused a shiver, even though she was no longer cold.

He took a seat across the table from her and they dined on beef jerky and canned peaches, washed down with hot, black coffee. As Amanda ate, she decided this was the finest meal she'd had in a very long time. A feeling of contentment washed over her.

Slade watched Amanda devour her peaches with unladylike grace, and smiled at her obvious delight. The tip of her tongue came out to catch the last drop of juice from her spoon.

Slade groaned inwardly as a sharp stab of desire coursed through him. He'd offered her the blanket for his own peace of mind as much as for her comfort. When she'd returned from her bath—her clothes damp and clinging, her hair wet, her face scrubbed and glowing—he'd felt his manhood begin to harden.

Quite unintentionally, the woman was slowly driving him insane.

He reached across the narrow table and ran a finger across her wet lips. He simply could not resist the urge to touch her.

"I do love to see a lady enjoy a meal," he whispered.

Amanda's pulse quickened at his touch. His eyes were dark, his expression warm. She understood his need to touch her—she had the overpowering desire to do the same thing. Why, she couldn't say, for she had never felt this need with any other man. The feeling frightened her.

"Do you?" Her words came out in a breathless gush. She stood, intending to put some distance between them. The blanket slid to the floor. And then he was there. His arms encircled her; his mouth descended to claim hers in a kiss that held such sweetness it took away what breath she still possessed.

She tasted like peaches and felt like heaven. Slade rejoiced in the feel of her body against his. They fit together perfectly. He wanted her so much, he shook with the need.

Her arms slipped around his neck and her mouth opened to admit his exploring tongue. He heard her soft moan and deepened the kiss, the need to make her his was a desperation that bordered on insanity.

His mouth left hers to rest against her cheek. When he could breathe again, he whispered, "You taste so good."

She backed away from him, and he saw the uncertainty in her eyes. He let her go. With an effort, he made his tone light. "I never could resist kissing a woman who tastes like peaches."

He glanced toward the bed with a sigh. Faith was sleeping peacefully in its middle. "Get your brush and come sit by the fire. I'll help you dry your hair."

With shaking hands, Amanda retrieved her brush from her saddlebags near the door. The diversion gave her time to compose her reeling emotions. She liked Slade's kiss, liked the feel of his hard, masculine body and the hot sensations that raced through her at his touch. Was this what it felt like to want a man? Lord, she marveled, a person could become addicted to this kind of thing. She hadn't wanted him to stop. Why *had* he?

She turned back, brush in hand, to find Slade sitting cross-legged on the floor before the stove. He patted the spot in front of him. She sat with her back to him and held up the brush, and he took it from her hand.

Amanda soon discovered that there was something very intimate in having one's hair brushed by a man. Her scalp tingled and her heart beat as rapidly as a hummingbird's wings.

Slade used the brush and his fingers to free the tangles from her long hair. He was slow and methodical, and she was lulled by a sense of contentment. This was something a man might do for his wife, she decided. Finally, he brushed the nearly dried mass forward over her shoulder and began to massage the back of her neck and her shoulders.

Long fingers and callused hands stroked and kneaded her tired, tense muscles, sending a tingle of warmth down her spine. She felt the need to stretch and purr as he stroked her. A sound of pleasure rose from her throat.

Slade spread his legs out on either side of her and

his arms circled her waist to pull her against his chest and groin. She could feel his hardened member press into the small of her back and his warm breath brush against her cheek. She allowed him the intimate contact, because she wanted it too.

"Slade."

"Yes."

"Why did you stop kissing me before? I liked it, you know."

"I know, but I didn't think you were ready for what comes next." He took a deep breath, and she felt his chest expand against her back. "I had to stop then, because I wouldn't have been able to later. I want you, Amanda." He pressed her more firmly against his arousal. "I want you so much I hurt."

Amanda turned and knelt between his knees. Her hands rested on his cheeks. Her eyes searched his. "How will you know when I'm ready?"

His hands moved to rest on her hips. Her fingers traced the line of his mouth.

"I'll know"—he breathed the words against her fingertips—"when you know." His voice was low and husky. The sound touched something deep inside her. The intensity of his gaze warmed her.

Before she had time to form a reply, he kissed her again, this time a hard, demanding kiss. She tensed. She liked it, but she liked the soft ones better.

As if reading her mind, Slade's mouth softened and he kissed her tenderly, exploring the corners of her mouth and the line of her lips with his tongue.

Amanda ceased to think. She could only feel the solid strength of his body as hers molded to it. Her hands found the soft hair at the back of his neck and lingered there. Her mouth opened to his insistent tongue.

Heat radiated out from the center of her body. She felt weak and clung to him for support as the world began to spin around her. His mouth left hers and she moaned "no" at the loss. He held her tight against himself as his lips teased her ear, and a shiver of pure pleasure coursed through her.

"Do you want me?" he asked.

Her mind understood the danger in his question, but her body would not obey its command to escape his sweet threat. "Please" was the only response she could make.

"Please what?"

"I don't know." Before she could think any further, his mouth found hers again in a long, mind-fogging kiss. Her breath, when she remembered to breathe, came in short little gasps. Her whole body throbbed with a painful ache.

"Open your eyes, Amanda. Look at me."

Slade's voice penetrated her muddled mind. She hadn't realized that her eyes were closed. Opening them was a mistake; she was immediately lost in the dark, passion-filled depths of his gaze.

"Say you want me, too." His voice sounded rough and strained.

"Yes . . . All right . . . Yes. I want you. I want the way you make me feel when you touch me. I want your kiss and your body touching mine. Only that isn't enough anymore." She paused, recalling the words he had spoken just minutes ago. "I hurt too," she said.

Her voice broke. Then she knew, and she smiled. "Make the hurt go away, Slade. Please."

Slade's raspy chuckle filled the small room. He got to his feet and offered her his hand. "Come to bed, love. I'll make it better, I promise."

He picked up Faith and placed her in her cradle beside the bed. Then he spread another blanket over the tick mattress as he slowly allowed himself time to calm down.

He wanted to go slowly and be gentle with her. It wouldn't be easy. He'd never wanted any woman as badly as he wanted her—not even his wife. That realization shook him. In fact, it scared the hell out of him.

He turned to her, and she moved into his embrace. Finding the top button on her shirt open, he lowered his head to kiss the swell of her breasts in the open vee. He felt her sharp intake of breath and his body surged with desire. His fingers found the other buttons on her shirt and worked them open, then untied the bows on her camisole and pushed it aside. He buried his face in the fragrant valley between her breasts and sighed with pure pleasure at the feel of her satiny skin.

His mouth nuzzled her right breast. Her nipple hardened. Desire, hot and demanding, twisted his gut at the evidence of her arousal. He ran the tip of his tongue over the sweet bud, and she pushed against him. He treated her other breast with the same intense care and felt her tremble.

Amanda's fingers found the buttons on Slade's shirt and worked them open. The need to touch him as he touched her was overwhelming. Her small hands caressed his crisp chest hair and his body jerked in response to the contact.

She was amazed at the sense of power it gave her to know he couldn't control his responses to her touch any more than she could restrain her responses to his. He wasn't overpowering her. They were equals. The knowledge made her bold. Her hands moved across his chest, followed by her mouth, as she learned the feel and taste of him.

"You're beautiful." She didn't realize she'd said the words aloud until he answered.

"*I'm* supposed to tell *you* that."

Her mouth found its way back to his, and she kissed him sweetly. "Then tell me," she whispered.

"Oh, Amanda," Slade chuckled against her cheek, "I'm glad you never do anything halfway."

He unbuttoned her skirt and untied her drawers and slid both garments over her hips and down her legs. Then he pulled off her boots. His hands explored her silky skin. His gaze roved over her nude body, committing it to memory. Her breasts were high and full, her waist tiny. The delicate flare of her hips and the flat plain of her belly were perfect. He dared not look lower, for fear of losing what little control he had left.

"You are beautiful, Amanda." He ran a hand over her, tracing a line from breast to thigh. "You're so beautiful you take my breath away." He lowered his head to kiss her navel and let his tongue dip inside. As her hips rose in invitation, his hand moved lower to caress the triangle of soft hair, and he felt her tense.

"It's all right, love. I won't hurt you." His fingers moved down. She was hot and slick and more than ready for him. He lifted her in his arms and placed her in the center of the bed.

With wide-eyed interest, Amanda watched Slade shuck his boots and pants. The sight of his nude body captured her attention entirely. His muscular arms and chest glistened in the light cast by the lamp on the table. The tan line at his waist told her he worked in the sun, without his shirt. Then her gaze dropped lower. His fully aroused state was . . . the only word that came to her mind was "majestic." She suppressed a nervous giggle and the nearly uncontrollable desire to touch him. She was sure no proper lady would ever be that bold.

Slade slid into bed beside her. Amanda's face was flushed, her eyes the deep green of spring meadows. His need was so deep it frightened him.

He watched her intently. The barest hint of a smile touched the corners of his mouth. For some reason, Amanda suspected, he was waiting for her to make the first move.

Just because she wanted to, she did what she thought no proper lady ever would—she allowed her fingers to brush across his erection. His body jerked at her touch.

"Did I hurt you?" she asked.

"No, love. It's just been a long time since a woman touched me there. I'd love to let you explore to your heart's content, but I'm very much afraid that if I do, this will be over before we really get started."

He drew her to him and kissed away her frown. Her warm breasts pressed against his chest. His rigid manhood rubbed against her thigh. She moved against him. "Please don't wiggle, love," he pleaded.

Rolling her onto her back, he knelt between her legs. She opened to him and he slowly slid inside her. He felt the fragile barrier of her virginity and groaned.

Amanda moaned and squirmed beneath the pressure of his invasion. With a thrust of his hips, he pushed deep inside her and silenced her small cry with his mouth. She was so hot and tight that for a moment he didn't dare move. "You feel so good, Amanda. Wrap your legs around me, love."

Slade's husky voice penetrated Amanda's senses. There was a storm building inside her; she could feel it. The only way to calm it would be for them to move together. She didn't know how she knew that, she just did.

Her hips pushed up against him as she wrapped her legs around his waist. He began to move then, and they rocked together. The feelings they created were so intense and powerful that she knew her body could not hold them. She screamed his name as her mind spun away on the wings of release.

Slade felt her body tighten around him, tugging at the last of his control. His climax was shattering in its intensity. A low growl of satisfaction escaped him. The words "I love you" rang in his head. Had Amanda screamed them, or had his mind cried out the words?

# 14

*Slade woke to the warmth* of Amanda's body. She was sleeping with her back to him, and his hand rested against the soft skin of her bare stomach.

Her hair brushed his face and he detected the faint scent of flowers. Breathing deeply, he savored the moment. The rise and fall of her belly beneath his hand and the feel of her warm, silky skin caused his body to respond with a need that threatened to consume him.

He had to get the hell out of this bed and away from the temptation this woman presented. Lydia's face appeared in his mind. He wasn't ready for this. Only a fool made the same mistake twice.

Still, he lingered, allowing his body to override his mind's command. He wanted desperately to wake her with kisses and see her eyes fill with passion. He wanted to make love to her until they were both exhausted. And he knew he could not have what he wanted. He rolled onto his back, being careful not to wake her, then slowly rose to sit on the edge of the bed.

The gray light of early morning allowed him a dim view of the shack. The fire in the stove was nearly out and the room was chilly. He bent down and tucked the covers around a sleeping Faith, then pulled a blanket up to cover Amanda's bare shoulder.

His mind was filled with pictures of a wife and child and a home. Anger and frustration ate at the pit of his stomach.

Damn it, he had to get up and get moving, he told himself. What he did last night was bad enough; there was no need to make it any worse. He had taken her virginity without planning to. He hadn't even been positive she was a virgin. If he woke her now and made love to her, he reasoned, it would mean making a commitment.

She would expect marriage, and he knew from experience that he couldn't make a life that included a woman. His work didn't allow it. But as things stood, he had taken advantage of her and was therefore responsible for her.

How the hell was he going to get out of the mess he'd created?

First things first, he told himself. Right now, he was going to get out of bed. His feet hit the cold floor and he dressed quickly, stuffed wood into the stove, and fixed Faith a bottle. She was beginning to squirm about in her cradle, so he changed her, then picked her up and sat on the floor near the stove's warmth to give her the bottle. He studied the baby as he fed her. Here was another thing he didn't need. So why did it feel so right to care for her? He shook his head at his lack of understanding.

He would get Amanda and the baby back to Three Wells, finish this assignment, and then get the hell away from them both.

Slade placed a contented, sleepy Faith back in her bed and left the shack to ready the horses. He tried to sort out his problems as he worked. This whole mess was as much Amanda's fault as his. She wasn't what she appeared. But then, what woman was? His wife certainly hadn't been.

Amanda awakened to soft, cooing sounds. She rolled to the side of the bed and peered down at Faith, who was staring at her tiny hands, which she seemed to do a lot, and making contented baby noises within the safe confines of her cradle.

Amanda smiled and rolled back to the center of the bed. She felt wonderful, and realized she was as content as Faith. Was this what it felt like to love and be loved? Images of Slade and last night's lovemaking filled her mind. Could that have been a dream?

No. Not even in her wildest dreams could she have imagined the sensations of last night. Her body grew warm as she remembered the things that she and Slade had done.

Amanda sat up, and a quick glance about the room told her Slade was gone. It was just as well, she decided. She didn't have a stitch of clothing on, and it would probably be best if she were dressed when he returned.

She was just pulling on her boots when the door opened and Slade entered. A smile spread across her face. "Good morning."

Her smile died at the sight of Slade's thundercloud expression. "What's the matter?"

She searched his face, hoping to find the reason for his ill humor, but could not. He didn't answer.

"Why didn't you wake me when you got up?"

"I should have, but I thought you might be overly tired this morning so I let you sleep."

Amanda thought she detected a bit of sarcasm in that remark. What had she done to cause this change in his attitude? To turn the subject away from herself, she asked, "Where have you been?"

"I went to saddle the horses. If we get started right away, we can reach Three Wells by noon. I already changed and fed the baby."

Amanda watched him fold the blankets they had slept under. He was all business as he gathered the few things in the shack and left to load them on the horses.

She stood alone in the middle of the room, wanting to cry. The realization that last night didn't mean the same thing to him that it did to her made her weak. She blinked back the tears that threatened, deciding that anger would be a better defense.

Composing herself, she picked up the baby. She wasn't ever going to allow Slade to see how hurt she felt. With Faith in one arm and the cradle in the other, she left the cabin.

Amanda rode beside Slade in silence. Faith slept peacefully in the cradleboard strapped to Slade's back, and that made the going easier. Still, it seemed like forever before they stopped to rest and water the horses.

Slade placed Faith on the ground beneath a tree and then led the animals to a small stream, where he allowed them to drink their fill. Amanda's anger had

grown as they'd traveled. She'd had just about enough
of his silent treatment. What was the matter with him,
anyway? He tied the horses to a small bush and came
to sit beside Faith in the shade of the only tree in sight.

Amanda decided that now was as good a time as any
to get whatever was bothering Slade out in the open.

"Slade," she began.

"What?" he snapped.

She folded her arms across her breasts. "That's
what I'd like to know. What the devil is the matter
with you? You act as though I've done something to
upset you, only I don't know what. I think we should
talk about whatever it is, don't you?"

Slade turned to face her, his anger showing in the
tight set of his jaw and his stiff posture.

"*You* might say that I'm upset," Slade spat out. "*I'd*
say I was damned good and mad. For God's sake,
Amanda, you should have told me."

Amanda gritted her teeth in frustration. "I don't
know what you're talking about. What didn't I tell you?"

"Damn it, Amanda!" Slade exploded. "You weren't
supposed to be a virgin." He was yelling now. "I don't
go around deflowering virgins!"

Amanda's hands came down to rest on her hips. "It
didn't seem to bother you last night! What was I supposed to be, McAllister," she yelled back, "a harlot
like my mother?"

"That's not what I mean and you know it. The least
you could have done was tell me."

"Don't be ridiculous. That isn't something a lady
talks about. I'm twenty-three years old, for heaven's
sake."

"My point exactly," Slade responded. "You're an

agent—a woman of the world, so to speak. Good Lord, most women are married by the time they're seventeen. How was I supposed to know you were inexperienced? Now I'm honor-bound to be responsible for you."

In that statement, Amanda thought, lay the problem. She was getting angrier by the minute. "And if I hadn't been inexperienced, what would you be feeling now?" She raised her chin in defiance and her voice rose. "Never mind—I don't want to know. You needn't worry yourself about me, McAllister. I'm just fine. I should even thank you for solving one of my little problems. I may still be an old maid, but now at least I'm not a virgin anymore."

"Lower your voice, Amanda, or you will wake Faith. If your father was alive, he'd likely stick a shotgun in my back and march me down the church aisle to you."

"Oh, my goodness." Sarcasm laced Amanda's voice. "What a horrid fate. Never fear, you're perfectly safe. My father is not a threat, and who would believe that the owner of a brothel was a virgin anyway? Besides, I wouldn't have you if you were the last man on God's green earth!"

"And why not? What's wrong with me?"

Amanda looked down her delicate nose at him. "Too many things to number, but that's not my reason. I don't want anyone who doesn't want me. So from now on, leave me alone!"

Slade stood and reached out to cup her chin in his large hand. "You got that all wrong, lady. God help me, but I do want you. After last night, it's going to be hell keeping my hands off you."

Amanda swung away from him to untie her horse.

"Well, hell is where you belong." She climbed into the saddle. "I think it's about time I went home. And when we get there, I want you to pack your belongings and get out of my house. You and your honor can both go to the devil, for all I care!"

Four silent hours later, Amanda rode beside Slade down the dusty main street of Three Wells. It looked the same as it had the day she'd arrived, the same weathered buildings and dirty windows. She didn't care if the town was rough and primitive—it was home. She could finally have a hot bath, a decent meal, and her own bed. And it didn't matter that her bed was in a house of ill repute. She was so glad to be back that even her anger at Slade was momentarily pushed aside.

When she sighted the house, she sighed. "I've never been so glad to see a place in my life."

If Slade heard her, he didn't acknowledge the comment.

Several buggies and a few horses were tied along the fence that separated the yard from the road. The buzz of voices could be heard through the open windows.

After they dismounted, Slade removed Faith from her cradleboard and handed her to Amanda. They climbed the steps together.

A wave of pain swept through Amanda as she remembered the first time she'd approached this door. If only Sampson were here to open it again, she thought with deep sadness. But he wasn't, and she would have to learn to live with that.

Amanda squared her shoulders and stepped into the entry hall ahead of Slade.

Roger Bennet, resplendent in a black suit, white shirt, and black string tie, stood at the bottom of the stairs looking up. Mattie, a vision in white lace, stood on the topmost step.

"Amanda!" Mattie cried as she flew down the steps. Roger took her hand when she reached the bottom. "Where have you been? We've been so worried."

Granny appeared in the hall just then. A wide smile lit her face. "I come to see what all the commotion was about out here. Lord, girl, you're a sight for sore eyes. And just what have you got there?" Granny reached out to take the baby from Amanda. "Land sakes, where did you get this little mite?"

"It's a long story, Granny," Amanda replied as she handed Faith over. "Would you mind finding her some milk and a dry nappy? I'll tell you all about it later." Amanda glanced at Slade. "We don't want to cause a fuss and spoil Mattie's wedding."

"Oh, Miss Amanda," Mattie exclaimed, "you could never do that." She held out the skirt of her white lace dress. "If it weren't for your help, I wouldn't be having this beautiful wedding."

Roger put an arm around Mattie's waist. "Miss Amanda's right, honey. There will be plenty of time to talk at the reception." He spoke to Slade. "We're having a party at my ranch after the ceremony. You and Miss Amanda must come."

"Oh, yes," Mattie added. "Please do." She smiled at Roger. "I'm ready. We really shouldn't keep the judge waiting any longer."

Roger led Mattie toward the parlor and Slade and Amanda followed, stopping just inside the door.

The bride and groom crossed the room and stopped before a nicely dressed man standing in front of the fireplace.

Amanda looked around the room. Jeanne, Wilma, and Rose were seated on the sofa. Lily and Buck were on the love seat. Two men she didn't recognize stood before the windows across the room. Vases of wild-flowers decorated the tables and adorned the fireplace mantel.

Mattie's smile was radiant as the judge read the words of the wedding ceremony. "Do you, Roger, take Mattie to be your lawfully wedded wife?"

"I do."

Roger held Mattie's hand and looked so proud that it made Amanda want to cry. Would a man ever look at her with that kind of love in his eyes?

"Do you, Mattie, take Roger to be your lawfully wedded husband?"

"I do." Mattie's smile was as bright as sunshine.

The judge smiled too. "I now pronounce you man and wife. You may kiss your bride."

Amanda watched through a film of tears as Roger took Mattie in his arms and kissed her reverently.

Sounds of happy congratulations filled the room. Amanda was tired and dirty and not at all up to facing the questions that were sure to come as soon as the din quieted. Feeling like a coward, she turned and fled the parlor, leaving Slade to fend for himself.

When she reached her room, she stripped off her dirty clothes and pulled on her robe. She wanted a hot bath desperately, but the big claw-footed tub was downstairs in the room off the kitchen. It was kept close to the stove so the hot water didn't have to be carried upstairs. She would have to wait until the house quieted before she could venture down.

Amanda slumped into the chair before the dressing

table and studied her reflection in the mirror. She was a mess. Fatigue had etched dark circles under her eyes. Her hair was a fright, and her face was wind-burned and weather-roughened. She touched her sore cheek. The swelling was gone, but a dark bruise still colored the area.

She wasn't sure she knew the woman in the glass anymore. The eyes that stared back at her were different. They had seen death, known passion, and learned regret. So much had happened to her in such a short time.

Amanda reflected on her situation. The guns had been recovered, so they would never reach the Knights of the Golden Circle in California, and the lawbreakers were in jail.

There was still her father's murder to solve. Maybe when she and Slade talked to the prisoners she would get some clue as to who was responsible.

And then there was Faith. What was she going to do about the baby? Amanda knew she positively could not give her up, that it would break her heart to part with the child she had tried so hard not to love.

If only Slade had wanted something from her other than a physical relationship. She could so easily have given him her heart, just as she had given it to Faith. Only he didn't want love. Well, she wasn't going to give him her body again. She had acted the fool once, and once was sufficient.

Voices from below her window finally drew her attention back to the present. Amanda rose from the vanity and went to the window to watch the guest-filled buggies depart for the wedding party at Roger's ranch. Mattie was sitting beside Roger in a buggy decorated with a Just Married sign.

Outside, Slade was assuring Mattie that he and Amanda would be along as soon as they were cleaned up. He waved them on their way, then turned to Buck and Lily on the porch steps.

Buck grinned and slapped Slade on the back. "You sure took your sweet time getting here. Run into some trouble, did you?"

"Some," Slade admitted. "But nothing I couldn't handle."

"Glad to hear it. I told Lily to stop worrying, but you know how women are." Buck turned serious. "I've got a favor to ask, friend. Since the judge is here, Lily and I have decided to get him to marry us. Would you stand up with me?"

Ten minutes later, Slade and Wilma put their names, as witnesses, to the marriage paper. Then Slade saw Lily and Buck to their buggy, watched until it was out of sight, and went back inside.

The house was quiet as Amanda made her way down the back stairs to the kitchen. Pans of steaming water stood on the stove. Granny sat at the kitchen table.

"I knowed you'd want to clean up, so I heated you some water, girl."

Amanda smiled. "Thank you, Granny. Where is Faith?"

"She's in my room with her tummy full and her bottom dry, sleeping like a little angel. Now, are you gonna tell me where she came from, before I die of curiosity?"

Amanda sank onto the hard wooden chair across the table from Granny, wondering where to begin. A picture of the burned cabin and its front yard flashed before her eyes.

"Slade and I came to a homestead that had been attacked by bandits." Amanda drew a shaky breath. "Granny, it was terrible. The poor woman had been . . . raped and murdered. The cabin was still smoldering. We found her husband behind the house. Slade dug a grave and we buried them. I was looking for stones to cover the grave when I heard crying. I found a hidden cellar, and the baby was in a cradle at the foot of the steps. She was cold, wet, hungry, and hoarse from crying. We had an awful time trying to figure out what to feed her."

Amanda paused and looked deep into Granny's compassionate brown eyes. "I'm going to keep her. I know it won't be easy, but I can do it."

"Lord, girl, you'll be setting up a hard row to hoe, just like your mama did, if you do."

"I'm not like my mother," Amanda shot back. "Faith and I will be fine."

"If'n you say so, Missy." The old woman sighed. "But you'd best figure on me tagging along to help ya."

Amanda rose, her heart full of gratitude, and moved around the table to give the woman a hug. "Thank you, Granny. I expect I'll need all the help I can get."

Together Granny and Amanda filled the tub, and then Granny went to her room to keep an eye on Faith.

Amanda tossed off her robe and stepped into the hot, rose-scented water with a sigh of pure pleasure. The warmth seeped into her tired body and began to ease away the discomfort left over from the arduous trek, not to mention Slade's lovemaking. She closed her eyes, allowing the feelings of peace and comfort to fill her mind.

A sudden draft of cold air caused goose bumps to rise on her wet skin. Her eyes popped open and she looked toward the door. Slade lounged against the doorframe, his arms folded across his chest. He'd shaved and dressed.

Amanda gasped and slid down in the tub. "Get out of here!" Her voice was a shocked squeak.

"I think not, love. We need to talk." Slade stepped into the room and closed the door.

"We have nothing more to say to each other, McAllister, and don't call me 'love'! Are you packed yet?"

Slade grinned. "You see, we do have something to talk about. No, I am not packed yet, and I'm not about to be anytime soon. I came to find you and tell you to hurry or you're going to miss Mattie's party. Only now I think I'd rather just look at you."

He took another step toward the tub. The gleam in his eyes made Amanda's pulse race.

"Stop right there or I'll scream," she threatened.

"No, Amanda, you won't. Everyone has gone to the party except Granny, and she is upstairs with Faith. You wouldn't want to upset her, now would you? Besides, you know that I would never hurt you."

"You already have." The words had just bubbled out; she hadn't meant to say them.

"I know, and I'm sorry." Slade knelt beside the tub.

"I'll just bet you are, Mister McAllister. You're sorry that I was innocent and you're sorry because you feel you owe me something for taking that innocence. Well, you can consider the debt paid, McAllister. You rescued me from Two Feathers and Loud Mouth and brought me safely home. I'd say we were even—but then again, I don't know how much whores get for a night's work, or how much value you put on virginity."

Slade shot to his feet and headed for the door, cursing with words that burned her ears. Halfway there, he stopped. Then he spun around and stomped back to her, reached down, and grabbed her by the upper arms. Water sloshed onto the floor as he dragged her out of the tub.

"You stupid little idiot. Don't belittle yourself like that ever again! You have to be the most exasperating woman I have ever known. I don't know whether to beat you or kiss you." His mouth was very close to hers. "Perhaps I'll do both," he whispered, just before his lips touched hers.

The kiss was long and deep. His tongue slid inside her mouth and made her tremble. The rough cloth of his coat against her bare breasts brought a heat to the center of her body that threatened to burn her alive.

"No . . . No . . . No . . ."

Slade released her, and she sucked air into her lungs. She staggered back against the tub, but his hand steadied her. He too was gasping for breath.

"Get dressed, you little witch, before I lose what control I have left." A wry smile touched his mouth. "It's damned little, so you had best hurry."

# 15

*Amanda and Slade rode* down the tree-lined drive to Roger Bennet's ranch in the buggy Slade had rented from the livery in Three Wells.

"You took your sweet time getting here," Buck said as he greeted them from the crowded porch. Leaving Lily's side, he came down the steps into the yard.

After Slade brought the buggy to a stop, Buck assisted Amanda from the buggy and told her, "You look as pretty as a litter of new pups."

Figuring that must be a compliment, Amanda smoothed the skirt of her emerald green dress and answered, "Thank you, Buck. You look well too."

Slade attempted to find a place to park the buggy among the twelve or so already lined up beside the house.

Stepping onto the porch, Amanda took Lily's hand. "Slade told me the good news. Congratulations."

Lily beamed. "I'm so happy I'm about to bust, but we're not going to make an official announcement until the party's about over. We don't want to intrude on Roger and Mattie."

"I don't care if another soul knows," Buck chimed in. "I've got the paper in my pocket and the lady is all mine."

He put his arm around Lily's waist. "Come dance with me, wife."

Lily laughed and allowed herself to be led into the house, where the sound of a fiddle could be heard.

Slade stepped onto the porch and took Amanda's arm, and they followed Buck and Lily.

The furniture had been cleared from the front room and the dining room. A long table filled with food and another with cake and punch stood in the middle of the front room. The fiddler was in the dining room and people were dancing there.

Roger and Mattie were greeting people as they came through the door. Amanda hugged Mattie, who was still wearing her wedding dress and still glowing with happiness. "You look beautiful, Mattie."

Mattie smiled. "Only because you helped with the dress. I've never worn anything this fine." She trailed her fingers across the bodice. "I'm not going to take it off until I have to. Oh my!" Mattie glanced at Roger and blushed. "I didn't mean that I didn't want to take it off. I—I—" Mattie placed a hand over her mouth to stop the stammer.

Roger pulled Mattie possessively against his side. "Hush, Mattie. I'm sure we all understand what you mean."

Amanda smiled and shook the hand Roger offered.

"Congratulations. I hope you will both be very happy."

Roger released Amanda's hand and shook Slade's. "I want to thank you and Amanda for being such good friends to Mattie. She's told me how kind you both were to her."

"We were glad to help," Slade answered. "I know you will take good care of her."

Slade drew Amanda away as another couple stepped up to offer congratulations. Amanda walked beside him, stiff and silent. She was, Slade knew, still angry with him for interrupting her bath, and for a few other things. They had exchanged only a few words during the ride out here.

"Can I get you some punch?" Slade asked, offering an olive branch.

"No!"

He tried again. "Would it help if I said I'm sorry?"

"No!"

"Have a heart, Amanda. It was as much your fault as mine. I wouldn't always be apologizing if you didn't make me crazy."

Amanda snorted. "So now it's my fault that you dragged me from my bath. My fault that you acted like a fool. Sorry, McAllister. You can't blame your bad behavior on me."

"Well then, let me make it up to you."

"You can't. But I suppose since I'm so hungry I could eat a horse, I might let you try."

Slade chuckled. "I don't think they have any horse on that table, but I do see some chicken. Will that do?"

Amanda smiled and nodded.

"I'll be right back." Slade headed for the food table.

Sheriff Davis took Slade's place beside Amanda. "Hello, Miss Jefferson. Captain Whitman told me about the Comanche dragging you off. Were you hurt?"

There was something about this man that Amanda didn't like. He smiled, and he was charming, but it was all on the surface. She just didn't trust him, and she didn't think her dislike stemmed from their first meeting when he had mistaken her for the girl from Baton Rouge.

"Not really, though it was a frightening experience. Thank you for asking."

"Would you mind telling me why you were traveling with McAllister and Emmerson? It seems strange to me that they would take you along on such a dangerous mission."

Slade arrived with the food, saving her from having to answer the question.

"I took her along because we thought Lily might need a woman to take care of her when we caught up with the guns, Sheriff. Miss Jefferson is very good with a gun, too, and handy to have around in a fight. But I think we should really wait and talk about all this tomorrow. I'll be in early in the morning to question Parker. Has he made any kind of statement yet?"

"No, he's not being very cooperative. Captain Whitman questioned him yesterday. He didn't get anywhere either."

Slade handed Amanda her plate. "Would you excuse us, Sheriff?" He steered Amanda toward a row of chairs against a far wall and seated her.

When Davis had left the room, Slade said, "I don't much like that man. When I told him I was a Texas Ranger and asked him to lock up the gunrunners, he got real hostile. He was mad as hell because I hadn't let him in on the case right from the first. I got the impression that he thought I had overstepped my bounds into his territory." Slade paused. "How's the chicken?"

Amanda took another bite, and sighed. "It's wonderful. I hope I never see another piece of beef jerky as long as I live." When her plate was empty, she turned to Slade.

"I'm glad you didn't tell Davis who I am. If we have to, we will, but not now."

Slade nodded. "All right. I'll question Parker tomorrow and see what I can find out. I've asked Captain Whitman and Ranger James to see that the guns get to Fort Worth. They're willing, if you give the word."

Amanda thought it over. "I don't see why not. I can give them the name of the man I was supposed to deliver them to if I found them. I'm sure Robert wouldn't object to the Rangers' seeing them safely there."

Slade studied her a moment. "Do you mean that you were not instructed to take them directly to the army?"

"That's right. Robert said that this man would take care of everything from that point on and I wouldn't have to deal with the military."

"You didn't find that a little unusual?" Slade asked.

"No. Robert said it was the best way. Is there a problem?"

"I guess not. He and your father must have made some special arrangements. Write down the man's name and I'll give it to Whitman."

"All right. With that taken care of I'll be able to concentrate on Parker to find out what he knows about my father's murder, and settle my affairs here."

Amanda paused, looking for the right words. "When I leave, I'm taking Faith and Granny back to Washington with me. I know how fond of Faith you are, so I will give you our address. You can come see her if you want."

"But, Amanda—"

She didn't let him finish. "I know it will be hard. People will talk. I don't care. I simply cannot give her up."

Slade understood the feeling. He had it too. "Then I insist on contributing to her care, and I'll see to it that her land is safe, so she will have something from her parents. When she's old enough, she can decide what she wants to do with it."

It was strange, Slade thought, that he had become so attached to the baby. He would miss her. There would be an empty spot in his life.

No, there would be two empty spots in his life.

He took Amanda's hand and tugged her to her feet. "Dance with me."

He led her into the other room and took her in his arms. The melody of a waltz filled the room. Slade relished the feel of her as she settled against him. They moved together perfectly. He felt that they were two parts of a whole that was soon to be split in half, and he didn't like the feeling.

He didn't want to think about it now, though. He would hold her while he could and be thankful for the moment.

A few minutes after the waltz ended, Amanda pleaded fatigue and asked Slade to take her back to the house. It was nearly dark by the time he let her off at the front gate and went to return the rented buggy.

Amanda went straight to the kitchen. Granny was at the stove, warming a bottle for the baby. Faith lay in her cradle near the table. Amanda picked her up.

Faith's chubby hand grabbed for the small emerald on the gold chain around Amanda's neck. She patiently disengaged the baby's fingers.

"Have you been a good baby today?" she asked. Faith gurgled, and Amanda laughed. "Does that mean yes?"

"Land sakes, of course she has. That baby ain't no more trouble than nothing." Granny handed Amanda the bottle of warmed milk. "A body just has to feed her and keep her dry and rock her a bit, and she act just like an angel."

"You are going to spoil her, Granny."

Amanda took a seat in the rocker that had somehow found its way to the kitchen, and set the chair to rocking with her foot.

Faith latched onto the bottle with her usual hearty appetite. The milk disappeared rapidly.

Amanda felt a sense of contentment flow through her.

"Where did the chair come from, Granny?"

"I got the boy what brings the wood in to lug it down from my room." Granny smiled. There was a strange gleam in her tired eyes. "You look just like your mama did when she sat in that chair and rocked you. I musta watched her do it a thousand times." Tears trickled down each of Granny's cheeks, and she brushed them away.

"Don't pay me no nevermind. I'm just an old woman." Granny took a seat at the kitchen table. She sighed. "It sure does feel good to have a little one to hold again. Makes me feel like I'm doing something important, instead of just getting through another day."

Amanda felt tears sting her eyes and blinked them away. She took the empty bottle from Faith's mouth and sat her up. A few pats on the back produced a healthy burp.

Slade came into the kitchen through the back door and stood silently watching Amanda rock her baby. A smile tugged at the corners of his mouth.

"Would you like to hold Faith a few minutes before we put her to bed?" Amanda asked.

Slade crossed the room and took the infant. Then Amanda vacated the chair and Slade took her place. Turning to Granny, she said, "Let me take Faith to my room for tonight. I wouldn't want you to have to get up with her."

"Land sakes, no! She won't be no trouble. Besides, old people like me don't sleep much. We'll get along fine."

"All right, if you're sure."

Amanda glanced at Slade. Faith was fast asleep in his arms. It was a sight Amanda was sure she would always remember. His man's hands seemed overly large as they cradled the tiny baby with delicate care. His expression could only be described as tender. She felt a stab of regret at the thought of taking Faith so far away.

He stood and handed the sleeping baby to Granny, who bade him and Amanda good night.

Amanda stepped to the stove and lifted the coffeepot. "There's some left. Do you want a cup?"

"No. It's been a long day; I think I'll go to bed early. I feel like I could sleep for a week. I thought you were tired."

"I am, but Faith was awake and I just had to hold her." She was sure they both understood that feeling.

They left the kitchen together and went up the stairs, stopping outside Amanda's door.

"Lily told me to tell you she and Buck will spend tonight at the hotel. She wanted you to know so you wouldn't worry."

It suddenly dawned on Amanda that Slade might not like the idea that Buck had married the girl from Baton Rouge. Slade didn't know about Lily. Did Buck know about Lily? Did it matter? It wasn't her place to tell Slade either way. She would have to ask Lily about it the next time she saw her.

Amanda placed a hand on Slade's arm. "I'm happy for them. They are both fine people."

Slade lifted his hand and brushed his fingers across her cheek. "I agree." One finger traced the outline of her mouth.

The sound of Amanda's heart beating was loud in her ears. The air in the hall suddenly seemed very warm. She was having a hard time concentrating on Slade's words.

"So are you."

"What?" Amanda tried to focus on his voice, and not on the shivers along her spine created by his touch.

Slade chuckled. "Pay attention, love."

"I am." She couldn't keep her eyes off his mouth. It was moving slowly closer.

Slade's lips, soft and warm, brushed hers. His tongue licked at the corners of her mouth. He used his body to pin her to the wall. Scenes of last night's love-making flashed across her mind.

He stepped back, freeing her. For a moment Amanda was sure she was going to slide down the wall. She didn't.

"Good night, love," Slade said suddenly, then crossed the hall and closed his door.

Thirty minutes later, after washing and putting on her nightdress, Amanda snuggled beneath the covers, determined to sleep. She was totally exhausted, but an hour later she was still awake, still thinking about Slade.

Finally, muttering in disgust, she left her bed and went to the window. The night was as black as ink. Stars, too numerous to count, twinkled in the velvet darkness. There was so much beauty here it left a person breathless. How could she have ever thought this place godforsaken?

Beauty was in the eye of the beholder—that was her answer. She had changed into an entirely different person. There were people here that she cared about, and would always remember fondly. Rose and Wilma and even Jeanne, though Jeanne was still a bit stand-offish, and Mattie. They were just women doing the best they could in a world where men made the rules.

Just as her mother had. That, Amanda decided, was one of the biggest changes in her attitude. She was sure she had finally put her bad feelings about her mother to rest. She still hurt, but she didn't hate.

Her anger had dissolved with understanding. She sighed. Slade had played a big part in that.

"You do what you have to do, and the sooner you understand that the better off you are." Amanda remembered Slade's words, and knew they were true. He had given her another motto besides "Confront and overcome" to help guide her life.

She and Granny and Faith would depart this place soon, leaving behind things dear to them. Sadness touched her heart.

It would always be hard to think of Sampson without a smile and a pang of guilt. She would have to savor the smiles and accept the guilt. Sometimes "Confront and overcome" were hard words to live up to.

Buck and Lily would always be a bright spot in her memories. And so would Wilma, and Jeanne, and Rose, and all the others.

And then there was Slade. He was her biggest regret. She loved him. She did not want to, had not thought she was capable of it, but she did and she was. Tears filled her eyes.

He wanted her body, but he had never mentioned love. Perhaps he wasn't capable of loving anyone after what his wife had done to him.

To isolate yourself to keep from being hurt was understandable; she had done it herself as a child. But now she knew that the inability to love could cripple a person.

If the trip here served no other purpose, she knew, it had opened her mind and her heart to love. She would try to find the man who murdered her father, because she owed him that. But, if she could not, she could live with the defeat. It was no longer the most important thing in her life.

Silent tears ran down Amanda's cheeks. She dried them with the hem of her nightdress and crawled back into bed. Tomorrow would be the beginning of the end of her time here. She would savor the moments.

It was nearly morning and Slade was still awake. From his bedroom window, he watched the first fingers of light creep across the eastern horizon. It had been a long night, a night of reflection and deep thought. His mind was still a confused mess. All he had managed to do was lose a lot of sleep.

His feelings were all jumbled—and feelings, he'd figured out, were his major problem. He'd thought he'd buried them with his wife, but now they were creeping back into him again.

Damn it, he had made a perfectly good life for himself. He had made his work the center of it and was well satisfied with it the way it was.

Slade rubbed a hand over his tired eyes. A man should not lie to himself, he decided. That thought caused him a moment's grief. How long had he been doing just that?

Maybe it was time to admit that his "perfectly good life" no longer suited him. That was Amanda's fault. The woman had turned his mind to mush and his well-ordered life upside down.

He was going to have to be honest with himself and face the feelings that were coming to life within him. It wasn't going to be a pleasant experience.

There were so many questions to be answered. Could he let Amanda and Faith walk out of his life? Could he go back to an existence of solitude and work? Did he want to?

He didn't know, and that made him feel like a fool.

But he did know that what he wanted most right now was to cross that dammed hall and make love to Amanda until they were both senseless. Christ, he was already senseless.

It was stupid to allow his body to rule his mind. Damn it to hell, that was what he had done with Lydia.

Amanda wasn't like Lydia, though. Somehow he

knew that deep in his soul. She was not self-centered. She was sweet and giving and capable. She was proud, and honest, and she cared. What had Buck called her? A "stand by your man" kind of woman. Slade smiled. Buck had an answer like that for everything.

Perhaps he could learn from Buck's example. He always gave everything he had to everything he did. If he got hurt, he just picked himself up and started over. He didn't hide behind pain or use it as a shield. Maybe Slade should talk over his Amanda problem with Buck. But first he needed to talk to Parker.

Slade had a bad feeling about Parker. The man was not alone in this gunrunning operation. He had been in Three Wells for years and was respected by the townspeople. As the owner of the bank, he was considered trustworthy. However, he was a Southerner and sympathetic to the rebel cause—a perfect tool in the hands of manipulative, unscrupulous people.

Parker would never have been implicated in the gunrunning if the transfer had gone off as planned. Amanda had been the downfall of that plan.

Slade had to find out who gave Parker his orders. It was someone with power and connections in Washington. He was sure of that.

There were still so many unanswered questions. Why had Three Wells been picked as the transfer point? Where had Griffin come from? Slade was sure he was a hireling; he wasn't smart enough to be anything else. Captain Whitman was still checking on him.

The men who were arrested the first time the guns were recovered had been questioned. Parker and Griffin had been their only contacts, so that was a dead end.

Slade ran a hand over the rough stubble on his cheeks. He needed a shave. It was early, but there was no hope of getting any sleep. He might as well make himself presentable and get his day started.

Parker held the key to this mess; Slade was sure of it. He had to find a way to persuade him to talk.

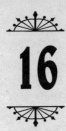

# 16

*"What the hell!" Slade muttered,* and broke into a run.

A crowd of townspeople milled about in front of the sheriff's office. Slade sprinted the last block and came to a halt just as Doctor Anderson was leaving the office, looking furious.

"What's the matter, Doc?"

"Slade! You saved somebody a trip. Sheriff Davis was about to send someone to get you."

"Why?" Slade's heart was beating double time from the run, and it was the only word he could get out between pants.

"'Cause that fool Parker tried to escape. Davis says Parker jumped him when he opened the door to give him breakfast. It's a hell of a mess in there. Blood and eggs are all over the damned floor."

"How could Davis be so stupid? Is either one of them hurt badly?"

"Davis ain't, but Parker is as bad as you can get. He's dead."

Slade shoved his way into the office. Davis was sitting behind his desk.

"I want to know what went on here. The Texas Rangers aren't going to be happy about you shooting my prisoner."

"Then you should have been here guarding him yourself. The man got a choke hold on me. What was I supposed to do, let him kill me?"

Slade was angry enough to kill the sheriff himself. "You know you're not supposed to open a cell without a deputy present. Where was he?"

"My deputy was too sick to work today. He has a bad case of stomach complaint. I couldn't just let the prisoner starve."

"He'd be better off hungry than dead," Slade snapped. He turned his attention to the cell.

It was a mess. The blanket from the cot covered Parker's body. Slade wondered what he was going to tell Amanda. Parker had been their most promising lead.

He swung back to Davis. "Did you get any kind of statement from Parker? Did he say anything that might implicate someone else?"

"Not a damned word; I told you that yesterday. Captain Whitman and Ranger James were here then and tried to talk to him. They didn't get anywhere either. Maybe you ought to go check with them instead of blaming this on me. Maybe that James fellah should have been here as an extra guard. Then this wouldn't have happened."

Slade stomped out of the office just as the under-taker and his wagon pulled up. Jess Tanner was a short, bald man of about fifty. He'd been helpful with both Anna Marie's and Sampson's funerals.

"Hello, Jess." Slade extended his hand and the undertaker shook it. "I have a favor to ask. Let me know if you find anything unusual when you lay Parker out. Check his pockets and the lining of his coat, and the heels of his boot, too. Sometimes they're hollow. They make a real good hiding place."

"Sure thing, Mister McAllister. I'll be glad to help any way I can."

Slade took a silver dollar from his pocket and handed it to Jess. "Thanks. I'll check with you later." Then he headed for the hotel, where he found Buck and Lily having breakfast with Captain Whitman.

"What brings you out so early?" Buck asked.

"Trouble!" Slade barked back. "Sheriff Davis shot Parker dead. Claimed he was trying to make a break."

Buck swore.

Lily blushed.

Whitman threw his napkin down beside his plate. His chair scraped the floor as he pushed away from the table and stood.

"Davis said you talked to Parker yesterday, Ed. Did you get anything out of him?" Slade asked.

"Hell, no! The man was as closemouthed as a corpse." Whitman's voice was filled with disgust. "Now he is one." Ed's gaze darted to Lily. "Sorry, ma'am, for the language."

"That's all right, Mister Whitman. I'm getting accus-tomed to Ranger talk."

Lily turned her face aside, but not before Slade saw the smile she was trying to hide.

Whitman turned on his heel and left the dining room.

"Sit down and have some coffee, Slade," Buck said.

Slade grinned and winked at Lily. "No, the two of you are on your honeymoon. You don't need me around. Besides, I've got to go break the news to Amanda. She's going to pitch a fit."

Amanda was giving Faith a bath when Slade entered the warm kitchen. Or maybe Faith was giving Amanda a bath. It was hard to tell, they were both so wet. Amanda laughed and Faith cooed and splashed.

Faith cooed, Amanda laughed, and Granny, who was standing near the table with a towel over her arm, eyed them with amusement. "Lord have mercy, you two are making a mess."

She turned to Slade. "Close the door. We don't want the child to take a chill."

Slade closed it with a chuckle. His gaze lingered on Amanda's wet shirtwaist. "Which one, Amanda or Faith?"

Amanda looked up at him and said, "If you came to make fun of me, McAllister, you can leave. This is serious business." Then she saw the amusement disappear from Slade's eyes.

"What's wrong?"

"Parker's dead."

"How? When?" Amanda wrapped the large towel Granny handed her around the baby and allowed Granny to dry and dress Faith while Slade told them the story.

Amanda waited until Granny left to take Faith

upstairs for a nap before collapsing into the rocker with a disappointed sigh. "I was sure Parker could have told us who my father's killer was."

"I think you were right, but now we will have to look elsewhere."

The sound of Buck's voice intruded. "Is anyone at home?" Buck and Lily entered the kitchen from the front hall. He looked Amanda over and grinned at her. "Who tried to drown you?"

A remark like that was to be expected, Amanda supposed, considering the source. She smiled fondly at Buck.

"I was hoping your wife might have settled you down some by now."

Buck grinned. "Lily likes me just the way I am."

"You are conceited," Lily put in.

"True, but I'm also lovable."

Lily rolled her eyes. "Oh! I do believe men are only little boys in long pants."

Amanda smiled at Lily in agreement.

"Lily told me something," Buck began as he and Lily sat down at the kitchen table, "that I think you should know, Slade. She didn't come here from Baton Rouge. She came from Washington, D.C. She told Amanda that Robert Commings sent her here to help her with the gun case. What she didn't tell her was that she was also to make reports on Amanda's progress and send them to him."

Lily looked pleadingly at Amanda. "I'm sorry, Amanda. I did send a report right after I got here and one after Sampson was killed. Then I got to know Buck, and you were so kind to me that I didn't send any more."

Amanda was too shocked to speak.

"I didn't tell Buck this until he got back from looking for you." Lily looked like she was going to cry. "I'm sorry, Amanda."

Amanda saw pain in Lily's eyes. They had become good friends. "I'm sure you thought you were doing your job, Lily, just as I was doing mine. I wrote Robert before you got here. I wondered why he never answered. Did he say why he wanted me watched?"

"Not exactly. He said he thought you wouldn't be able to handle the situation here and that you would likely be ready to return home by the time I got here. If you were, I was to accompany you back. If by some chance you were not, I was to send him word of your progress. He also wanted the identity of your contact here. That was the piece of information he wanted most. I didn't learn it was Slade until after I stopped sending the reports. So if he knows, he didn't get the information from me."

Amanda turned to Slade. "My father had your code name in his files, but not your real identity. Why would that be important to Robert?"

Slade mulled that over for a long moment. "I don't know, unless he has someone else here in Three Wells, or hereabouts, that he could pass the information to. Someone like Griffin . . . or maybe Parker."

"Are you implying that Robert was in on the gun theft, Slade? If you are, I don't believe it. He was my father's lifelong friend. They owned the business together for years. He may not have had much faith in me and my abilities, but I don't question his."

"I didn't say he was involved, Amanda; I said he might have known Parker. If he knew your father for as long as you seem to think, he probably knew your mother as well. He could have been in Three Wells at some point. Did your father ever say how he discovered you were at the convent?"

"No. I never thought to ask."

"Did Anna Marie ever say anything to you about Commings or Amanda's father, Slade?" Buck asked.

Slade shook his head.

"Then perhaps you should ask Granny. If anyone here would have that information, it would be her. Where is she?"

"Upstairs putting Faith down for a nap. I'll go get her."

Amanda got up from the rocker and left the kitchen. She found Granny tucking in the edges of a patchwork baby quilt around a sleeping Faith.

Since bringing Faith to the house, Amanda had noticed that the baby had a great many changes of clothes. She had been meaning to ask Granny about it.

Amanda moved to stand next to the cradle. "Did you send someone to town to buy clothes for Faith, Granny? If you did, I want to pay for them. She's my responsibility."

"I didn't buy them, honey. I went up to the attic and got them out of the trunk your mama packed them away in."

Granny ran a finger over the tiny pink flowers embroidered around the neck of the white flannel gown Faith wore.

"If I close my eyes, I can see your mama and me sitting together sewing these on. Anna Marie saved all your things. If you want to see them I'll take you up to the attic the first chance we get."

Amanda felt a wave of sadness sweep over her.

Once she would have rejected the idea that her mother had cared enough to keep such things. Now she knew better.

"I'd like that, Granny, but not right now. Slade wants to speak to you downstairs. I came to get you."

When Amanda and Granny entered the kitchen, Lily was pouring coffee for Slade and Buck. "Can I get either of you a cup?"

Granny shook her head and took a seat in the rocker.

"No thank you, Lily," Amanda replied, taking a seat at the table.

"Granny," Slade began, "we need you to answer some questions for us. Do you know if a man named Robert Commings ever came to see Anna Marie?"

"No, he didn't. I know the man, though. Anna Marie got letters from him inquiring about Amanda. I don't know how he found out where we were or that Amanda existed. Amanda's mama never wanted him to know about the baby."

Granny gave Amanda an imploring look. "Anna Marie was going to come get you as soon as we had enough money saved for her to go into some other business. Your father found you before she got the chance. She knew she couldn't fight him to get you back. It was the only time I ever saw her give up on anything. I think she convinced herself that Cecil could give you all the things she was never going to be able to."

Granny looked so sad it made Amanda want to cry. She went to the old woman and gave her a hug. "It's all right, Granny. I know now that you both did the best you could."

Granny patted Amanda's hand. "Anna Marie had a special account at the bank. She put money there to

pay for your keep at the convent. I do remember that
Frank Parker asked her about that once."

"You mean that Parker knew who I was and where
I was?"

"Of course, child. He was your mama's banker for
years."

Amanda directed her next question at Slade. "Do
you think Robert found out where I was from Parker?"

"I think that once Robert Commings traced your
mother here, Amanda, it would be logical to assume he
would check the bank and anyplace else in town—say,
the sheriff's office—to learn what he could. In a town
this size, it wouldn't be hard to find out what he wanted
to know." Slade paused to take a swig of his coffee.

"The fact that Commings knew Parker gives us
something to think about. I know you don't want to
believe Commings could be involved with Parker, but
I'm going to get Captain Whitman to check him out
anyway. Do you want to come with me, Buck?"

"I would rather go upstairs and help Lily pack, but
I'd probably keep her from getting it done, so I'd best
go with you."

Lily smiled. "Go. I'll wait right here until you get
back."

Slade and Buck left, Lily went upstairs to pack, and
Amanda helped Granny wash the cups and peel potatoes to cook with the roast beef that was already in the
oven.

Thirty minutes later, Amanda went upstairs and
knocked on Wilma's door.

"Come in."

Amanda opened the door and stepped into the
room. Wilma was sitting before her dressing table

putting up her hair. Amanda took a seat in a chair beside the bed.

"You know you gave me an awful fright, Amanda. When Buck came back and said the Comanche had you, I thought you were gone for good. Buck said Slade would find you and bring you back, but I wasn't so sure. Are you all right?"

"I'm fine, Wilma. I do need your advice about something, though. I'm going to be leaving here as soon as I can get my business affairs in order. I've been worried about what to do with the house. I don't want you, and Rose, and Jeanne to lose your home. I talked to Slade about that, and we decided, if the three of you agree, to put the house in all your names. If you want to make changes, that will be a matter for the three of you to decide." Amanda secretly hoped that pride of ownership might be enough to encourage them to find a more reputable line of work.

Wilma looked stunned. Then her mouth turned up at the corners in a smile. "I should have known you would think of us before you just up and sold the house. It's what your mama would have done. You're very much like her in so many ways."

She rose and went to Amanda. "I think we should pay you something for the house. We have money in the bank that your mama put there for us. I believe Rose and Jeanne would agree to that."

"I don't want your money, Wilma; it belongs to the three of you. Will you speak to Rose and Jeanne?"

"I will, and I'm sure they will be agreeable. We were all worried about what to do if you sold out to someone else."

Tears formed in Wilma's eyes. "I moved into this place the day your mama and Granny and you did. It's my home." She grasped Amanda's hand and tugged her from her chair to hug her. "Thank you."

"You don't need to thank me, Wilma. I have a home in Washington. Granny and Faith and I are going to return there. I just want what's best for everyone."

Amanda stood and went to the door. "Talk to the others and let me know what you decide, and then we can go to the land office and have the deed changed."

She left the room. Her mind was made up now; all she had to do was tie all the loose ends together. In a week she would be finished here.

Slowly she walked down the hall to Granny's room to check on Faith. The baby was sleeping with a fat little thumb stuck in her mouth. Amanda stood and gazed at her for a moment. Her face was peaceful in sleep, and so dear to Amanda that her heart swelled inside her.

Even if she didn't find her father's killer, the time here had been well spent. She had Faith and Granny to love now. Taking care of them would give meaning and direction to her life. It was time to get on with the business of living.

The next morning Amanda stood in the front hall waiting for the ladies to come downstairs. Last night over dinner, she had talked with them about arrangements. Wilma, Rose, and Jeanne had all agreed with Amanda on one point: They wanted to remain at the house. But all three had disagreed with Amanda on another point: They wanted to pay for it in some manner.

After lengthy discussion, it was decided that each

woman would deposit one hundred dollars from her savings in an account at the bank in Faith's name. When Faith was old enough, it would be hers. That arrangement allowed the ladies to keep their pride intact.

Amanda smiled as the three women descended the stairs dressed in their bright silks and satins. Rose wore yellow, Jeanne was dressed in a grass green gown that matched her eyes, and Wilma's gown was a rust color, nearly the same shade as her hair. Amanda felt almost dowdy in her pale lavender skirt and fitted jacket.

"Good morning, ladies." Amanda opened the front door and ushered them out onto the porch.

"I'll drive," Wilma announced as they headed for the buggy the hired boy had readied for them. It stood just beyond the gate. Amanda assumed that since Wilma was the oldest, she had the seniority to assume driving duties, and Wilma insisted she was the most qualified of the three to handle the horses. Amanda didn't know about Jeanne and Rose, but she knew she wasn't much of a driver.

Amid a flutter of skirts, they seated themselves. Wilma twitched the reins over the horses' backs with the command "Gettie-up," and the buggy lurched forward. The others all held on to their hats as the vehicle rolled down the street at a steady clip.

A number of the men and woman along the street stared at them openly. A few of the braver men tipped their hats.

Amanda wanted to laugh with delight. What a sight they must make, she thought amusedly. A month ago she would have been shocked at seeing a buggy full of prostitutes driving down Main Street. A month ago she would not have understood that these women were doing what they had to do to survive. Now, she not only understood them, she admired them.

Wilma brought the buggy to a halt in front of the land office. Two very young cowboys stepped off the walk and offered to help them down.

Amanda allowed one, several years her junior, to take her hand and assist her.

"Thank you, sir," she said with a smile.

The cowboy stammered, "Yes, ma'am," and turned a bright shade of red. Still, he gamely offered a hand to Jeanne while his friend assisted Wilma and then Rose on the other side of the buggy.

Amanda thought they would undoubtedly have a fine time recounting this tale around the bunkhouse table.

The ladies followed her into the land office. The man behind the counter looked a bit intimidated by the group.

"May I help you?" he asked.

Amanda favored him with a brilliant smile. "I believe you can. I need to transfer the title of this property"—she laid the deed to the house and grounds on the counter—"to these ladies."

It took only a few minutes to change the deed. They all signed their names in the proper places and Amanda breathed a sigh of relief as she paid the transfer fees. She was sure she would recount this experience to Faith years from now with laughter and fond memories, but for now she was simply glad to be free of the house.

They left the land office and walked the short distance to the general store. Amanda withdrew from her reticule a list of supplies Granny needed and handed it to Jeanne.

"Would you and Rose mind getting these? I promised Wilma I would go to the dress shop with her to pick up her new outfit."

"We would be happy to," Jeanne replied. "I need some things there myself."

Amanda and Wilma continued on down the block to the dress shop. The proprietress greeted them warmly. Evidently, Amanda mused, their money was as welcome as that of the more respectable ladies of the town.

The woman showed Wilma her finished dress. It was a bright shade of pink that would clash horribly with her coppery hair. But apparently, Wilma loved it. She turned to Amanda.

"Well, what do you think?"

The proprietress gave Amanda a worried look.

Amanda smiled. "I think it's lovely, Wilma. If it pleases you, that's all that matters."

Amanda noticed the shop owner's relief as she scurried to wrap the dress in tissue and brown paper.

A bright pink cloth rose in a display counter caught Amanda's eye. It would be the perfect thing to replace the broken feather on her gray traveling hat. She realized that a month ago she would have picked out something much more sedate. She faltered a moment over her choice, then followed her heart. The rose pleased her, so she bought it, feeling content with herself.

With their packages wrapped in brown paper and tied with string, Amanda and Wilma headed back to the general store. Rose and Jeanne waited on the boardwalk with packages of their own.

When they reached their buggy, the two cowboys were gone, so they climbed up unassisted, storing their packages under the buggy seat. The ride back to the house passed pleasantly and when they got there, the hired boy was waiting by the gate to take the buggy to the barn.

"There are some supplies under the seat, Ben. Please bring them to the kitchen after you unhitch the buggy," Amanda said.

"Yes, ma'am," the boy replied, and headed the team toward the barn.

The ladies went to their rooms. After laying her reticule on the hall table, Amanda went to the kitchen to find Granny and Faith. The room smelled like chocolate. Granny was just putting the finishing touches on a cake at the kitchen table.

Faith was in her cradle, staring at her own hands with such intensity that her eyes crossed. Amanda giggled at the sight.

Granny offered Amanda the icing bowl and spoon and Amanda took a seat at the table to enjoy the remains.

Ben came in the back door and deposited an armload of packages on the table.

"Thank you, Ben," Granny said. "After you fill the wood box you can have a piece of this here cake and a glass of milk, if you want."

"Sure enough," Ben grinned. "I'll be right back." He rushed out the door to do Granny's bidding and earn his treat.

Amanda sorted through the packages, looking for the one containing her pink rose. It wasn't there.

"Ben must have overlooked my package, Granny. I bought a rose to put on my gray hat. I'll just run out to the buggy and get it."

# 17

*What a beautiful day, Amanda* thought as she made her way to the barn. The sky was a deep robin-egg blue. There wasn't a cloud in sight. It was hot, but she was becoming accustomed to that. After all, this was Texas.

The barn smelled of freshly sawed wood and new paint. Slade had set men to work on it the day they'd left to find Lily. It was larger than the one that had burned.

Amanda slipped into the barn and waited for her eyes to adjust to the dimness. The buggy was to her right, the horse stalls to her left. She lifted her skirt and climbed into the buggy. Dropping to her knees, she searched beneath the seat for her package. It was at the very back, almost beyond her reach. With her fingertips, she snagged the string that bound the package and tugged it out.

She stood, dusted off the front of her skirt, then turned to step down. A figure standing in the barn doorway stopped her just as she'd put one foot on the step. The light was at his back and his face was in shadow. Amanda's heart began to pound rapidly.

"Who's there? Slade? Buck?"

"No, Amanda." The man stepped to the side of the buggy.

"Robert!" Her first reaction was surprise, her second panic. She must not let either show. Robert had no way of knowing she'd learned of his treachery from Lily. "Oh! You startled me." She stepped to the ground, clutching her package. "What are you doing here?"

"I came to see you, my dear. You've caused me no end of trouble, you know."

"I? In what way, Robert?" Amanda didn't like the look in Robert's eyes. She tried to step away from him. He put out a hand to stop her and grasped her arm.

"I sent Griffin to clear up matters here, but he botched the job. Parker didn't fare much better, and Lily is a turncoat. You, my dear, are a nuisance. I intend to see that you and Lily pay for the inconvenience you have caused me."

He pushed her backward against the buggy. "I only allowed you to come here because I was sure if you remained in Washington, your meddling would have caused questions to be asked that I didn't want to answer.

"I thought when you arrived here and realized who and what your mother was, you would turn tail and run. You really should have, you know. Now you are forcing me to take drastic measures."

Amanda began to struggle and managed to loosen Robert's grip on her arm. She made a quick move toward the barn door. Robert was quicker. He blocked her exit and shoved her against one of the horse stalls. Amanda tasted fear. Don't panic, she told herself. Find out what he wants.

"I don't understand, Robert. What have you to do with Griffin and Parker?"

Robert's smile was so evil it made Amanda's knees weak. "Don't play at being dense, Amanda—I know you're smarter than that. I underestimated you; I won't do that again. You are going into town with me. You are going to persuade Ed Whitman to turn over the gun shipment to me. You will tell him who I am, that I am from Washington, and that I am authorized to take charge of the guns."

He grabbed her arm in a painful grip, and again she twisted and tried to break free.

"No! I won't."

"You will, or both you and Whitman will end up dead, just like your father did."

Amanda's mind focused on Roberts words. Slade was right. "Oh my God, Robert! Why! Why did you kill him?"

"Why? You're being muddleheaded again, Amanda, and foolish. Gold, Amanda. Supplying weapons to the Knights in California will make me as rich as Midas."

Amanda felt tears fill her eyes and hate harden her heart. "But my father was your friend."

"Yes, he was. Only he was a bigger fool than you. I didn't want to kill him, but he wouldn't listen to reason when he found out I was behind the plot. I offered to cut him in on the deal. The stupid man thought he was a patriot. The Union, he said, must prevail. That is rubbish, Amanda. Money is power, and I intend to be powerful."

He yanked Amanda forward. "Now, my dear, it's time to go."

Amanda dug her heels into the soft earth floor and opened her mouth to scream. Robert's hand covered it before she could utter a sound.

"Don't push me, Amanda," Robert warned.

Over Robert's shoulder, Amanda saw Lily standing just inside the barn door. How long had she been there? Hope sprang to life inside Amanda. She had to keep Robert talking long enough for Lily to go for help.

Amanda nodded her head and Robert slowly removed his hand from over her mouth. "I won't scream, Robert. If you will answer some questions for me first, I'll help you."

He didn't look like he believed her.

"Make it fast," he growled.

Amanda fought down panic when she saw Lily pick up a shovel from the floor. Dear God! Amanda realized in horror. Lily wasn't going for help. She was going to try to help *herself*.

"I can understand a man like Griffin working for you, but not Parker. How did you get him to cooperate?"

Robert sneered. "He was a true southerner, Amanda. I appealed to his sense of duty. He still has family in Virginia."

Amanda watched Lily creep forward, the shovel raised like a club above her head.

"Parker can't help you with the guns now, Robert. He's dead. The sheriff shot him."

"I know that, Amanda. I'm not stupid." Robert sounded a bit annoyed. "I had him killed. His usefulness was over."

Amanda's heart was pounding so hard, she could barely hear. Robert loomed over her. He jerked her toward him just as Lily brought the shovel down hard on his head.

Robert grunted in pain. His hands went to his head. He started to turn.

Amanda screamed.

Lily hit Robert again, and he crumpled to the floor at Amanda's feet.

Lily threw down the shovel. "Are you hurt, Amanda?"

Amanda shook her head. "Did you hear?"

"Enough," Lily responded. She looked at the man on the floor. "Do you think I killed him?"

Amanda felt Robert's neck for a pulse. "He's alive. What are we going to do?"

"Tie him up so he can't get away," Lily advised as she searched the tack on the wall for a rope. "Then send someone to find Buck or Slade. I think they are at the hotel talking to Captain Whitman."

Together they rolled Robert over on his stomach and tied his hands and feet. He groaned, but didn't open his eyes. Blood soaked the back of his head, staining his salt-and-pepper hair.

When they were done, Lily hugged Amanda tightly. She was trembling. "I was afraid he was going to hurt you. I think he planned to kill us both."

"I believe he must be a bit mad, to do the things he has." She stepped away from Lily's embrace and took her hands. "If you hadn't come to help me, I don't know what I would have done. How did you know I was here?"

"Granny told me. Slade and Buck were busy talking to Captain Whitman about moving the gun shipment to Fort Worth. I decided to come visit. She said you'd gone to the barn to get a package left in the buggy. When you didn't come back, we started to worry, so I came to see what was taking you so long."

Amanda released Lily's hands. "Do you think you can guard Robert while I send someone to town for help?"

"I think so." Lily gave Amanda a weak grin and bent to retrieve the shovel. "I don't really think I'll need this, but it will make me feel better to hold on to it."

Amanda ran all the way to the house and went in the back door. Ben looked up from his place at the table. A half-eaten slab of chocolate cake was on the plate before him. Granny turned from the pot she was stirring on the stove to stare at Amanda. The wood box beside the stove was filled to overflowing.

"Land sakes! What's all the rush?" Granny asked. "Where's Lily?"

Amanda had to take a second to regain enough breath to speak. "Ben," she panted, "I need you to run to town and find Slade or Buck. Get both if you can. Tell them I need them to come to the barn right away. Tell them to hurry."

Ben was out the door in a flash, and Amanda immediately collapsed in his vacant chair. Granny towered over her, waving the wooden spoon clutched in her hand.

"Are you going to tell me what all the commotion is, girl? Or do I go see for myself?"

"Lily and I have Robert Commings tied up in the barn. Granny, he killed my father. He admitted it. I'll explain everything later. I need to get back to Lily."

When Amanda reached the barn, Lily was perched on a bale of straw, the shovel across her lap. Amanda sat down beside her. "Are you all right?"

"Sure. He hasn't moved." Lily managed a light laugh. "There's nothing to this guarding business."

As they waited, it seemed to Amanda as if the minutes were as long as hours.

When Slade finally ran through the barn doorway, she felt like shouting with joy. Buck was so close on Slade's heels that he plowed into him before he could stop.

"Sorry, Slade."

Slade regained his balance as he stared at the man lying on the ground, bound hand and foot. He glanced at Lily. Buck was prying a shovel from her hands. Amanda stood beside Lily, looking rumpled and a bit worn.

"What the hell's going on here? Who is that, Amanda?"

Slade went to his knees beside the man and felt for a pulse.

"That's Robert Commings. He wanted me to help him get the gun shipment back. He was going to take it to California himself. You were right, Slade: He masterminded the whole thing. He even admitted killing my father."

Slade stood and placed an arm around Amanda, then turned her toward the door. "I think you two have had enough excitement for one day. I want you and Lily to go to the house. Have Granny fix you some coffee. You both look like you could use some."

He gave Amanda a nudge toward the door. "Go! Buck and I can take care of things here."

Amanda had almost reached the door when she suddenly turned back. "Slade, I just remembered something Robert said. He said he knew Parker was dead."

Slade pondered that a moment. "He probably heard about it in town."

"No, I told him Parker couldn't help him anymore because he was dead. He said he knew that because he'd had him killed. My God, Slade. That means Sheriff Davis is working for Robert."

"It would seem so. Buck, you ride to town and ask Doc Anderson, quiet-like, to come out here. Then find Captain Whitman and Hank James and tell them what we know about Davis, Parker, and Commings. Ed has the authority to arrest Davis on suspicion of murder. Tell him I'll be along as soon as Doc tells me it's all right to move Commings to town."

Buck helped Slade carry Commings upstairs to Lily's room and place him on the bed. Lily and Amanda stood just inside the door.

"On your way out, Buck, ask Granny to heat some water for Doc. He'll probably need it."

Buck grabbed Lily by the hand as he passed and they left the room together.

Slade took a seat in the bedside chair, and Amanda went into the room to stand at the foot of the bed. She felt the need to make conversation to fill the time until Doc could get there. All this waiting was starting to drive her crazy.

"What was your meeting with Captain Whitman about?"

"I had him check out the man in Fort Worth. It turned out that he is a known outlaw. If we had delivered the guns to him they would have been headed for California again." Slade glanced at the man on the bed. "He made sure he had every possibility covered."

Amanda stared at Robert. A wave of anger washed over her. She had trusted him. "I've been stupid and foolish. I thought I could accomplish everything I set out to do here, just because I believed I could. And if I had, Commings would still have won. If it weren't for you, I would have botched the whole thing."

Slade grinned at her. "Not true, Amanda. Without you and your interference, we wouldn't have discovered Parker's part in this. Commings wouldn't have come here to finish the job himself and he might never have been found out.

"You might not have training and knowledge on your side, but you do have determination and grit. Don't sell yourself short. Your father would be proud of you."

Amanda gazed at Robert with distaste. "You can't trust anyone anymore. When I got back to Washington, I was going to have him help me find a man to do my half of the agency's work. I suppose I own the whole business now. Maybe I'll sell it and live on the money while I figure out what to do with my life."

Slade left his chair and came to stand behind her. His breath tickled her ear when he spoke.

"You don't have to go. You can stay here and let me help you. We can hire a lawyer in Washington to sort out your affairs. You can trust me, Amanda."

Amanda turned. Slade's eyes held sincerity. "I know I can, but staying here won't solve my problems." Amanda knew the pain in her chest was her heart breaking. "I don't belong here. My mother was right about one thing: A brothel is no place to raise a baby. Besides, I have already signed the house over to the ladies."

They both turned at the sound of a soft knock on the open door. Doc grinned at them from the doorway.

"Sorry. I didn't mean to interrupt you two, but Granny said my patient was in here."

Slade moved to the side of the bed. "Right here, Doc."

Amanda left the room. In the hall she met Granny, who had a pan of water in one hand and several pieces of white cloth in the other.

"Where is Faith, Granny?"

"Lily's got her in the kitchen. That woman is plum took with that baby. It's a good thing she got herself married, 'cause I think she wants a bunch of her own."

Granny stepped into the bedroom and Amanda continued on to the kitchen.

There, Lily was rocking Faith and talking nonsense to her. Faith was cooing and waving her chubby arm in the air. Both appeared to be quite content. Lily smiled at her in greeting and continued to play with the baby.

Amanda crossed the room to the stove to check on dinner. The chicken stewing in the pot smelled wonderful. She wondered if Ben had gotten to finish his cake. She would have to make sure he was given extra money for going to town to find Slade.

She sat down at the table and spoke to Lily. "What have you and Buck decided to do now that you are married?"

Faith had fallen asleep on Lily's shoulder. Lily shifted her to the crook of her arm.

"We've talked a lot about that. We've decided to put our money together and buy a ranch. We will raise cattle, horses, and children." Lily ran a finger over Faith's soft cheek. "We want a dozen."

"I'm glad you're happy, Lily. I know Buck adores you. You're both very lucky."

Lily's smile was replaced by a look of concern. "You know that Buck and I would gladly take Faith and raise her as our own, if you don't want her."

Amanda sighed. "I know, and I thank you for the offer, but I think God brought us together because she is probably the only child I will ever have. She and Granny and I will get along just fine." She rose and took the sleeping baby from Lily. "I'll take her upstairs and put her to bed."

Granny entered the kitchen then, talking a mile a minute. "You really gave that man a smack on the head, Lily. He's coming around, but Doc said he was going to have a whopper of a headache for a while. Slade and Doc are going to put him in Doc's buggy and get him a room at the jail where he belongs." Granny turned to Amanda, wagging a finger. "You'd better go put that baby down. You're going to spoil her with all that holding."

Lily laughed.

"Me!" Amanda exclaimed. "You know what I think, Granny? I think you're the pot calling the kettle black." Amanda giggled. "And you're probably right."

Granny's laughter followed Amanda all the way down the hall to the stairs.

Slade and Doc were on their way down, supporting Robert between them. The look Robert gave her when he passed made tiny prickles of fear run along her spine. The man was surely mad. Amanda waited until the front door had closed behind them before climbing the stairs.

Slade sat in the study downing a glass of fine Kentucky whiskey. He grimaced as the fiery liquid burned his throat and warmed his stomach.

The house was finally quiet. He grinned. What an unusual evening it had been. The news about The House changing hands had spread like wildfire. That was to be expected, since the land office man was an even bigger gossip than the one at the stage office.

Nearly every client on The House's list had shown up to congratulate the three new owners. Most of the men only wanted a drink and to be reassured by the ladies that The House would continue to operate as usual.

Wilma, Rose, and Jeanne were delighted by the attention and their acceptance as the new owners. The announcement that a new girl would be hired to "help out," as Wilma so delicately put it, was greeted with enthusiasm.

Slade chuckled and took another sip of whiskey. The men had swarmed to the house like bees to a hive to be sure their supply of honey wouldn't be interrupted.

Amanda had made a final appearance, wearing that

damned green dress again. Slade wondered how a man could love and hate something at the same time. The dress, with Amanda in it, would live in his memory forever.

He wondered if she was sleeping. She would be leaving in a few days. That knowledge brought a chill to his heart that even whiskey couldn't warm. He had tried to get her to change her mind. He'd asked her to trust him. She said she did. He'd asked her to stay. She said she couldn't. What more could he do?

The image of Amanda cuddling Faith in her arms amid the ruins of the burned homestead came to his mind. If he was ever going to contemplate taking another wife, she was the kind he would want.

He wanted her all right. The tightness in his groin every time he thought about her attested to that. But that was lust, not love. Did he love her? He knew Amanda would never settle for less.

Slade swallowed the last of the whiskey and set the glass aside. He'd finally gotten around to talking to Buck. He had asked him how he'd been sure he loved Lily.

Buck, in one of his rare serious moments, had replied, "She makes me feel ten feet tall and like I could lick the whole world in a fair fight. The first time we made love, I knew no other woman had ever made me feel the way she did, and I knew no other woman ever would. Love isn't something you can see or touch or taste, and it sure as hell doesn't make any sense. You just know."

Slade thought back to the night in the line shack. He remembered the feel of Amanda's body, soft and willing beneath his, with such clarity that it made him hard with need. There had been a oneness between them then. Together, they'd reached for heaven. Together, they'd found it. He'd heard the words "I love you." He thought she'd said them. The words rang in his head like a song. Making love to Amanda had felt so right. No woman had ever made him feel like that. He hadn't been just satisfying his own yearnings; rather, together they had satisfied a mutual desire.

Did he dare believe that with Amanda it was love, not lust? He was beginning to think just that. A painful kind of joy filled him. It stole his breath away. Dear God, why had it taken him so long to realize it?

Slade took the stairs two at a time. When he reached Amanda's door he knocked softly, and waited. She couldn't be sleeping, when he was so wide awake. He knew that was a stupid premise, but he was too excited to care. He had to talk to her.

It seemed to take forever before the door opened a crack. Amanda peeked around its edge. "Do you know what time it is?"

"No, and I don't care. I've got to talk to you, Amanda."

"Now?"

"Yes, now. You weren't asleep, were you?"

"Of course not. It's only three in the morning."

Slade thought she sounded a bit annoyed. "Amanda, let me in. This is important." He gave the door a little nudge, forcing her to step back as it opened.

Her hair was mussed from sleep. A soft white gown covered her from chin to toes. She looked like a sleepy angel. Slade grabbed her around the waist and swung her off the floor.

"Slade, put me down! What the devil is the matter with you?"

He laughed as he set her on her feet. Tipping up her chin, he kissed her with all the pent-up emotion coursing through his body. He crushed her to him. Her body beneath the gown was soft and unrestricted. Slade groaned.

Amanda began to struggle, and he released her.

She glared at him. "You're drunk."

"No I'm not," he answered, taken aback.

"You taste like whiskey, you smell like whiskey, and you're acting crazy." She placed a hand on each hip. "You're drunk."

"Amanda," Slade said, using his most patient tone. "I had one drink, and I am not crazy."

"Then why are you here?"

"If you will just shut up, I'll tell you."

Amanda clamped her mouth shut and waited. Slade wanted to laugh at the picture of impatience she made. He stifled the urge and smiled at her instead.

Now that he had her complete attention, he wasn't sure where to start. "I've been doing a lot of thinking." She looked like she might be forming a reply to that, so he hurried on. "I want you and Faith to stay. I think I'm in love with you. I want you to marry me." Slade took a deep breath and sighed with satisfaction. He knew there was a silly grin on his face, but he didn't care.

Amanda looked shocked. Her green eyes were wide with surprise, her beautiful mouth hung open. Slade reached for her to kiss it closed.

She backed away, shaking her head. What the hell was the matter with her? Slade wondered. She looked as if she might cry.

"Amanda, did you hear what I said?"

"I heard! What makes you think you can come in here and tell me what you've decided? You 'think' you love me." Her eyes were bright with unshed tears. "Don't do me any favors, McAllister."

Slade felt like he'd been punched in the stomach and doused with ice water. What the hell was going on here? Her words cut him to the core. He felt like a bomb ready to explode.

"I believe you think you love me," she went in a small, tight voice, "but I think you're feeling guilty. I don't regret the night we spent in the line shack, Slade. I don't want to ever forget it. I was willing. You don't owe me. I'm all grown up. I can handle this."

She moved to the door to usher him out. "Good night, Slade."

"Oh no, lady. I'm not leaving until this is settled."

"It is settled. You said, you 'think' you love me. That's not good enough. I'm keeping you from making a terrible mistake, one that would only cause us both pain."

Slade watched a tear trickle down each of Amanda's cheeks. She looked so small, so sad, and so damned determined. She was breaking his heart.

"You're the one making the mistake, Amanda." Slade brushed past her. When he reached the hall, he turned back. "You're going to regret this."

"I know," she whispered, and quietly closed the door.

Slade crossed the hall to his room. He sat down heavily on the edge of his bed and pulled off his boots. She was convinced that she was keeping him from making a mistake. She had a lot of nerve to assume that she knew his mind better than he did. He did love her. "I think" had been a poor choice of words. But hell, wasn't everyone entitled to one mistake?

He would give her a little time and a bit of room. She would come around as soon as she realized he was right. Slade stripped off his clothes and crawled into bed. It was almost dawn again. He chuckled ruefully. He was going to have to marry the lady in order to get a decent night's sleep.

Across the hall, Amanda sat huddled in the middle of her bed, with tears running down her cheeks. She had done what was best for them both. But dear God, the decision hurt, and she was afraid it was always going to hurt. Her only comfort was that it would hurt more if she agreed to marry him and they found out, too late, that he didn't love her. That would destroy her totally.

Amanda slid under the covers and hugged her pillow to her chest, crying silently, as she waited for sleep.

# 18

*Amanda checked her reflection* in the dressing table mirror. Her gray traveling suit had been cleaned and pressed. The pink rose now added a touch of color to the matching hat.

Her trunk was already at the stage office, along with Granny's box and Faith's small satchel. She knew Granny and Faith were waiting downstairs for her. Still, she lingered.

Amanda allowed herself one last look at the room. Her room, her mother's room. She was aware of why she felt reluctant to leave this place: It felt like home—something she'd never really had before. But she knew that leave it she must.

It had been two days since she'd seen Slade. He wasn't even going to let her say good-bye; she had hurt him too much. She wished desperately that things had turned out differently.

Amanda moved around the bedroom, touching things, committing them to memory. Memories were all that she was taking with her. She stopped before the dressing table and ran her hand over the glass surface. She swallowed the lump that formed in her throat. She was absolutely not going to cry.

She left the bedroom, and entered the sitting room where she knew her mother must have spent much of her time. If only Amanda could see her, just once, relaxing in the chaise or sitting at the writing desk. *I love you, Mother.* The thought came unbidden, but she knew it was true.

"Good-bye, Mother." She blinked back the tears she had promised herself she wouldn't shed. "I'm glad I came."

Picking up her reticule from the chair in front of the desk, she walked slowly to the door and opened it. She didn't look back as she softly closed it behind her.

The ladies were waiting in the hall, along with Granny and Faith. They smiled up at her as she descended the stairs. Wilma, wearing her extraordinary pink gown, had tears in her eyes. She took Amanda's hand when she reached the bottom step.

"You'll come back to see us sometime, won't you? You know you will always be welcome here."

Amanda hugged her. "I know, and we will try to come visit."

Rose extended her hand. Amanda took it.

"It has been a pleasure to know you, Amanda. We will all miss you."

Amanda smiled and released Rose's hand. "I will miss you too, and I will never, ever, forget our first meeting."

Jeanne, in a rare show of emotion, gave Amanda a hug, then quickly stepped aside.

Amanda watched Granny embrace each of the three women. She chuckled when Granny instructed Wilma to hire a cook who would appreciate and take proper care of her kitchen.

Amid tears and laughter, the ladies escorted them to the buggy, which was waiting before the open gate. Amanda held Faith while Rose helped Granny into the buggy. When Faith was settled on Granny's lap, Amanda climbed up.

She picked up the reins and, after a final wave to her ladies, she gave a flick of the lines over the horse's back. The buggy began to roll at a slow, careful pace toward town.

They hadn't gone a block when three men stepped off the walk. One of them went to the horse's head and took hold of its bridle, bringing the buggy to a stop.

Amanda reached for her reticule, and remembered that her derringer was packed in her trunk.

"Let go of the horse!" she demanded as she reached for the buggy whip instead.

A bearded man grabbed the whip before she could reach it. "Sorry, ma'am. We got instructions to take you someplace."

"Where, and what the devil for?"

The bearded man grinned. "Sit still and be quiet— we ain't going to hurt you none. We're just getting paid to do a job, ma'am. I wasn't told why."

"Who's paying you?"

"I'm not at liberty to say, ma'am."

The man holding the horse's bridle gave it a tug

and began to turn the buggy around. Amanda held on to the seat for balance. The buggy was being led down the road leading out of town.

She glanced at Granny, who was being unusually quiet. Amanda's mind worked frantically. She addressed the man with the beard.

"Is McAllister paying you?" The man didn't answer. "I'll give you double what he's paying if you will take us to the stage office instead."

"That's a mighty generous offer, ma'am, but we done made a deal. We'd likely get shot if we didn't keep to it."

The sound of approaching riders caused Amanda to glance over her shoulder. Two men on horseback drew up alongside the buggy. A rangy cowpoke with carrot red hair shouted at the man with the beard.

"What the heck are you doing, John? Me and Bud here was supposed to stop this here buggy before it got to the stage office. It's a mite unfriendly of you to take over a job we was going to get paid to do."

"I don't know nothing about that, Red, but you're welcome to tag along if you want."

"You're darn tootin' we will! We expect to be paid for our time. It ain't our fault you got them first."

Amanda felt like a bone in a dogfight. Damnation!

The buggy, surrounded by the five rough men, came to a halt before the church. Amanda stared at the square white building. A feeling of excitement and expectation began to grow inside her.

"Is this where you're taking us?" she asked the man named John.

"Yes, ma'am."

Amanda was quiet as she watched him take Faith from Granny and help the old woman down.

"Granny," she finally questioned, "what do you know about this?"

Granny smiled a secret kind of smile and answered, "I'm not at liberty to say, girl. Why don't we go inside?"

Amanda was beginning to understand the method to this madness. "Oh no, I'm not about to be forced into anything."

John reached up and grabbed Amanda around the waist. "Sorry, ma'am, I've got my orders." He pulled her, fighting and kicking, from the buggy and carried her to the church door.

"It won't do you no good to fight me," he told her as he waited for one of the other men to open the door. He followed Granny inside, and the other men trailed in their wake.

Slade McAllister stood at the altar with the minister. He was dressed in a black jacket and pants, a white shirt, and a black string tie. He was so handsome it made her heart almost break.

John set her on her feet, but blocked her path when she tried to scamper back through the open door. When she turned toward the front of the church again, McAllister was striding down the aisle toward her. She glared at him.

"Did you pay these men to bring me here?" she demanded.

Slade glanced at John and his two companions. "Nope." He chuckled. "I sure didn't."

Red and his sidekick shoved their way forward. "Well, you owe us!" He pointed a finger at John. "We can't help it if they got there first."

McAllister grinned. He seemed to be enjoying all

this nonsense a great deal, Amanda thought. "Well, boys," he said, "you might have a legitimate gripe there. I suppose we could talk about it."

Amanda was becoming more confused by the minute. If Slade hadn't hired John and his men, who had? Her gaze roamed the church in search of Granny and Faith. She found them sitting in a pew at the front. Surely not Granny, she thought, but she would bet her last penny that Granny knew more than she was telling.

Amanda grabbed Slade's arm and yelled to make herself heard over the arguing men. "You tell these men to let me go. I'm going to miss my stage."

Slade glanced from Amanda to John. "Since they are not in my employ, I don't think it's likely that they'll take orders from me."

Amanda stomped her foot in frustration. "This isn't going to do you a bit of good, McAllister. I'll just have to take the next stage if I miss this one."

"Amanda, honey, calm down." He took her hand and tugged her along the aisle toward the front of the church and away from the five men arguing over who was to be paid for what.

Amanda tried to free herself from his grip, but she could not match his strength or determination.

When they reached the front of the room, he pinned her in a corner with his body. She could feel his heat seep into her. It was a good feeling, and it made her sad.

"Let me go."

"Amanda, be reasonable. I thought if I gave you some room and some time, you would see that marrying me is what we both want. I can't let you go. Why are you being so stubborn? Damn it, Amanda, I love you."

"You think! I don't—"

"No, Amanda," Slade interrupted. "That was just a poor choice of words on my part. You can't hold it against me."

"And don't cuss in church," Amanda continued as if she hadn't been interrupted.

A commotion at the back of the church caused Slade to turn toward the door. Amanda peeked around him and saw Buck and Lily push their way into the church, with Rose, Jeanne, and Wilma following close behind them. The three women threaded their way through the group of hired men and joined Granny in the front pew.

Slade left Amanda to talk to Buck. She stood with her mouth open, observing the chaotic activity around her.

Buck was handing money to the three men who had brought her to the church. So he had hired them!

Slade was talking a mile a minute to the two other men. He finally dug into his pocket and gave Red some money.

Faith was screaming at the top of her lungs. It was past her feeding time, she was probably wet and Amanda had no doubt that all the noise was upsetting her.

Granny was cooing soft words of comfort to her, but not making much headway.

The minister, standing at the altar with a Bible in his hand, looked about ready to have a fit.

Lily was grinning widely and Rose, Wilma, and Jeanne also appeared to be enjoying all the excitement.

It was, Amanda decided, the biggest, noisiest, most unorganized conspiracy she'd ever been involved in—and all because Slade loved her. That thought vibrated in her mind like a clap of thunder.

*He loved her.*

Amanda began to smile. The smile turned into a laugh. She couldn't help it. This was the strangest assortment of people she'd ever seen in a church, or anywhere else for that matter. And they were all there because Slade loved her. She was suddenly filled to overflowing with delight. Her laughter rippled through the room.

Slade approached her, looking at her as if she'd lost her mind. His comic expression made her laugh harder. Tears of amusement filled her eyes.

The five men still arguing in the church aisle turned and stared at her.

Amanda was laughing so hard her stomach hurt. She collapsed onto a pew and tried to regain control over her surging emotions.

Slade towered over her. "What the devil is the matter with you?"

Amanda giggled.

"Stop that!"

"I can't . . . can't . . . help it," Amanda got out between giggles. "You look so silly."

"Silly!" Slade shouted, glancing around the church. "I don't think this is a laughing matter, Amanda. I love you. I've never been more serious about anything in my whole life."

The minister approached. "If there isn't to be a wedding, Mister McAllister, I request that you get those men and their guns out of my church."

Amanda's fit of giggles finally stopped. She stood and turned to Slade. After probing the velvet softness of his intense brown eyes with a steady gaze, she smiled at him.

"Ask me again."

"Ask you what?"

Amanda sighed at his lack of comprehension. "Never mind, I'll do it. Will you marry me, McAllister?"

Slade grabbed her around the waist and swung her off the floor. "Yahoo!" His yell shook the rafters. "Yes! Yes! Yes!" he shouted as he whirled her around.

A dozen voices raised in laughter filled every corner of the church. The reverend asked for order.

"Really, Mister McAllister, you must practice a little restraint. After all, this is a church."

Slade allowed Amanda's feet to touch the floor and drew her against his side. "My Bible says to make a joyful noise unto the Lord, Reverend. If I get any more joyful, I'm apt to raise the roof."

Buck and Lily came to stand beside Slade and Amanda. Buck winked at Amanda, then said to the minister, "Do you think we could get on with this so I can go eat some cake? When I left the house Mattie and Roger were setting out the refreshments."

Slade took Amanda's hand. "Are you ready, love?"

"Yes, McAllister. Yes."

Their vows were exchanged with solemn ceremony. Amanda thought her heart might burst with happiness when Slade produced a wide gold band from his pocket and slid it onto her finger.

"With this ring I thee wed." His words, clear and filled with love, would be etched in her heart forever.

When he kissed her, the world began to spin. Then

she was jerked back to reality as Slade rushed her down the aisle and out the door. The buggy ride to the house took only minutes.

Slade held up his arms to assist her from the buggy. She smiled at him. She was so happy she felt giddy with it. He lifted her down, his hands firm but gentle on her waist. He walked beside her along the walk and up the steps. The rest of the wedding party followed close behind.

Amanda was filled with delight at the sight of a dozen white satin ribbons tied to the heart-shaped door knocker, fluttering in the early evening breeze.

She glanced at Slade. "Who did this?"

He shrugged, then chuckled. "I don't know. You'll have to ask Buck. I think he probably masterminded most of what's happened today." Slade opened the door and before she could move, he'd swept her up in his arms to carry her over the threshold.

After setting her on her feet in the hall, he grabbed her hand and hurried her into the parlor as the wedding guests poured through the door behind them.

Mattie and Roger, Ed Whitman and Hank James, and Ben rushed in to offer them congratulations. Slade shook hands with the men while Amanda hugged Mattie.

"How did you manage all this?"

A table, covered with a snowy white cloth, stood in the middle of the room. It held a cake, frosted white, on a gleaming glass pedestal plate, a vase of Granny's roses from the bush out back, and a punch bowl filled with lemonade and surrounded by shiny glasses.

Buck moved to Amanda's side and kissed her on the cheek. He looked about to burst with pride.

"Lily and I plotted the whole thing. Of course, Lily

and Mattie did all the hard work—making the cake and all the rest. I only hired the men to bring you to the church and talked the reverend into doing the service. We had to tell Granny, because we didn't want her scared witless when the men stopped the buggy. We didn't tell Wilma, Rose, and Jeanne, though until we came to pick them up after you left."

Buck grinned at Slade and clasped his hand with vigor. "If you'd a-told me you were planning the same thing, we wouldn't have had to hire so many men and could have saved a little money."

Slade laughed at Buck's remark, then smiled fondly at Amanda. "I wasn't as sure as you were that the lady would agree so quickly. I thought I might have to drag her off someplace for the night and compromise her until she said yes." He grinned mischievously. "I was kind of looking forward to that."

Amanda gave an exaggerated sigh and smiled at the two men. "Thank you, Buck, for everything."

She spoke to the group clustered around her. "Thank you all."

Then she stood on tiptoes to whisper into Slade's ear. "And you, Mister McAllister, will have the rest of your life to compromise me."

Slade drew her into his arms and kissed her soundly.

Amanda's body warmed with a blush that must have turned her face the same shade of pink as Wilma's dress. It was caused, she was sure, partly from the passionate public kiss, but more so from her outrageous comment and the delightful image it projected in her mind.

Mattie and the ladies cut the cake and filled the glasses.

Ed Whitman made a toast that included all three newly married couples, wishing them long life, happiness, and a goodly number of children.

Amanda, standing beside Slade, thought that a wedding reception held in the parlor of a bordello, with three lovely ladies of the evening, five roughly dressed and armed men, a fussy baby, a black nanny, two Texas Rangers, a hired boy, and two couples still on their own honeymoons would live in her memory as one of the most treasured moments of her life. She also decided that love does sometimes bloom in the strangest places. Her gaze rested on Mattie and Lily for a moment. She was sure they would agree.

Three hours later the house was finally quiet. The cake had been reduced to crumbs. The last wedding guest had departed. Granny had taken Faith to her room, and the ladies had all retired early. Another conspiracy, Amanda supposed.

Slade, leaning against the fireplace mantel, looked at her with a strange gleam in his eyes. Amanda felt a shiver of sweet anticipation race along her spine. He walked across the room to her side with predatory grace.

Silently he took her hand and led her from the parlor, up the stairs, and along the hall to her room. He paused before her door and opened it. Picking her up, he carried her over the threshold and let her slide slowly down his body until her feet touched the floor.

"I love you, Amanda McAllister."

Her new name sounded strange but sweet to Amanda's ears. She didn't have much time to ponder it, though, because Slade was busy pulling the pins from her hair and tossing them onto the desk.

When he had her hair free, he dragged his fingers through it. She sighed with pleasure as he massaged her scalp and the back of her neck.

"That feels wonderful," she murmured.

"I know something that will feel even better," he whispered against her ear.

"Really." She gave him a smile she hoped was seductive, and asked, "What?"

Taking her hand, Slade led her into the bedroom and stopped in the middle. His hands moved to the front of her jacket and began to work the buttons free of their holes. Amanda's heart was beating as fast as a hummingbird's wings.

She shrugged off the jacket while Slade unbuttoned her skirt and untied her slip, which fell to the floor, along with her jacket.

Slade untied the blue bows down the front of her camisole and brushed the straps off her shoulders, baring her breasts.

His eyes dark and intense, he gazed at her. Amanda's breath caught as he lowered his head and brushed his mouth over each nipple. She dropped her arms to her sides and the camisole joined her skirt on the floor.

She grasped Slade's arms to steady herself as he continued to kiss and caress her. She began to tremble.

Slade lifted her, freeing her from the pile of garments at her feet, and carried her to the bed. Laying her across it, he began to remove what was left of her clothing.

His hands caressed her hips as her pantalets slid off. His fingers teased the inside of her thighs and the back of her knees, then he rolled down her stockings, and when her feet were finally as bare as the rest of her he raised them to his mouth and kissed each of her toes.

It was an outrageous thing to do, Amanda thought, and she loved it. She was surprised that she still had the presence of mind to think at all. She shivered with pleasure.

Slade let her go, and she moved to the middle of the bed to watch his body appear as he removed his clothes. He was all hard muscle, sun-browned skin, and soft black hair. He was beautiful. She didn't suppose, even if she lived to be a hundred, that she would ever tire of looking at him.

When he was as naked as she was, she held out her arms to him. He settled over her like a warm blanket and kissed her until she could hardly think. The feel of him against her was too wonderful for words.

He took his weight from her and onto his elbows, the look of love in his eyes melting her heart. Then he grinned.

"Are you sure you wouldn't rather have spent tonight at the hotel?"

Amanda giggled. "I'm positive. I want to be able to tell our daughters, when they are old enough to appreciate the fact, that I spent my honeymoon in a house of ill repute."

Slade chuckled. "Then you won't mind if I tell our sons that I'm probably the only man alive to make love to his wife in a brothel?"

Their laughter mingled and became a sigh as their bodies joined, and then, in the big canopied brothel bed, they found the sweet joy in each other that only love can bring.

### *Someday Soon* by Debbie Macomber

A beautiful widow unwillingly falls for the worst possible new suitor: a man with a dangerous mission that he must complete—even if it means putting love on hold. Another heartwarming tale from bestselling author Debbie Macomber.

### *The Bride Wore Spurs* by Sharon Ihle

When Lacey O'Carroll arrives in Wyoming as a mail-order bride for the unsettlingly handsome John Winterhawke, she is in for a surprise: he doesn't want a wife. But once the determined Lacey senses his rough kindness and simmering hunger for her, she challenges Hawke with a passion of her own.

### *Legacy of Dreams* by Martha Johnson

Gillian Lang arrives at Lake House, a Victorian resort hotel in upstate New York, determined to get answers to questions about the past that have haunted her. As she is drawn to the hotel's owner Matt O'Donnell, her search for the truth unfolds a thirty-year-old tragedy involving both their families and ignites a dangerous passion that could lead to heartbreak.

### *Bridge to Yesterday* by Stephanie Mittman

After falling from a bridge in Arizona, investigator Mary Grace O'Reilly is stunned to find she has been transported one hundred years into the past to help hell-raising cowboy Sloan Westin free his son from an outlaw gang. They face a perilous mission ahead, but no amount of danger will stop them from defying fate for the love of a lifetime.

### *Fool of Hearts* by Terri Lynn Wilhelm

Upon the untimely death of her father, Lady Gillian finds herself at the mercy of her mysterious new guardian Calum, Marquess of Iolar. While each attempts to outwit the other to become sole heir to her father's fortune, they cannot resist the undeniable desire blazing between them. A witty and romantic novel.

### *The Lady and the Lawman* by Betty Winslow

Amanda is ready to do whatever it takes to uncover the mystery behind her father's death—even live in a brothel in a rugged backwater town in Texas. More disturbing than her new lodgings is the undercover Texas Ranger assigned to help her, with his daring and hungry kisses proving to be the most dangerous obstacle of all.

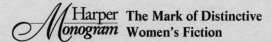

GLORY IN THE SPLENDOR OF SUMMER WITH

# HarperMonogram's

# *101* Days of Romance

# BUY 3 BOOKS, GET 1 FREE!

Take a book to the beach, relax by
the pool, or read in the most quiet
and romantic spot in your home. You
can live through love all summer long
when you redeem this exciting offer
from HarperMonogram. Buy any three
HarperMonogram romances in June,
July, or August, and get a fourth book
sent to you for FREE. See next page for
the list of top-selling novels and
romances by your favorite authors that
you can choose from for your premium!

# 101 DAYS OF ROMANCE
## BUY 3 BOOKS, GET 1 FREE!

CHOOSE A FREE BOOK FROM THIS OUTSTANDING
LIST OF AUTHORS AND TITLES:

## HARPERMONOGRAM

____LORD OF THE NIGHT  Susan Wiggs  0-06-108052-7
____ORCHIDS IN MOONLIGHT  Patricia Hagan  0-06-108038-1
____TEARS OF JADE  Leigh Riker  0-06-108047-0
____DIAMOND IN THE ROUGH  Millie Criswell  0-06-108093-4
____HIGHLAND LOVE SONG  Constance O'Banyon  0-06-108121-3
____CHEYENNE AMBER  Catherine Anderson  0-06-108061-6
____OUTRAGEOUS  Christina Dodd  0-06-108151-5
____THE COURT OF THREE SISTERS  Marianne Willman  0-06-108053-5
____DIAMOND  Sharon Sala  0-06-108196-5
____MOMENTS  Georgia Bockoven  0-06-108164-7

## HARPERPAPERBACKS

____THE SECRET SISTERS  Ann Maxwell  0-06-104236-6
____EVERYWHERE THAT MARY WENT  Lisa Scottoline  0-06-104293-5
____NOTHING PERSONAL  Eileen Dreyer  0-06-104275-7
____OTHER LOVERS  Erin Pizzey  0-06-109032-8
____MAGIC HOUR  Susan Isaacs  0-06-109948-1
____A WOMAN BETRAYED  Barbara Delinsky  0-06-104034-7
____OUTER BANKS  Anne Rivers Siddons  0-06-109973-2
____KEEPER OF THE LIGHT  Diane Chamberlain  0-06-109040-9
____ALMONDS AND RAISINS  Maisie Mosco  0-06-100142-2
____HERE I STAY  Barbara Michaels  0-06-100726-9

To receive your free book, simply send in this coupon **and** your store
receipt with the purchase prices circled. You may take part in this exclusive
offer as many times as you wish, but all qualifying purchases must be made
by September 4, 1995, and all requests must be postmarked by October 4,
1995. Please allow 6-8 weeks for delivery.

MAIL TO: HarperCollins Publishers
          P.O. Box 588 Dunmore, PA  18512-0588

Name_____

Address_____

City_____State_____Zip_____

Offer is subject to availability. HarperPaperbacks may make substitutions for
requested titles.                                                H09511